THE CHEERFUL CAPTIVE

by the same author

THE LIGHTED BOX
DEER ON THE STAIRS
LOVE AND ADMIRATION
SUMMER STRANGER
THE BOYS FROM SHARON

LOUISE FIELD COOPER

The Cheerful Captive

OR THE NINE DAYS' ASTONISHMENT

Illustrated by Paul Galdone

HARCOURT, BRACE AND COMPANY
NEW YORK

COPYRIGHT, 1954, BY LOUISE FIELD COOPER

All rights reserved, including the right to reproduce this book or portions thereof in any form.

first edition

LIBRARY OF CONGRESS CATALOG CARD NUMBER: 54-9719

PRINTED IN THE UNITED STATES OF AMERICA

THE CHEERFUL CAPTIVE

CHAPTER ONE

"Here they come, madam," a voice called, and an avalanche of cotton rugs descended from an upstairs window. Hennie, standing on the cottage lawn in afternoon sunshine, turned in time to see the rugs falling to a heap and not an instant later Agnes arriving to snatch them apart and spread them out.

Hennie on the grass gave a flap or two of a duster to imply she too might be working, and a very little dust floated away on the blue fall air. As always, when she brought Agnes and Gino over from town for a day in late September or early October to clean and close the cottage for the winter, when five o'clock approached she wished those two would climb into the station wagon and go back to town without her.

In just the weeks since she had left, the cottage had

got away from her; it had a life of its own and didn't want her back. She had supposed it was a friend, and she turned around to look at its simple gray-shingled exterior, but the windows were eyes that would not meet her eyes.

The sky and air and the spread-out sea were never bluer than the one day in each fall she came to close down; and the flowers in the narrow garden across the front of the cottage were never, in July and August, so velvet-blooming, larger than life, and extravagantly scented, lolling out over the edge of the garden into grass, as they were the last day she would ever see them. If she sent Agnes and Gino home and stayed on, she deluded herself, each day the dark velvet flowers would grow larger and larger, lolling at her feet until snow came to surround them and bear them up.

"Seems a waste of time to go way over there to clean now, and then all over again in the spring," Laurence had observed that morning at breakfast, but every September he said this. The first ten years they had had the sea cottage he had said it at breakfast and ten times she had listened, looking doubtful, and then explained why she must, but nowadays she paid no heed.

"Now, madam," Agnes said from behind her, "now what? The china cupboard," she said, and marched away. Agnes MacGilvray was a woman who was never a prey of self-doubt, and that made life even easier for Hennie, whose life was very easy anyway.

Mid-afternoon on cottage closing days always found her idling about, neither one thing nor the other, mistress nor servant, but a creature subject to fits and starts of work which sometimes promised to rise to orgiastic fervor but soon slowed down, slowed down like a motor barely ticking over. "You do it," she would say to whomever else was there, smiling warmly, "you do it better than I do," and everyone knew how true this was. She always ended the day with a reluctance to shut down the windows on the finished rooms and turn the key in the door, though when she had, she never thought of the place again until the following June. For three summer months these windows had stood open letting in sun, fog, rain, and salty gusts; curtains had blown into the rooms carrying furlings of fog in their floating hems, flapped and twisted, and then on stormy nights shot wildly out again into the darkness and rain. Now the curtains were down, aired and folded away, and the windows were larger, innocent and bare and sad, and it was a treachery to them to rattle down the sash and snap the lock. She idled along the flower border. It was such a pity to shut inside for those many months to come only today's air, which, however blue and gentle and gold-flecked like goldwasser now, would become colder and grayer day by day and month by month until inside the cottage all would be heavy, damp, still, and repellent.

A thudding at the back must be Gino stowing away the long chairs and the lawn mower. She intended to go around and ask if he had remembered to bring the rowboat up from the beach in the station wagon to store in the garage, but without actually sitting down on them she continued to hang around the front steps, blinking off at the water between the swoops of honeysuckle racing up the porch pillars and flowering now for the last time. "If I did stay here for a while, I'd need that rowboat," she said, "if I wanted to go out and row around the islands." Without giving up for a minute an engagement to have luncheon tomorrow with Olivia in what she and her friends called the Dark Bar of the hotel in town, she stared at the shimmering blinding blue September sea, glittering with a skim of silver and gold, and knew the way the oars would be in her hands, the soft heavy warm gray wood, dipping gently, awkwardly perhaps, but no matter into that blue dazzle. She had meant to go rowing a good deal that summer, but the fact was she hadn't once set foot in the boat. If she stayed on she would make up for such indolence; she could see herself in the boat, rounding the bare stone island where terns laid eggs, herself a tiny figure in all that blue. She must wear dark glasses against the glare there would be—no, no; tomorrow she would be wearing her new feather hat to show Olivia. "They don't lay now anyway!" she said. "Nearly winter as it is. Gino," she called, "what about the boat?"

But to ask any question of Gino was a waste of time and sometimes it was faintly humiliating as well, because all he ever said in reply was "Hunk," with his face held down and if possible averted. "Hunk," the Stacpoles had learned, could mean either yes or no, and in the end one went to see for oneself, quietly and furtively, to glance, as if but in passing, through the garage window and see if the boat was there, tipped on its side, or, at other moments, in other circumstances, one took an artless-seem-ing stroll through a hall to learn if he had indeed moved the potted camellia or yet waxed the hall floor. Whether he had, and most times out of a hundred he had or was just about to, his answer to questions was always the same, and affronted-sounding, and observations and random remarks made nervously to fill a momentary vacuum he never replied to at all. Moreover, for ten Septembers he had remembered the rowboat. She folded herself down on the warm top step.

Agnes was back upstairs again, her steps audible on the bare wood floor, but her duster got away from her and came floating down past Hennie to snare on a barberry bush and almost at the same instant it settled over the sharp twigs Agnes arrived and tweaked it up, her mouth pursed. "Shall I just take yours in too, madam?" She relieved Hennie of her cloth.

"Now don't hurry," Hennie said. "There's no rush. Isn't it lovely here! But I'll be in in a minute and help."

Nevertheless, she sat on, pinioned by the sun, looking across the lawn and down over the rough meadow that rolled away to the shore; no other house or rooftop showed; the Stacpoles might have owned the whole of Long Island Sound and all adjacent territory. Summers I do, she thought; winters, of course, the whole place isn't here at all but simply vanishes into nothing; it gets hauled up into the sky on cords until June, when we get it let down again for us. She thought she would go and give the basking rugs a shake and turn them over and Agnes would see her from an upper window and say to herself, "Now what a *good* Mrs. Stacpole; working!" But she sat on, aching comfortably from what little work she had done, her hands idle in her blue denim lap, her face raised to let the sun burn her cheeks salmon pink for the last time this year. There had been this summer; and now it was over. It had been delightful; nothing any different from a dozen other summers. With the best intentions, in June, she had packed all the many, many white paper volumes of *Les Hommes de Bonne Volonté*, announcing to Laurence and the children, "These I am going to read between now and September, every word. I am going to spend the summer steeping myself in it and if I unconsciously break out into French at the table, though not breakfast probably, but luncheon and dinner, you'll just have to forgive me." The long row of books, fresh and uncut as the day she had bought them, waited now in the room behind her to be packed for town. "This winter, then," she said aloud, "by the fire, evenings we don't do anything else." She recalled and brushed aside a recollection of *The Intelligent Woman's Guide to Socialism*, which she had repeatedly brought to Flanders Point, summers, and in the end had decided was better suited to winter reading. "Did I?" She squinted up into the sun. "I did, didn't I? I certainly think I did. I may quite possibly save *Les Hommes* for next summer and in that case I might as well leave them here." Laurence had laughed at her, back in June, when he carried the box in and set it on the living-room table. "Wait a minute while I find volume one for you," he had said, looking at her over the loaded box, mocking, but she, stretching and yawning, had gone to a window to gaze out on the sea and the summer to come. "Just leave them; I'll find it when I want it," she had said, and yawned again. "Ah-h-h—this wonderful air undoes me, like a doll with limp elastic. I may not begin serious reading for a day or two." And all summer long she had lain around on the sand and on the grass, ripening like a fruit, growing gold all over like a peach on a wall, reading *The New Yorker* if anything, or *Newsweek*, but not regularly.

Gino, who hadn't hurried even on the day years before when the laundry basket caught fire, came with his steady pace around the corner of the cottage and crossed the grass to the bird bath on a rock. He took the long steps short men do, misbelieving it gives them stature. "Oh, Gino," she called, "did you—" but in one motion he raised the bird bath to the exact level on himself where he could best carry it and continued on his way around the far corner and never looked back and said nothing. Her shoulder settled against a pillar; the sun battened down her lashes and she felt the day slip sideways, this moment worth the whole summer. Indeed, it became her whole summer, concentrated. In a high, rearing wave of light it crashed silently down over her.

For long moments she swung in this golden undertow, her eyes closed, no sound in her ears except the high scree of slow gulls circling and sailing the blue air—no sound until the bang of a window in the house behind her brought her back to today.

Through the stripped living room, already beginning to be cold and ugly, the sofas and chairs revealing their real selves of henna and nasty green where all summer long the flowered linen covered them, now bare, and resigned to winter, marched Agnes, bound upstairs with the armful of rugs. Hennie, looking through a desk drawer, was apologetic. "I was meaning, as soon as I had finished neatening this drawer, I was going to pick up those rugs." To show her heart was in the right place, her intentions unexceptionable, and only lack of time her enemy, she left the desk and fell on a rank of sofa pillows and began shaking them and gathering them up. "Hadn't these better go out in the sun too till just before we leave?"

"They were out all morning, madam." Agnes's voice was not impatient at all. "They had a thurrel airing." She added, with kindness, that Mrs. Stacpole hadn't noticed because she had been so busy. They both loved this fiction; each in her different way forgave Hennie for never lifting a finger if she could help it. "She's so easygoing," her many friends often said. "I do think it's wonderful. So relaxed, though do you suppose Laurence really likes it when his shirt buttons come popping off? But it must be wonderful to be so easygoing. You'd think she'd be fat, wouldn't you?" they asked each other, with a little something in their voices that sounded like regret, "but she isn't." Now Agnes said everything was getting done in good time today.

How nice she is, thought Hennie; she actually doesn't want me to feel I'm not working just as hard as she is, and of course I am, from time to time, in my way; and besides, I've always noticed she admires me most when

I'm being most myself, and that's *not* when I'm exerting myself. The two tall women smiled at each other and Agnes went on her way with her armful.

It never pays to leave postage stamps in a drawer at the sea over the winter. No matter how pleased and surprised one may cunningly plan to be upon finding them there the following June, stamps themselves can't be trusted and will stick to anything, even to each other, in order to cause annoyance. Hennie gathered hers up and put them in her handbag. She straightened piles of Peru, Indiana, letter paper with "Mrs. Laurence Stacpole, Rambler Cottage, Flanders Point, Connecticut" printed in deepest ultramarine, observing how far fewer envelopes remained than sheets—one of the simple facts of life, this. She savingly wound up short lengths of string and then dropped them idly in the scrap basket. The drawer needed dusting out, but the day was nearly over; one can't do everything, and who would notice—not even Agnes—and with a feeling of comfortable guilt she bent her bright head and blew. She smiled; she was really a very pretty woman. She scraped up a thin pile of Laurence's summer letters; very few they were because he came over from town every week end, and mostly they said only, "Tuthill has been at the house this week and fixed that back banister and the cellar door," or "Remind me on Friday the cottage is out of gin or maybe you'd get it if you think of it?" And because, as it happened, he had not met with some terrible accident on the forty-five miles of road between their two houses, neither coming up on the Friday afternoon nor on the return trip early Monday morning, she now felt it safe to drop these letters in the scrap basket on top of the string, whereas if anything had happened to him on Route 80 she would have preserved them forever; each one so dear and ordinary would have been a springboard for tears. The papers slid with a thin slithery whisper down the basket Agnes had already emptied for the winter. Dear Laurence. She hoped she had remembered to buy the gin, that time.

If she had been alone she would have drifted back into the sun, out of the sullen cottage, but with the servants there she had to appear to do her share. "Me, the last Puritan," she said, though it was the last thing she believed, and went to start in on the bedroom off back beyond the kitchen which was occupied by a maid, every year a different one, who came to her for the summer from New London and in September vanished thither, while Agnes and Gino, though they hadn't spoken to each other for eleven years, stayed in town together to look after Laurence and the house. Delicacy caused Hennie, every year at cottage closing time, to assign the final picking up of this room to herself; Agnes always offered to; Hennie always replied, "Oh, thank you very much; no. I will."

She called upstairs to the trotting feet, "I'll be out in the back bedroom downstairs if you want me."

"I can see to that one, madam, when I'm through up here."

"I'll do. Goodness knows what's out there, she was such an odd soul, and I never did find out anything about her, all summer."

"Know nothing—fear nothing," Agnes intoned, passing the head of the stairs, her arms brackets for a pile of folded chintz.

"Yes, I suppose that's true. Oh, I hate to have to close up this place, a day like this."

"It's the warmpth."

"The what?"

"It's just the warmpth," Agnes repeated tenderly, peering down through the banisters, "just like summer."

The maid's bedroom smelled cold when she opened the door and walked in. On the north side, it was never entered by the sun that poured all summer down the face of the cottage. There was little to be done here; nothing, really. Irma from New London, like the Irmas and Berthas of other years, had removed all trace of herself. The room smelled like cold soapsuds and, mysteriously, like faint cigars. "Couldn't be, though," Hennie said. "That is, I hope not." She pushed shut a top drawer with her hip, and pulled down the one window shade. What had the woman thought about all that long summer, this summer's Irma? Already Hennie could scarcely recall the blunt features. There was no clue in this room. Know nothing—fear nothing. She picked up the scrap basket and peered solemnly in, thinking to find there some revealing spoor, but what was in it was simply nothing, not even a hairpin or a chewing-gum wrapper, only a floating sweetish smell. If she had expected to come on Latvian love letters, she was disappointed. Setting the basket back on the floor she jostled the spindly, painted summer-cottage bedside table, and at once a big tin alarm clock tottered a few eager steps forward and started itself up in a loud sycophant flurry of ticks and hiccoughs. "Pressed for time?" she inquired. She stood looking down at it. "Nasty thing that you are, so sly and shiny." Faster and faster it went, beneath her scrutiny, getting itself all worked up. What had this clock been to Irma, half-friend, half-enemy, or all enemy, screaming her out of her sleep in the early mornings? Quarter past five, it chattered, and she glanced at her gold wrist watch; quarter past five too; what an odd thing!

Hennie was visited with a sadness for her own fine, empty summer, so recently over. "Or did I have it at all?" Oh, the fine, empty summer she had had, or supposed she had had. All at once she found herself remembering what she had criminally forgotten, or ignored, since childhood—a conviction that by some very simple act of faith or disdain one could spread out one's living sideways so that instead of having to move relentlessly into the narrow banked-up walls of the future, the tunnel of time, with one's past out behind in a snail trail, one could travel sideways too, running freely in meadows beside the path. There was no tunnel. "We make our own tunnel. My life's slipping sideways," she had called this feeling when she was ten; it included an amused belief in one's limitless power, the ability to do anything at all no matter how unlikely or dangerous, the power to perform magic, and was always accompanied in its early moments by a joyful trembling in the abdomen.

"Why has it come back now?" she wondered, and at once relentlessly it began fading; that gay irradiation of body and spirits faded, faded. What was it, exactly, that had just been? Gone, whatever it was. "But don't I want it back?" She frowned in the effort of recapture, and the effort made her frown, and frowning made her put up her hands to smooth away the furrow. "Wrinkles," she rebuked herself.

The cold stale block of air that was this maid's room left her no hope but that the great, gold-colored months were gone. What a mistake for the sycophant clock to imply it thought it was continuing a job she or anyone else wanted done, but its word had been heeded so long and now here it was, and it must become reconciled to neglect for nine months until another Irma came who would jump to its command; its voice would be ignored now for a while, and for it there would be no tomorrow morning. "I must say I shouldn't blame it if its alarm went off *whang,* any minute now, out of exasperation; or perhaps it will wait slyly and do it the exact moment, pretty soon now, when the car turns out of the drive. I fear it will. It will scream with pique in the empty house; that I couldn't bear."

Hennie seized up the chattering cold thing and shook it; it clacked hysterically back at her. She flipped up the window shade, pushed the window full open, and hurled it out into the blue day. Oh, what a fine cast, the best and truest she had ever seen a woman do! The clock sailed through the air to crash square against the trunk of a tree and burst. Parts went tinkling into the grass, sounding like the death of a thousand Christmas tree ornaments. Gino, his face questioning and shocked, appeared in the doorway.

"Hello there, Gino," Hennie greeted him, very gay. His head lowered and he turned away. She called after him that they were going now.

The station wagon hummed its way westward carrying three people with work-dry hands and tired shoulders; tomorrow their hips would ache, Hennie's more out of sympathy than because of actual toil in which, she would be the first to admit, she had not seriously indulged. Gino drove. It was fair to ask this of him as Hennie had driven over in the morning, and presumably, because he was a man, though a very small one, he wasn't now as tired as she should have been. The protocol of motoring with these two was complicated by their not speaking, so she always drew Agnes after her into the middle seat, because of a clear recollection of one drive, years ago, of mile after mile of nervously watching the backs of their two heads not once turning to each other in friendly talk, not one word escaping out of either of them, even by chance; they were so wary-jealous; it had been too much for Hennie. Which of them had come first into the Stacpoles' service she had by now forgotten and would by no means have dared to inquire of either of them because of the fifty per cent chance of hurt feelings, and which of them it had been who decided the other was not fit to be spoken to, either at once upon first meeting, or shortly thereafter when some quarrel had touched off the long silence, the family had never known. "A state of armed neutrality," she sometimes explained to her friends, unaware of the pleasures of the live, bitter feud wordlessly flourishing belowstairs in quarrels that were born, lived, and slowly died, but left, each succeeding one, a bitter rime like receding liquid in a dish that is often filled and never washed.

Agnes's garbage tin, just emptied, would be returned to the kitchen too soon and mar the still damp, scrubbed linoleum floor—Gino's ploy; a window screen fitted in at spring cleaning time and induced to stick just enough so an average woman could never open it without tearing her fingernails—Gino again; the tin from the cat's food thrown into the garbage instead of the trash, whence it must loathesomely be fished out—that was Agnes's inspiration, as was the cellar door left bolted from the kitchen side so Gino, arriving at eight in the morning had to go the long way around to get in the house because nothing on earth would make him call to Agnes to let him through. Oh, the materials and opportunities for annoyance were wonderfully endless—the pantry window left unlocked after washing; *any*body could crawl in and murder Agnes from behind as she sat at the kitchen table with her cup of tea! They never spoke of each other to the Stacpoles. One would have supposed each ran the house singlehanded.

Sometimes the Stacpoles decided they wouldn't stand it another minute. "It's a lucky thing you're home with a cold," Hennie had said once to her son Will, who was sitting up in bed with a huge glass of lemonade, running a dinky toy truck along the gentle curved complaisant spine and tail of his best friend, Stockinette, drowsing on the bed beside him. "I have to go to New York tomorrow, and if the upholstery man calls you answer it, will you, and ask him to come and pick up the library sofa, because if Agnes answered Gino would never be told to help, and he's lame. The man, I mean. So you tell Gino. It's intolerable, really, isn't it? Only, they're both so wonderful."

Will had said, with a glance upward, at the same time running the truck all the way down to the tip of Stockinette's extended tail, "It's because he's shorter'n she is."

Hennie ran the house by blandly telling everybody in it, as though they were all half-witted, all the same things, days before they were due to occur and whether or not all of them needed to know.

"Why should I care if Pearl is coming an extra half-day next week?" Laurence would demand, with lifted eyebrows. "I'll be at the bank and what possible—"

"But, darling, you never know; there just might be some chain of circumstances, I can't think what, but there might. Say Agnes was the only one home and no one had remembered to tell Gino to go to the Green to meet Pearl on her bus and you just happened to be home for some reason, *you* could tell him to!"

"Where would you be?"

"I might be upstairs lying down," she answered, feeling sorry for herself, "with a blinding headache, unable to speak."

"Look, we've been married twenty-one years and I've never yet known a time when you were—when you had a blinding headache."

"I know; isn't it almost miraculous, when so many poor people do? I do think I'm terribly lucky. Well, then, does everyone know Pearl is coming an extra half-day next week to iron the guest-room counterpanes?"

Sometimes the maneuver of total alerting resulted in cases of numb nonlistening by the family, so that each one quite honestly believed, nor hesitated to assert, that he hadn't been told a word about where to have the big potted camellia set down if he happened to be the one to open the door to the nurseryman's ring. But with Agnes and Gino the system worked closer to perfection; neither of them ever forgot anything, as it would have been too much of a triumph for the other, the enemy; neither one could endure the thought of the quiet smile of triumph the other might be seen giving. Hennie said she believed this system was the only way to manage. "But sometimes the silence frets me," she said. "It's as though I were going deaf."

"But they both talk to you," Laurence said, "so it isn't really like being deaf at all."

"Deaf as a post," said she.

Sometimes, just before taking her afternoon off, Agnes would have to write a little note to Mrs. Stacpole, and this she would leave on the hall table, and Gino, passing through on his way to polish doorknobs would see it and smile a secret, small, triumphant smile. "Hunk," he would murmur to himself, delighted.

This evening the station wagon purred along smoothly in the dampening air. Hennie felt terribly well. From a condition of delicious slight aching she looked out with renewed admiration upon the sunset-lighted fields fleeing past. She knew quite well that if she took the trouble to she could stretch out an arm that would be twenty yards long and run the inside of her fingers over a space of marsh grass as soft as plush, or, from rising ground, nip up between delicate giant thumb and finger a whole tree growing isolated, nip it up by its trunk, its top a vast bouquet; it would come up out of the ground as easily as weeding up a piece of sorrel in the spring, and with the same sound, the faintest tearing. The nameless organ in the throat that trembles and dilates when one is overtaken with unreasonable joy swelled up in her. She laid her hand across where she thought it was, but there was nothing to feel; it was all inside. To herself she said, "It seems to me—haven't I been missing something, and wasting time? I'm stodgy. Oh dear, stodgy. We both are, Laurence and me both. We take everything for granted and I believe that's what is meant when people speak of the unforgivable sin. I've always supposed it had something to do with sex and was a secret everybody knew but me. Now I see it's merely not seizing the world with glee. I must immediately tell Laurence."

Her stomach muscles commenced to tremble and if alone she would have sung, but the proximity to her knee of Agnes's suitable light gray tweed coat and the so-well-known back of Gino—thick black hair cut short on a round head, a rim of leather collar around a small neck, small neat brown leather shoulders—all these accustomed sights inhibited song.

"—What was that?"

"What was what, madam?"

"I thought I saw a shadow of something on the road." She glanced behind; nothing. It had been a giant's shadow, striding. When she looked ahead the air and sky were more brilliant than ever, the air palpitating pink over the evening mist rising along the land.

"Nothing there, madam."

And, of course, there wasn't. Hennie glanced apologetically at the stiff back of Gino, who never apologized. All at once she laughed out, remembering the clock sailing through the air, ticking away at five-fifteen. I tried to throw away time, she marveled, and Gino, hearing that laugh, became, if possible, even more motionless, silent, and disapproving, and Agnes turned politely toward her, waiting to be told the joke, if there was one. When no words followed the peal of laughter, Agnes turned back and gazed out the window, acquiescent to silence. "Oh, the hell with them; I believe I could fly," Hennie said to herself, "if only these two weren't here. The car and I together, tired as I am, could take off from right here in the road, and go sailing over the countryside, swooping toward the West; the wheels would start whirring faster, and then up we'd go. I've always been able to fly; I've never worked at it, that's all. All my life I could have been flying."

The sun, sinking fast, sheened through plumes of milkweed floss on ends of sticks, then struck only in the tops of trees, and then, higher up, on a plane's wing, a single sequin. The cooling air poured in the windows past Hennie's sun-dried and reddened cheeks. She turned to Agnes and embarrassed her. "When you were a child didn't *you* believe you could fly, if you tried?"

"Fly, madam?" The scanty eyebrows climbed the candid brow. She made a token effort to recall any such delusion, failed, and was not surprised. "I can't say as I ever reelly thought about any such thing," she said. "In Perth," she explained kindly, "there never was so much talk about aireoplanes, that I can remember."

In the living room Laurence Stacpole, in the absence of his wife and entire domestic staff, thought to let down the slatted blinds through which no one would ever glimpse Venice, nor anything like her, but before he could recall which way it was Hennie insisted the slats must be—whether overlapping like the plates on an armadillo or flat open like the blinds of restaurants with liquor licenses—and as he was manipulating the cord this way and that, he observed the return of the station wagon.

"We're dead," Hennie announced, coming in. He smiled, seeing how lively she looked, and wondering how it was possible anyone could. The very idea of cleaning out a summer cottage tired him. Close the door and come away would be his method of dealing with the inevitable end of summer. Kissing her, he felt the day's golden bloom and some little house dust on her skin; knowing her, he knew she had spent most of the day doing nothing, and if tired, was so only in sympathy with Agnes and Gino. "Completely dead." She collapsed slowly backward into a soft chair as if to remain for hours, groaned, and placed her tired long legs, toes up, aching heels to the floor, straight out in front of her. "It *was* a long day. I'm not really tired, only Agnes always politely tells me I must be. Oh, it was lovely! I hated to come away. The garden looked better than it did all summer, deceiving wretch; you never saw so many petunias, and they've grown huge since we left. If I take a bath now I'll fall asleep in the hot water, but anyway dinner will be late, so—" She glanced around, but her dazzled eyes still saw only the beds of glistening sprawling purple flowers, and the sun-struck sea. For a moment she leaned forward, observing him closely, with her long golden dusty fingers clasped in her lap. Then she struggled up and went away. "I must tell you something," she called back.

"Tell me what?"

"I'll tell you later. We're going to make our life over. Got to."

He was glad dinner would be late. It would give him an unforeseen space of time in which to write a long-overdue letter to his pair of great-aunts in Vermont. "Dear Aunt Effie and Aunt Sadie, or Dear, dear Aunts, Effie and Sadie," he said, moving toward the desk. And after that? One couldn't say, "I often think how remarkable it is of both of you to still be alive; how do you do it?" though that was what came into his mind whenever he thought of them at all. He and Hennie always told the children it was weak-minded and essentially rude, too, to begin letters with apologies, so he must not start off "I've been meaning to write you but." The Stacpoles had an English friend who always began her letters with the desperate phrase, "I am determined to finish this letter before tea!" He paused by the table and selected a pipe from a Lowestoft bowl and set to filling it. Would they like to hear about the current loan his bank was contemplating granting in order to expedite the happy merger of two shaving-soap companies? Or how his new stenographer was working out? Not too well, he would have to report; she giggled in the back office. Or, on a strictly personal level, that he was very much afraid he ought to buy a new brown hat before winter set in? But they lived so far away they hadn't seen his old one yet. He tamped in the tobacco and veered off on a search for matches. How pleasant to have this unexpected interval toward the end of a busy day. He might tell them about one of his more emotional depositors who had planned to cut his lady love right out of his will with a pair of scissors until persuaded otherwise by the bank's new trust officer, Edward Latham; but after a little consideration, he decided not to. "Dear Aunt Effie and Aunt Sadie, The weather here is being surprisingly normal for late September. Hennie has been over at Flanders Point cleaning the cottage all day and has returned full of mysteries and secrets. How is it with you two in Center Sandwich? Cold yet? I don't suppose the maples have begun to turn color yet, have they?" No, no, no. Better not to write at all.

Not even looking toward the desk again he took up a book, sat where Hennie had briefly sat, and flipped up and over the ribbon marker. The lending club they belonged to glued a length of red ribbon in each of their books. This looked well but tended to cause some trouble, some acrimony, when two members of a family were simultaneously reading the same book, one daytime, the other in the evening. He thought he might suggest to the committee they glue in two ribbons, blue for the wife and red for the husband, and this would eliminate the irritating question "Have you come to the part yet where the younger son has to leave—but perhaps you haven't, so I had better not say anything to spoil it, or the awful part where—no, no, I won't ask." "Ask me!" was the invariable reply. Two ribbons would do away with all this.

His pipe traveled slowly across from one corner of his mouth to the other. He settled deeper and found his place, page ninety, near the bottom. A door upstairs opened and shut, and in the brief interval he heard a loud hot waterfall rushing into a bathtub. The children were somewhere in the house, but silent, and silently, in established mutual acrimony, in the back premises Agnes and Gino went about their evening jobs.

The pages of the book turned calmly, regularly; the younger son left home, thereby earning Laurence's approval though the boy's mother was in floods of tears for half a chapter. Upstairs Hennie slid deeper into hot water where a scent of lavender rose with the steam, and closing her eyes saw colored pictures of blue and purple flowers larger than life, and beyond them meadows, a countryside she had never known, wide and inviting slopes peopled by giants and lovely strangers. Agnes stalked into the pantry to leave the picnic basket, the thermos bottles washed and laid on their sides to dry beside their corks, and Gino, happening through on his way to the cellar saw them, and his eyes brightened and he rammed in the corks, a thing absolutely forbidden in that household, and put them away in their cupboard; when next they were wanted their insides would smell old. He continued on his way, happy, and Agnes smiled to see him, knowing that when he reached the foot of the cellar stairs he would come on the vacuum cleaner with its bag a great bloat of dust. She had left it there early in the morning of that very busy day. "Ah-ha," she now said, within, "all right for him!" and clapped five lamb chops on the broiler.

"But you have no normal curiosity," Hennie complained, wielding her hairbrush, yawning into her dressing-table mirror, which had a frame of Venetian glass, blue blown lilies and green leaves and little nameless flowers in amethyst and amber.

"About what? Yes, I think I have."

"I told you when I came in I had something to tell you. I had some kind of a mystic revelation today at Flanders Point; almost mystic. I shouldn't wonder if I weren't mystic myself, a bit." She leaned to peer at her sun-reddened cheeks and then turned solemnly and gazed at him as he slowly, yawning too, divested himself of his long brown trousers and started in on his shirt buttons. "I know it's hard to understand when I'm not explaining very well because of being sleepy, but all of a sudden I simply hurled the cook's clock outdoors and remembered how wonderful it felt to be a child with everything, everything still possible. Don't you remember that feeling? And whatever I've looked at since then has looked much brighter; I noticed kind of a halo around a hydrant as we came along State Street. We lead terribly quiet lives, don't we? Oh, we do—when all the time we could be living sideways."

"How long did you say you'd been having this uncomfortable feeling?"

"I told you! Just since I threw Bessie's clock. Irma's. It was five-fifteen. And years ago, of course, and so must you have, once. It isn't uncomfortable, and it's not a disease after all, and now it will last forever, because the fact is, my eyes have been opened." When he asked to what as he took out his cuff links, she said it was to the fact she was a captive, and went on, a shade impatiently, "I may hardly know what to do with my eyes open but I thought surely you'd help me. I'm trapped, unless I can learn how to use them; you can see that, I hope. I did think you'd be fascinated! I can't discuss it with the children, not with Clare mooning after her loved one; and Will's too young. But I'm going to do something about it, even if you are only a stick-in-the-mud." Laurence saw himself, a dry limb off a tree, probably an elm, upended in a brown sea. "I have plans," she went on. "Or if they aren't plans, they're intentions," she said, looking at him through the neck of her nightgown.

"Ah," he said. He sat down and removed his brown socks.

"*Well?*"

He regarded her gravely, and then the look of speculation softened down, slowly, like a heap of brown sugar on a plate, into amusement and love. "Don't let's reform the world."

"I wasn't going to," she assured him, reasonably. "I have *no* desire to do good. I only want you and me to live more fully."

"Ah," he said again, and padded into his clothes closet after his pajamas. From the depths his voice came, comfortable and quiet. "This won't last."

"Forever!" Sharply she put down her hairbrush. "Oh, I do think men are extraordinary."

He emerged. "All men or just me?"

But how could *all* men be, she asked crossly, and hopped into bed. "It would be a mathematical impossibility."

A quarter-hour passed before she waked him up.

"Darling, you need stirring up," she whispered lovingly, urgently. There was no reply. She waited a moment and then she was considerably surprised to hear what she said next, that perhaps she would leave him for a while because they had become so used to each other. "We might as well be a hundred years old."

"We nearly are—our combined ages."

"Oh, don't say so!" she cried, hiding her face with her hand in the dark. "That I can't bear to hear," came out from between her fingers. "We must try—"

But he interrupted. "I had supposed we were going to have a good, quiet fall," he complained from his bed.

"Quieter than other falls?"

"No, no; just a nice ordinary quiet fall."

She sighed with gusto. "And we already so sot, and

dull. What have we got between us? Comfort only. I've been thinking about it *all evening,* and the fact undeniably is we don't lead life to the full. We need romance, and tragedy, and a stirring up. How can you bear to keep on coming back to me every evening? I don't see how you can stand it, frankly. Don't you ever—"

He said no, he never did.

"You don't know what I was going to say."

"Nevertheless I— What's got into you?"

All at once she gave a tremendous long yawn. Then she laughed sleepily, turned over, and buried her face in her pillow. "Tomorrow," she promised.

CHAPTER TWO

There it was still, an unaccountable elation welling up in that organ unknown to science, situated at the base of the throat, generating glee that went spreading and spreading and glowing through the body that lay so flat in bed. She had wondered, rather hoped it might drain away in the night, but she had no more than opened her eyes, certainly had not yet managed to focus them, and for the second time in twenty-four hours she was seized; not since adolescence nor before, she thought; so why now, this year, this September, again this morning?

In a minute she was wide-awake and dying for the day to begin, hankering for its delights, for the laminated multitudinous doings of her very simple life, which she had every intention now of complicating to bursting point. The blind-pull wagged in the window in the early breeze. Over in the next bed was the hump, the long barrow, that she had every reason to suppose was Laurence. Far from being a partner in her pristine elation, he appeared to be not even awake, and she reached a stealthy hand and as quietly as possible clicked off his electric blanket, thus disposing in the one gesture of a shred of treachery in having switched him on in the middle of the night when he had begun to snore, for she maintained she was the discoverer of a new etiological principle—that electric blankets can quell the human snore, and occasionally she speculated aloud about selling her discovery to General Electric for some vast sum. Laurence had said if this would entail a full-page colored photograph of himself in bed in the advertising pages of *Good Housekeeping* he would prefer to increase her allowance right away now, even retroactively, he said, back to the moment when she had been taken with this preposterous belief, because, of course, there was nothing in it; had she observed, he asked, how having the blanket turned on under Stockinette made her purr all the harder? The principle must be the same; in fact the human snore was nothing more nor less than a lovable sort of great human purr denoting comfort and well-being. Hennie had replied how kind and generous of him, though perhaps kindness was not his motive, but she thought her allowance was really sufficient for her few and simple wants. "Not but what it is true about your snoring," she had said. "I've proved it time and again. You don't snore a bit like purring, either, if you must know; it's more as though you might be strangling; and isn't it my duty to bequeath this piece of new knowledge to the world? Think of all the wives—oh," she had said, her blue eyes large and philanthropic, "*think* of all the wives!" This morning she stretched, sloping her toes away beneath the far reaches of pale blue China silk crisscrossed with lace; she yawned with anticipation; her cream-pink arms rose up in the cool early air, and waved about. When he woke she would try him again; last evening's unresponsiveness had been only normal, banker's fatigue.

The alarm in Laurence's clock sprang off with its insane rattle, and he reared up, dealt with it, staggered in sleepy half-circles, and disappeared to shave. She got up then to pursue him, though customarily she lay dozing until he was fully dressed and going out the door into the hall. "I'm awake," she would say as he carefully folded his fingers around the china doorknob painted with violets and roses. "You don't need to creep."

But this morning she rose at once and sailed after him to the bathroom, the cool air from the windows buoying out her thin nightgown behind her; it swayed and danced behind her legs. Laurence was leaning, yawning, propped up against the bowl; just above the porcelain rim a tiny convexity showed; perhaps it was only his pajamas; forty-five is *nothing*. "Whereas in our grandparents' day, it was so different," she said. "No longer young, the phrase was." Above a soap beard, untimely white, his sleepy eyes looked out at her, reproachfully. What are *you* so brisk about, so early, they seemed to ask. Even to her, so full of blind enthusiasm, he scarcely seemed in receptive mood at all; best to postpone philosophic discussion.

She wondered if, perhaps, all these years he had preferred her to stay late in bed; all these years she needn't have been feeling guilty about not getting up when his clock yelled at him. Looking at his long cheek, sloped away from her, it seemed he'd prefer she was a slugabed and left the bathroom to him. I suppose I do look unnaturally lively this morning, for so early in the day. Poor Laurence. She merrily drew a bath and let her nightgown fall. He closed his eyes and yawned, a yawn so vast the razor had to wait a while, suspended in air. Seeing this, she too yawned, she couldn't help it, a long deep refreshing satisfying gape before she stepped into the tub.

"What—" she began before the yawn was quite finished with her, "what do you think we—" but Laurence might just as well have been not there, or still sleeping in his bed. In and out of the shower cabinet he plodded and back to the bedroom to dress. She slid herself down long in the tub and lay musing at her bobbing, floating feet far away down by the silver taps, hearing him pull open drawers and cupboard doors; presently he began to hum in an early-morning monotone, so she roused up to dry herself and soon, stark naked except for the layer of cold cream she was applying to her face and throat she opened the door into the bedroom and emerged, inquiring, "Well now, if you're awake, how much *do* you think we ought to let your mother pay for Clare's beaver jacket?"—straight into the bright aghast stare of Gino, bent over, trapped, emptying morning wastebaskets; but as for Laurence, he was nowhere to be seen.

Hennie stood at an upstairs window and watched Laurence's long back going down the early-morning street. Well-tailored, she always thought; extremely well-tailored, and then wondered why she was compelled to qualify perfectly good adjectives with "extremely" and "awfully" and "very." "But," she argued aloud to the retreating brown sharkskin shoulders, "if I said about you 'I have a well-tailored husband,' just like that, *tout court*, it sounds so halfhearted; it sounds derogatory, even. But I am an *extremely* happy woman," she said, knowing it to be true, "a very, very, very, very happy woman, only—" She leaned her forehead against the water-blue-white of the glass and smiled at the last of Laurence going off to the bank down the sunny street. She felt as warm and silky and lithe as Stockinette. "But I could love several husbands all at once, all at the same time, and do it very well. It's terrible, how satisfied I've been and not known it. I must go away. Oh, I'm fit to fly. What shall I do with myself? I'm fit to be tied, as Granny used to say," she went on extravagantly. "Is this, am I, me?" Her brow was bent to the glass.

Am I me? She had speculated about that long ago in school days but not recently, not since she could recall. How do I know, she used to demand, standing half-dressed in the bathroom thirty years ago, early mornings; how do I know I'm Hennie? Was that person me yesterday who roller-skated home from school? It may be, she had slyly said, standing outside herself, that child was some other child tearing along with her blue and white checked skirt whipping out behind, some other child, perhaps a dummy who looks exactly like me so even the family couldn't tell who was coming back from school with her skate wheels sounding like turning pumice stones, and later last evening was that I, me, Hennie, who did all that algebra homework? How do I know? What way is there to be sure? There may be a conspiracy, she used to warn herself, leaning limp and suspicious against the tepid bathroom radiator, with long brown ribbed lisle stockings dangling, one in each hand. Everybody else knows about who I really am except me, *and I amn't me*; what's more, I never have been, but they aren't going to tell me so. Who, then? Do I exist at all or have I merely made myself up? It may be that I am me only to myself and if I ran away this morning, if I simply did not appear at breakfast no one would say anything because the table isn't set up with a place for me unless I go to the dining room, and then it is, magically, in an instant, by unseen hands. But if I went, the hole where I am would close over. She would bend over and sadly draw on the long, long, odious stocking, a trickle of tears running down inside her throat. Maybe they want me to go; maybe they're just waiting.

There was also the distinct possibility, gayer and more plausible, that she was a princess, but they weren't going to tell her for a while; for some royal reason she was being tried in the comfortable crucible of ordinary upper middle-class American life; she was captive, and hadn't till now suspected it. But by the time she had arrived at that phase of brooding the very suggestion she was a changeling had displaced and dissipated the earlier, emptier, more mystical wondering, and she would go down to breakfast smug and merry, as befitted a future queen who already knew a thing or two unsuspected by her subjects. If the family she lived with wasn't going to tell her she was royalty in ambush, she wasn't going to tell them she knew it.

When she was younger still her best friend had been an ancient trolley conductor, and she had kept a nickel sternly inviolate for years in her couchant camel china bank, ready for running away with him from her perfectly happy home, when need arose. What the need might be she never stopped to think, but it was always possible her family might begin treating her like the Poor Little Match Girl. She had been accustomed to dally on the granite curb at the corner where the end of the line was, on the lookout for Tom O'Shea, planning: Naturally, I won't go away today, but tomorrow I will. She would loiter there, bending first one and then the other toe into the gutter to wet the leather in the shallow stream that sometimes ran there carrying along with it elm twigs, or yellow-green ailerons from maples; an occasional dry curled brown beech leaf veered by like a ship, and she would squint, seeing herself tiny, and say, "I'll go off on that and not wait for the trolley." Winters, the stream had ice on it and she would slide, though forbidden, waiting for the huge high ocher car to charge up the avenue and come to its screeching stop. Tom O'Shea, with sparse silver hair and a thousand red threads in the cheeks below his watery blue eyes, would descend, and limp over, watch in hand, to spend his five minutes with her. The motorman would come out too, and switch around the pole preparatory to the trip back downtown, but without speaking to the two friends on the curb. She never told Tom about the nickel she had at home, and the red necktie she gave him every Christmas she gave out of pure love, but she kept the possibility always in mind that circumstances might bring on the moment when she would turn to him to be her confederate, when she would take the hand that did not hold the watch and mount the three trolley steps at his side, not even looking back at the house she had been born in.

All these artificially induced alarms and unconsummated excursions had been so long ago they might have been in another life, a low-ceilinged life of simple red and blue, trolley-car yellow, snow white, right and wrong, early bed, an intimate tent of sky encompassing all, a faraway-back small life with a dignity of its own and its days as long as weeks were now, an existence tucked off safely forever behind the long-legged years of adolescence and a twenty-year stretch of marriage—so what was there about the last twenty-four hours to call back these old emotions, all that illogical wondering, and particularly, how now account for her glee that had been pouring back over her, taking away her breath, ever since the bursting of the cook's clock?

"I should have gone with Tom O'Shea. One adventure per life is not too many."

Possibly she was now experiencing a premature second childhood; second childhood brought the picture of old men with walking sticks sitting in the sun on benches by the doors of alehouses—always alehouses—and aching bones and witless giggling and fast-falling teeth, and truisms propounded in a Yorkshire dialect. Forty-three, in Connecticut, was surely far too young for all that, though next year it was quite possible she might begin to fade off. She looked ahead; in the spring she would be forty-four. The erect, forbidding, identical numerals, like a section of fencing, stood there already, a barrier, waiting for her to come up to them. If she put her finger on one of them, any one at random, which year would it have been? 1939, say. She couldn't for the life of her recollect one minute of it; or had it been the year she had planted lilacs beyond the garden in the back yard? But that could have taken scarcely more than one afternoon, not even that if she had had Gino to help her, but whether he had been with them then she couldn't say.

If it can't be premature second childhood beginning, then it must be an unfinished figment of one of my previous early selves floating up to the surface like a floating rib. How she and her friends had gone on when, in an elementary physiology class in the sixth grade, they had first heard of floating ribs. "Oh horrors!" they had said, turning, appalled, to look at each other. "What if it floats off and gets jammed in crosswise among the other parts of you? How do you feel today? I'm beginning to feel funny; I think I am." They had laid their hands against their navy-blue serge middy blouses and waited gravely to hear the first, faint grinding of their wandering bones.

"But I don't want to recall my entire past this morning." She moved away from the window. Clare came along the hall and she called her in. "I'm frightfully energetic," she said, beginning to pick up and deal with clothes and pillows. "I'm going to lead a much broader life from now on, darling; see more and stranger people, really *live*, so let's do something different with ourselves today. I'm lunching with Olivia, but when I come back let's get in the car and drive to—oh, Danbury, for instance, for tea." Danbury, forty miles away, sounded as remote and romantic as Florence.

"*Dan*bury?" Clare looked doubtful. "Why there, especially?"

"No reason. Or anywhere. Something wonderful might happen to us. I must set about seeing life, and I feel *capable of change*." She paused with a folded sweater held against her breast and looked hopefully at her child. Maybe Clare, delicately approached, would be more understanding than Laurence. She was younger, but wasn't she more subtle of mind? Only a few years, a scarce handful, intervened between now and those same relative years of childhood and adolescence that Hennie had been recalling, and as she remembered herself at those ages she had been so sensitive anybody could have snapped her like a twig.

"Mummy, is there some specially good tea place there, that you know about, or what?"

"Who knows? There might be or there might not be,

but we could go and see. I am so very foot-free. Yes, I remember, there is a tea sort of place, an old mill, out beyond in the country."

Clare then asked relentlessly if they would be home by five o'clock.

"Of course not." Hennie laid the folded apricot sweater on a shelf.

"Then I'm afraid I can't go. I'm awfully sorry. It sounds fun, but there's a film club showing of Emil Jannings I happen to be going to."

"Then I'll go to that instead. No, no I won't," she quickly said, seeing Joseph Wood, three dimensional and carrying a brief case full of homework, in Clare's round brown eyes. "I won't go near the place," she promised. "Quite the opposite, whatever that may be. Dear, dear," she sighed, as she treed some lizard pumps, "I don't know what's got into me as my grandmother used to say. 'What's got *into* you, deary?' she used to say, and if I did something really wicked, like kicking your uncles, who were so much smaller, she would say, 'What *made* you do that, deary?' In a way, people weren't thought to be as responsible for themselves in those days as they are now. Perhaps Granny believed in the devil." She wasn't surprised to have Clare observe that must have had its advantages. "Oh, I don't know. People were no wiser then than now. As for me, I am merely slightly frantic and can't think what to do about it. It's just this feeling I could move mountains; you know?" Her voice was apologetic. "I do hope you never have this trouble, my poppet. I do apologize for this absorption in myself, and

I know it's unbecoming in a middle-aged woman, but what can I do about it?"

In her flower-wreathed mirror, in a flash no longer than a wink of light on the top of her gold lipstick case, she saw Clare at forty-five; saw her absolutely. She was quite handsome. And you too, Hennie thought, you too, my darling, will then be going through exactly the uneasiness I am now. The wink of light was gone, and Clare's face was a young girl's face and the voice that said, "Rest," to her mother was charming and solicitous, and a child's voice, uncomprehending and sweet.

"Rest! I don't want to rest! That's the *last* thing! Anyway, from what, I should like to know?" She upended her red calfskin handbag on the dressing table, and everything cascaded out—change purse, billfold, lipsticks, and pencils and little pads of paper; she scooped them all up, blew on them, and transferred them to another handbag.

"Have you told Daddy about this—this upsettedness?"

"Oh, him! He. Yes, I did, twice last evening, especially when we were undressing, and he just yawned and yawned and as much as scratched his stomach in that awful avaricious way he does when he's sleepy, so lux*u*riously, and got into bed."

Clare said then she couldn't suggest anything to her mother at all but just to try and take it easy.

Hennie repeated bitterly, "Take it easy. That's what policemen say to crowds if they've studied psychology—you know what I mean."

"And it always works."

"But I'm not one."

Clare did not reply; someday she was going to grow into a very tactful woman. The idea of Danbury died its natural death.

Hennie sat down on the bench before the dressing table, with her back to the wreathed mirror. "Darling, I've been meaning to say this for some time, but don't you think you are awfully solemn lately? When you were a little girl you were quite a cheery type, but now we do notice, Daddy and I, that you're becoming awfully serious and solemn," Laurence's approval had hitherto been Clare's greatest guerdon; now, his name might not have been spoken. The king is dead, thought Hennie; there is a new king, with a crew cut.

"But things are solemn, aren't they, Mummy? Things that matter, I mean. Jo says they are; things that matter, the way the world *is*, nowadays."

"Yes—no!" From lowered brows they stared at each other, wondering which of them was right, two simple-minded charming women neither one sharp enough to see they both were, as well as both wrong, too. "Well, that's that. I just thought I'd mention it, in case you hadn't noticed." Hennie rose and went deep in among the racks of dresses in her cupboard. "Have a good time at the movies." She covered her ears with a beige dress so she wouldn't have to hear her darling child say she had been told the film was very significant. "There's such a thing as being altogether too significant, and superior, and high-minded," she murmured into the dress, and aloud she called, defiant, from the muting depths of sweet-smelling silk, "Danny Kaye's the man I love," but Clare had gone.

Later that morning Hennie walked downtown for luncheon. The Stacpoles' square white clapboard house, flanked by new three-story apartment houses and Classic Revival mansions stranded from the middle of the last century and now converted to the use of doctors, was only half a dozen blocks from the Green, which was the spiritual if no longer the geographical center of the city. Hennie had left the house earlier than was necessary because she kept encountering Gino and could not bear to meet his eye. She had no way of knowing that neither by any means could he meet hers. Every time they encountered each other there occurred a startling silence. She tried to speak to him about polishing the andirons, glancing away, her eyebrows raised. "Hunk," he said, and she fled, not caring whether the brass were polished or not. By tomorrow he would have forgotten, she assured herself, knowing quite well that he never in this world would. Probably, she humbly thought, he would have preferred catching a glimpse of a short, wide, and swarthy woman with low hips and no waist rather than one who was long and sandy-gold—but he'd hardly had any choice in the matter, poor boy. And I am as I am and no need to feel guilty; quite the contrary, or so Laurence used to imply, and not so long ago either. Now, of course, he's just a stick-in-the-mud.

She walked along briskly, but dreaming, not noticing people or buildings. It can't be, she speculated in a reasonable internal voice, that I am the only person alive who feels like this. I hope it's not merely a form of softening of the brain I've never heard of because I don't keep up with medical discoveries. Her regard lifted and she stared far off as along she went, down one curbstone and up another with no attention for her surroundings but an unconscious twentieth-century respect for the menace of traffic.

"Life going sideways," she muttered, aloud, to the surprise of a boy on a bicycle. I should have kept hard hold of that lovely feeling all the intervening years between childhood and now; if I had, how very, very different my life and my family's life would have been. Freer. But it's wicked, how one is let forget—made to forget. Our days would have been full and golden, and floating half in and half out of reality. She narrowly missed being slain by a Buick. "Oh, don't kill me now," she said to it reproachfully, "not now when I've just had some kind of revelation and am going to redo my entire self. I must find out if anybody else I know ever gets taken this way, if other people are seized this way, and what they do about it, and if they feel like someone *captured*." And she wavered between pride at being bewildered at her time of life and regret at the inconvenience of not knowing what ailed her. She would catechize her friends. She would tell them what she had just learned and they would all follow her.

But when she was seated opposite Olivia in the dimness of the black oak bar of the hotel, she couldn't begin. Olivia's narrow sharkskin suit, her narrow, pale but healthy face and kind dark eyes were so utterly familiar to the regard of her friend that it was ridiculous to suppose she thought of herself as the victim of circumstance. Though one never knew, of course, so Hennie smiled at her with more than usual warmth.

"How are you?" she asked, with an extra degree of significance, lost on Olivia and instantly dissipated, soaked up by the surrounding synthetic, black, black Elizabethan woodwork, beams, tables, rafters, and carvings.

"Fine, I guess, though I thought I had a tickle in my throat earlier this morning. However, all gone now. Two Martinis, please, John; no olive. Did you get the cottage all cleaned and put away?"

Hennie was aware as never before of the shiny brush stroke of the eyebrows across the table, the texture of the throat. Does she see me as sharply, I wonder? I'll never know. It's a terrible thing, but I'll never know. "Clean as a snail shell with the snail gone. Frightfully clean. Horrid. You'd never suspect Clare spent the summer in it getting engaged, if she is engaged, or how Will had been whittling airplanes in every room for months upstairs and down and never picking up one single splinter of them. Isn't balsa wood splendid stuff, though? Never anything like it when we were children."

"Is she, do you think?"

"I'd be the last to know," the girl's mother said, "frankly. Oh, of course that isn't true. I'm fairly sure she is, or not far from it, because she goes around looking glazed, if you know what I mean. She looks as though she were taking in the whole visible world in one great bite, but I believe the absolutely one and only thing she does see is that mouse-colored crew cut, either right before her sitting in a chair a large part of the time, or miles away at law school—a mile and a half, actually."

"You don't like him! I thought you did!"

"Very much indeed; why?"

"Well—*mouse*-colored."

Hennie leaned a patient cheek on her hand. "I think he's divine," she said, taking the liveliest pleasure in supporting her child, "if but a wee bit forbidding, but I daresay he'll mellow in the next forty years. He's extremely worthy, you know. Tidy-minded. Not but what I envy that quality more than I can say, heaven knows. Shall we have chicken sandwiches? Sliced or salad?"

"Not salad. The mayonnaise."

"Of course," agreed Hennie, whose figure could scarcely have been prettier, and, if anything, Olivia was too thin.

"And no top slice of bread," Olivia adjured John the waiter, who had been lurking by for some time. Not many people had been taken that noon with the idea of lunching in that dark bar; even if it had been full it was easy to ignore everyone but one's vis-à-vis across the coarse-grained black wood of the table. "Tell me more," Olivia suggested, full of friendly interest, but Hennie asked what more was there to tell. He was still in law school; there could be no question of their marrying until after he graduated. She eyed the quiet face from across the chilled rim of her glass.

"You tell *me* something," she said quickly, surprised to find her breath a traitor in such a little matter; it had withdrawn itself, now when she needed it. She set down her glass and took a long swallow of air before she was able to ask, "Tell me if you've ever had a most peculiar sensation—" here she gave a too-quick laugh, instantly regretted—"I don't suppose you ever possibly have, but about the way we live, that you and I and everybody in the world, *Persians* even—I know you'll say I'm insane and tell everyone—but could it be that we are all too much, much too terribly tight and small, but that really, right alongside us, but unseen, there are possibilities, like meadows stretching out sideways—" She leaned her rosy tweed elbows on the table and held Olivia's face sternly with her eyes. "Have you? Of course what I'm trying to say is, what do we know about anything? There must be so much floating about that we don't begin to understand. Just lately, actually just since late yesterday afternoon, I have felt capable of finding out more, and so much of what we do, we don't need to, though perhaps that's far off the point of what I—" She was running down. "Or am I merely going mad, do you suppose?"

"Tired, probably," Olivia said, knowing her friend well enough to know how unlikely it would be, and by picking up her fork and delicately nipping out the olive in her glass detaching herself from what Hennie had been hoping all along was a hypnotizing stare.

Hennie cried she wasn't in the least tired; not tired at all; not tired enough; she was searching for something to expend herself on.

"Public service."

"Not that kind of thing. I mean that wouldn't solve

my present problem, present since yesterday, and of course I do do that kind of thing somewhat, collect for the Community Chest, and so on." She turned her water glass by its stem with her finger guiding the base. "And let us never forget the only speech I ever made."

"I have forgotten," her friend told her tranquilly.

"Why, birth control! In Naugatuck. Years ago one horrible hot day in June."

Olivia appeared interested, or if not interested then very polite. "With what result?" she inquired, but Hennie stared at her.

"Would I know? No, none of this is what I'm trying to tell you, you being my dearest friend. We must cause romance to happen, if I make myself clear. I've decided just to go off, right away from everything familiar, for a trial flight." She enveloped Olivia with her smile. "Laurence doesn't believe I will, but I will. You come with me," she urged.

Olivia gave her a grudging, amused, "It sounds nice." Then, sounding almost sarcastic, though that was one thing she never was, "That *would* be wonderful, wouldn't it!"

"Well, if you won't do that, then think, darling, think! Two bright women, we ought to be able to think of something. I don't at all mean opening a shop. But we might take a lover."

"A lover?"

"Two then. It's just a suggestion," she protested.

"No. Impossible. It would take one out of the house so much, wouldn't it; I should suppose so; and my family says I'm never home anyway. No. I think your trouble is you're simply overtired, exhausted from watching Agnes and Gino clean the cottage. All that sand people bring in on their feet all summer, hiding in the cracks. Look, he brought them with olives after all." She neatly ate hers. "Though, of course, don't think I don't know exactly what you mean. I often get so frustrated that I'm fit to be tied. Oh, I think if I have to tell Bertha just one more time to make out two laundry lists! Wouldn't you think she'd do it without being told, considering how many perfect strangers' socks come home every week? But no. And when she cleaned the children's medicine cabinet do you know what she did?" She leaned forward over the table, recounting her life to the absorbed-looking face of her friend, a light-skinned woman in early middle age, to the face tipped sideways, most attentive appearing, of Hennie Stacpole, who was actually hearing not one single word. "You know what she did, she poured all together into the same bottle everything that smelled like cinnamon. Can you imagine? Mouth wash and cough mixture! Neatening up was what she called it." To the waiter, coming along from the kitchen passage with his sparsely filled tray, they appeared equally interested in Olivia's spate of words. "Oh, yak-yak-yak," he murmured tolerantly over the open sandwiches.

Clare, who had been the exact center of the universe for nineteen years, the cast, unique pebble causing surrounding circles to widen in the pool whose edges are eternity, but she, the pebble remaining the only center, beamed across an inconsiderable space of living-room air at the center of his own universe, Joseph Wood, who had dropped in almost unexpectedly after luncheon, and said, "I'm sure, but are *you* sure, Jo?" The space between them closed gradually, the crew cut bent down against the smooth brown hair she had inherited from her father, and he said with conviction, "I have been since way back last June when I was only twenty-three. You know perfectly well!"

"I know," she slowly said, smiling.

Seeing nothing, they gazed together out the living-room window, and if they had been focusing they would have observed brownstone mansions across the street, where black and gold names of otolaryngologists ran down the porch columns, the letters of each name the exact size of all the others, lest jealousy seep in among the swabs and tongue depressors. The only names these two had in mind were their own and each other's, and jealousy with them did not exist. Within themselves, separately, they were marveling—how precarious that they had met at a law school dance far away back one Saturday evening in June; they might so easily not have gone to it; or only one of them might have! She had worn a long pink dress, but who had taken her, and what if he hadn't? Jo couldn't have said who did, and she would have replied, "Well, then, who was it?" if anyone asked her now, and it was nearly true that she couldn't recall that instrumental him; in any case she would have given him absolutely no credit for being fate's instrument. It was inevitable that she and Joseph Wood were to meet, but a matter for catching the breath over still; it was ungrateful to imagine they would not have met, but they were touched at fate's goodness on their behalf, and turning to each other said as much, out loud.

"But have you ever thought," she whispered, "what if we had met all right, in the course of the centuries, but one of us had been terribly much older than the other, what would we have done then? What if you had been in your forties?" She nearly swooned to hear herself, but he stopped her at once, imploring her not to be morbid. He said that was the most completely morbid idea he had ever heard, but when she asked him hadn't he had it too, since meeting her, he said yes, and worse, but what those were he would not say. Then they sighed luxuriously together and pointed out to each other all over again how benevolent Providence could be when she put her mind to it. Then, rather meanly, they said: But Providence had to recognize the inevitable when she saw it.

"But will your family?" he asked, presently.

Her hand slid away from the bare back of his neck. "They'll be very much surprised," she replied, not without a becoming smirk of complacency, "but I'm sure it will be all right because everybody does get married, more or less, so it can't be too frightfully surprising for them, and anyway it won't be for ages—*will it?*"

He shook his head and then reversed its motion and nodded it. "No. I mean, yes, it won't. Have to get those bar exams out of the way first."

"Of course," she agreed, her eyes looking down into her striped gingham lap, her fingers laid alongside his hand, measuring. "Naturally. Look how big your paws are," she said with admiration. "Twice the size of mine. Of course people do get married while they're still in college or law school, or medical school, or wherever. Actually I've known thousands, haven't you?"

He said sternly that indeed he had but, nevertheless, it made for a very poor start in life, a hand-to-mouth start, he said. She tipped her head sideways, a reasonable young woman with an open, inquiring mind. "What is hand to mouth, exactly? It sounds only like someone hiding yawns and so on."

"It must mean living in such small cramped-up space you're all hunched over all the time and uncomfortable and probably you only have room to eat by keeping your elbows on the table and slooping up the food." For some reason this miserable picture brought on both a laughing fit.

"In a cave."

"In a hut!"

"In a pup tent! How would you like me to come crawling home to you every night into a—"

A step crossed the hall, and instantly they became grave. She gave him back his hand at once as though she had no further use for it, smoothed out the gingham lap, and they both sat straight and still, waiting, wary as birds; but the steps came no nearer.

"I guess it was just Mummy back from her luncheon, going into the library. Shall we tell her what we've— we've decided, or shall we wait till Daddy is home too?"

"I think I'd rather wait until I've written my father

about it. I'd much rather, if you don't mind. Anyway, it won't be bothering your family any to wait to hear, seeing they don't suspect."

"Very true. All right. But let's go across and at least tell her you're coming back after the movies for dinner." Clare was so recently delivered from her adolescent self, when to disagree had been instinctive, that to hear herself agreeing with Jo was a positive, conscious pleasure, like getting into a warm deep bath, or like growing tall all at once, and straight.

In the little library Hennie looked around from her desk and greeted Jo with the blend of pleasure, surprise, and matter-of-factness she had hit upon early in the summer when it had become clear to the whole household, even to Gino, even to Stockinette the cat, that this young man had come into their lives to stay. Hennie and Laurence had seen with compassion that he wasn't entirely aware of this himself, but dating from his first elaborate dropping in on the cottage at Flanders Point from town some forty-five miles away—"I was driving around near here, just happened to be," he had said—they had treated him as though he were at one and the same time an old shoe, a member of visiting royalty in disguise, a candidate for the next vacancy in the Supreme Court, and a neighbor child known and borne with through sling shooting and voice changing.

"Will you just look at my desk," Hennie complained. "Mail a foot high. When I was young I used to love writing letters, all about my self and my soul, and sunsets, but nowadays I absolutely abominate the mere sight and sound of paper and envelopes." She started to laugh as she leafed through the pile. "Did I show you this, these two? They came a while back, this one first." She passed across for their inspection a pamphlet edged in tricolor stripes setting forth the advantages both to Mrs. Stacpole and the French Republic if she could see her way clear to sending a monthly parcel of food or clothing or both to a child in Brittany, the offspring of a Frenchman who had died in the Resistance. "*Amis de la France*" was printed across the top, and a thoughtful committee had caused "Friends of France" to appear directly beneath. "Read that first, and then I'll show you what came next. Of course I sent off a parcel to them in their New York office right away, before even being assigned a child, and enough airmail stamps, at killing expense, so they could send it right on. I always think it's so awful to have to wait for treats." She smiled, and watched her child reading.

Clare, wondering what seemed so amusing to her mother, flipped over the pamphlet. "I see you've put Will's name on the row of little dots."

"I know," her mother acknowledged. "So easy to sign a name; easier than not, in a way. Anyway this is so worthy and," she went on rather more energetically, "it'll be good for his French. How he's arrived at the fifth grade knowing as near nothing as makes no difference is a constant wonder to me, but this will give him just that little impetus to learn that he needs."

"Putting his finger on the knot once a month when you tie up the bundle?"

"Darling, what have you got to be waspish about? You won't be the one to pack and stuff and pull out and repack and then go off desperately to buy that one little thing more to fill a gap because you're so afraid the gap will hurt the feelings of the person opening. God knows I spent the war years floundering on my knees with brown paper and balls of stout string, and I daresay your mother did too, Jo, in Dayton."

"Denver, Mrs. Stacpole. Yes, she did."

"Of course, I mean Denver. No, I'd see to the parcels and Will would correspond with the child, the son of a hero, or so I supposed." Here she laughed. "But wait. It was a very nice arrangement really, because he'd increase his vocabulary and at the same time *not* acquire a Breton accent, which would be disastrous. So I asked them to give me a twelve- or fifteen-year-old boy so his grammar would be good and yet he not be so much older than Will but that they'd have interests in common." She sat and smiled at the letter in her hand.

Clare said she believed French boys flew kites a great deal and Will didn't even own one, and her reading mother murmured why would he, a town child, and in any case she would never allow him to go running along streets backward.

Joseph Wood said he thought the whole thing a fine idea. "I wish I'd had the opportunity to do something like it when I was Will's age, Mrs. Stacpole, but as a matter of fact I didn't start French till I was fifteen. The son of a hero," he said, wagging his head; "understanding between nations."

"Then listen to this," Hennie crowed, and reading from the letter in her lap, passed over to them a photograph that had accompanied it, of a boy with thick colorless hair truculantly *en brosse*, spectacles, a small mouth and chin. " 'Paul Mésurier,' " Hennie read out to them, "sixteen, older than I'd asked for, 'son of Widow Berthe Mésurier,' *that* was all right, 'mother works as laundress to support her son and daughter Geneviève and aged mother because Mésurier senior died in 1932.' Neatest trick of the week, wouldn't you say?"

Clare handed back the picture and Jo looked aside. "I see," he said, and cleared his throat.

Clare was counting on her fingers, and when she was through she said, "Mummy! So what did you do?"

Hennie folded the letter and tucked it away. "I simply wrote the committee and said it was only because I found it a little difficult to explain to my young son that not only was Monsieur Mésurier not killed in the Resistance as I had every right to expect but indeed that he—and so on and so on. Do you think," she inquired with a serious mouth but a glint in the voice, "that I was narrow-minded?"

"Certainly not," Clare said, and Jo nodded his sympathy. "Quite a situation," he said with careful nonchalance, "misrepresentation," but later, in the hall, on their way to ask Agnes if there was enough dinner for him to come back to after the film showing, he said to his love, "You know, I think your mother thought that was funny." She was aware of a speculative look in his eyes. "I guess I don't know her very well."

If a girl as quiet as Clare could be said to bridle, Clare bridled. "Mummy is going through some phase the last day or so, and I prefer not to discuss it."

Laurence, mindful of low rumblings from his sacroiliac joint, walked slowly home at the end of the afternoon. He had a theory about the sacroiliac: keep moving, but softly, don't bend over, and don't speak about it, and it will go away. The last of these strictures to himself he was seldom able to obey and he went back on it yet again when, after mounting, nobly erect and suffering, the one red sandstone step flanked with green iron urns of ivy before his front door, he came on his wife and son, one at either end of a sofa, tugging and nudging it away from the living-room wall.

"Don't do that; you'll strain yourselves. Here, let me—no! My back's bad today."

"My new super-jet," explained Will, a hatchet-faced boy of ten with the brown hair and eyes of his father. "I zoomed her down the stairs and she came in here somewhere and I'm afraid Stockinette'll find her and play with her." He disappeared on hands and knees behind the sofa, and Hennie reached a yardstick to him.

"Steady twinges all day long," said Laurence, modestly. He seated himself with more evidences of care and concern than he had exercised at the bank at any time. "Considerable discomfort," he said, and waited for sympathy.

"Old age," she suggested, calmly enough.

"Hardly that. I've had it off and on ever since the day

I tried a double back flip at Camp Beaver, and that was when I was nine."

Hennie said she didn't approve of summer camps, all that moss and bark, and handicrafts. "Burnt leather book ends. And I detest things with bark on them; it's so affected."

"Here she is!" cried Will, emerging. "*Dr-r-r-r-r, r-r-r-r,*" he went, like a droning, insane bee. Rapidly he circled the room, ignoring his parents, holding his plane up and ahead of himself with one outstretched hand. "*Dr-r-r-r, dr-r-r-r.* High-powered-super-jet-supersonic-electronic," he intoned and disappeared out the door. He did not hear his father's "Come back here," and Hennie said, "I can, perfectly well," and nudged the sofa into position against the wall.

"I'd help you if I could."

"Perfectly all right." She sank down on the sofa, ran her fingers through the short ash-blond curls above an ear and continued on around to shape upward the shorter hair at the back. "The fact is there is nothing I can't do these days. I do try to tell you, but you don't listen, you just look fondly at me as if I'd lost my wits."

"Darling, don't you want me to be fond of you?"

"Yes, yes. I want you to be fond—and listen!"

"Tell me now, then, in words of one syllable." He shifted in his seat a trifle, so she wouldn't forget how sitting still for any length of time was for him, in his present condition, torture—that is, torture almost.

So she folded her hands in her lap and looked across at him. "Did you ever hear of anyone getting stronger than ever before in all her life, suddenly, like a *giant?* I have this conviction I could pick up anything with one hand, houses, and trees. It's more than that though. I mean the powerful part is not what is making me—"

"Unstrung?" he suggested. She had such a lovely voice, all bells and warm icicles, it was a pleasure to listen to her, no matter what she was saying.

"Oh, no, not at all! How can you think such a thing, let alone say it?" She was resentful. "What is disturbing me is a sudden realization that all this time, all my life, I could have been living more widely; that's perhaps the way to put it; more widely. We just poke along, happy and comfortable, everybody does, but all this time we could have been—"

"Uncomfortable?"

"Exploring! That's it, exploring." She beamed at him. "Furthermore, I believe the world, the earth, all the airs and objects that surround us all the time want us to live more acutely. Don't raise those banker's eyebrows at me! Weather and animals would be delighted to co-operate with us, if we only had the sense to know it."

"I don't quite get it."

"I know." She refolded her hands. "It's not easy to explain, but, for instance, why does the syringa suddenly, and what we think of as unnaturally, shoot forth one perfect scented white blossom *in the fall* when it's supposed to be all through blooming in June? On the tip end of a twig; it did it today, practically while I watched. I could go out and lie on my stomach on the grass all day and simply gaze and gaze at it, but how would I look doing that? What would Agnes say? But if I could get Agnes to do it with me, that would be really something."

She ignored his agreeing that it would indeed, and she went on to suggest they might begin a new life by some very slight but token rebellion against the tyranny of time. "You could take a few days off from the bank, unexpectedly, and we could go up to Center Sandwich and visit your aunts. It wouldn't be a very spectacular thing to do, but it would have the virtue of being unexpected."

He stiffened at the very idea of the long drive, the frequent stops at antique shops and roadside stands which, fatally, he always caught sight of a split second before she did and he would make the mistake of stepping on the accelerator, thus giving himself away, as sometimes she might not have glimpsed them at all if she had not felt the telltale spurt, so small, shabby, and unassuming these shops sometimes were, lurking there by the roadside—three ginger jars and a spindly rocker in the long grass of the verge, but she was always convinced there would be Lowestoft within. Worse than antique shops he dreaded hamburger and coffee meals on the way.

"It's too early. After Thanksgiving," he said craftily, "will be better for them, liven up the beginning of winter for 'em. I shouldn't wonder if they aren't pretty busy this time of year." Doing what, she enviously demanded, and he was visited by inspiration. "Making jelly. Grape, quince, plum, ah—pickled pears."

She sighed. "Actually, I don't think you get my idea exactly. It was not so much of them I was thinking, but of some way to utilize the new, powerful strength I have."

He said how lucky she was to have this feeling of strength, but as for himself, with his back the way it was, a man who, he said with dignity, got normally tired— Then he gave a grimace which the likelihood is he would have called wry if anyone had asked him; but she didn't; she was lying back on the sofa looking up and away, beyond his head, and the cluck she gave, though wifely-prompt, was not enough in his opinion. Still, if men were called on to suffer more than women, and at the moment he was convinced this was so, then also it was incumbent on them to be more stoic, so he was a little bit surprised at hearing himself say, "Bending, they say, is the worst thing in the world." It wouldn't hurt her to sympathize a little more! Watching her draped along the sofa, brooding away to herself about her own abounding health, even gloating maybe, he pictured how an old-fashioned wife, a Biblical or early New England woman, would be running around with bottles of liniment for him, and jars of salve and soft cloths. But she just sits there oblivious to all the discomfort I'm in; I bet we haven't even got any liniment in the house. "Have we?" he demanded.

Her idle, woman's mind was elsewhere. "Have we what?" she idly asked.

"Any liniment," he said, patient. How any bystander would admire his patience in the face of all this fecklessness!

"Bottles and bottles, but it's the worst thing in the world for a sacroiliac." He asked how could she know, never having suffered from it herself, and that brought back her wandering mind at once. "But of course I have, don't you remember? Awfully, both times, before Clare and Will were born. It was much worse than yours; must have been, considering." He went *m'mn'm* in a doubting sort of way. Then he unbent to inquire what she had done about it. "Simply reefed up my horrible maternity girdle another notch. Don't you remember it? Maybe what you need—" She smiled over at him at last, a perfectly heartless smile. "It's probably still around somewhere, up in the attic. It's not so long ago, those days, after all. In a way they seem just like yesterday, don't they, in a way?"

Nothing was plainer than that she was not roused about his discomfort. He forbore to smile at her reminiscences, but then he was stricken to see an almost unprecedented thing, tears welling slowly up into her blue eyes, and she turned her face against the back of the sofa. Tears for his sacroiliac! Oh, how sweet of her! He had been misjudging. He leaped up without a single twinge and hurried to her side. "Darling, don't! It's not so bad as all that, really." He sank down with his arms around her and his cheek against her hair.

"Oh," she wailed, "why didn't we have ten children while we were at it? We could have perfectly well. I like having hard things to do, and now what good am I? I feel so terribly, terribly, terribly full of life I've gone around all day *trembling*."

He detached himself and sat back, and a twinge like the bite of a bulldog shot across his lumbar region. "If you insist," he said. "I suppose we are still reasonably fertile."

"But not *now*; it's too late. With Clare just about ready to be getting married how would it look?" She wiped her eyes on the chintz cover and gazed around at him reproachfully. "I have my own ideas about what the mother of the bride should wear and it's not flowered chiffon cut full and it's not a great swatch of orchids either, covering up something. No; never." Reflectively running one finger along the piping on the sofa arm, she quieted. Her tears had not been for him, and she still remained absorbed with something he could know nothing of, even had he been willing to try.

"Afraid I don't know exactly what a swatch is," he said, moving stiffly off to the door, and she fetched another great trembling sigh, but not, as he flattered himself she did, at his masculine ignorance.

"Oh, I'm glad you're here," Hennie said that evening, as though she hadn't seen him for a month, walking into their room to find Laurence standing before his open closet door, looking in. She went up from behind and wrapped her long arms around him.

"Yes, I do love you," he said at once, but she said no, it wasn't that; what was he doing?

"Trying to decide if that old brown tweed is ready for the Goodwill Industries bag." He plucked out a sleeve from the hanging suit and examined the edge of the cuff. She squinted sideways along the back of his neck, so clean, a city man's neck, with a neatly clipped platoon of short hair; the hard gray stuff of his jacket shoulders smelled like what it was. With some difficulty, because of her embrace, he managed to get his fingers into the inside pocket of the brown jacket and turn the label to read it. "What are you trying to do, garrote me? Good God, nineteen-forty-three."

"So old? Into the Goodwill bag."

"Practically brand new," he countered briskly. "Wouldn't think of it, but here goes this old navy blue."

Hennie hugged him tighter. "Oh, I wish we had a longer time to live," she said.

"Good God." He searchingly scrutinized the shine on the seat of the navy-blue trousers, turning it in the light from the hanging bulb. "Isn't enough enough?"

"No-o-o." Lingeringly, she let go. "Not nearly. Come and sit down." A rising excitement shivered into her voice. "Nobody pays any attention to how terribly exciting simply existing is! It's all whirled up inside me. Oh, come and sit down!" She subsided backward onto the tufted green velvet of her dressing-table bench; her eyes were shining up at him, but he took the change from his pocket the way he did every evening and stacked it methodically on his chest of drawers and said he'd listen while he got undressed, but he doubted if he had anything to offer in the way of a solution.

"Well then!" She whisked around and seized her brush and began running it up through her hair so she began to look like a maenad. "Say we took a bird's-eye view of our life, our life and times and circumstances, what would we see? Say we soared contemplatively around looking down at *us*, what would we see? Oh," she waggled her hairbrush at him, "I'm not a discontented woman, as you very well know. Don't think that."

Laurence, slowly unbuttoning the gray vest, said he didn't. She eyed him sharply.

"Are you yawning? Because if you're yawning I'll kill you. Well, what we should see from up there would be two perfectly happy, contented, well-adjusted, well-off *blind* people." Laurence stepped backward out of his trousers. "Absolutely blind to nine-tenths of what is going on in the world. There are forces at work on the earth, in the air. I don't mean current events or international affairs or anything of that nature, but the wonderful odd things all around us; they don't bother to explain themselves to us; inexplicable things. I want to burst my bonds."

"It's too bad my sacroiliac's coinciding with your feeling so extra spry."

While he peeled off his underwear and stalked naked to the closet for his pajamas she took a moment to consider a reply and should have taken two for it accomplished nothing when she said, "But your back is such a small thing, relatively, and this discovery of mine is so big."

He said, as he evened the ends of his pajama cord by holding both far out in front of himself like reins, then tying a single-ply knot in them and sharply jerking it back against his stomach which he tensed to receive the shock, that the word "relatively" happened to have absolutely no meaning for him and, curiously enough, never had had, since a child.

"But that's absurd! Oh, well, we can forget that. I'm sorry about your back but it really doesn't signify, as my grandfather used to say. What does matter is this sudden exultation, exaltation, and I want *you* to suffer from it too, darling. I tried to explain it to Olivia at luncheon, and she couldn't have been stupider, dear as she is." Hennie brushed her hair with abandon, until she exactly resembled a Blake angel, though healthier. "We lead such tiny lives," she said enthusiastically, "but we could spread out. That's why I must leave home for a while, to explore." She was surprised to hear how sure she sounded. "There's a lot more goes on than we take any account of; there are forces," she plunged on. "What makes a curtain move when there's no wind, for instance? And faces you think you see for a minute in tree trunks, I bet they *are* faces! And what's Stockinette laughing about, half the time, behind our backs? Just off somewhere for a week or ten days, darling; you'll hardly know I'm gone. What do you suppose Stockinette honestly thinks of us? Tell me that," she demanded, and as silently as nothing at all she turned and laid the brush back on the dressing table and fixed him with her large blue eyes.

"I don't doubt for a minute that you're right, but I'd like to know why going off for a week would improve matters?"

"That's easy to say. And you don't believe I'm going, but I am. If you felt the way I do, then everything could become so much more interesting."

"They're interesting enough now; I wouldn't want them to be any more interesting. Anyway, what exactly do you mean by 'things' and 'everything.' And 'it.' What do you mean by 'it'? You keep saying 'everything' all the time," he complained, and moving to his chest of drawers he began building a little rampart on the top of piles of nickels, piles of brown and gray pennies; the gray pennies he then dropped with distaste through a slot in the lid of a small wooden box; when he had accumulated a boxful he always gave it to some worthwhile charity he was indifferent to. "When you say 'it' you mean life, don't you?" He watched her in his square mirror, and when she made a face and said she supposed so, he nodded, his worst or best suspicions confirmed. "That's what I thought you did. Well, I find life plenty interesting as it is and I wouldn't want it any more so. Couldn't stand it, in fact. Good God," he mused, "as if there weren't enough to do already without thinking up other—up other— Oh, the hell with it," he finished very cheerfully indeed, tightened the sash of his dressing gown, and stepped into his bedroom slippers. "I guess I'm a born Philistine," he said with the utmost unconcern. "Come kiss me."

But she would not. Why kiss a man who didn't believe her when she said she was going to leave him? "I pity you for your obtuseness," she announced. "There is a world of whirling wonder, but you—"

"But me, I have my own self-centeredness to consider," he said not without dignity, and stalking past into the bathroom he could be heard turning on the hot water full and then the cold in a rush and thunder into the washbowl.

She began brushing her hair again, slowly. Why was it so hard, so impossible, to make him understand? Here she knew Laurence better than anyone living, and yet it seemed he couldn't be made to attend to what she was trying so hard to tell him. Perhaps in her absence he would begin to reflect.

He came back into the room, looking very bland. "My sacroiliac's not *too* bad," he murmured.

Later, in entire absent-mindedness, trying still to think of some way to communicate, she lay and drew small precise geometric designs on the small of his back.

"Really," he sighed into her ear, sleepy and content, at peace, unregenerate, "sometimes I wonder if you're playing ticktacktoe back there."

"Never! All by myself, why should I?" and she kissed him and tapped a sudden brisk row, like buttons, right up his long spine.

CHAPTER THREE

"If you're restless why don't you go to the mountains for a week," Laurence had suggested next morning, while shaving. "You've been at the sea all summer, and mountain air's so bracing," but *bracing*'s not the word he should have used, he knew, even before she spoke.

"Bracing! That's the last thing! Anyway, this is an experimental trying my wings so what does it matter where I go?"

"Perhaps we might take a week end and run up and visit the aunts in Center Sandwich," he had pleaded.

"Yes indeed; turncoat, whatever a turncoat is." She sounded ironical, and her glance was straying.

"When, then?"

"Well, when would be the question. Except, I've been

reflecting and now I scarcely think a trip to Center Sandwich would embark us on the full life."

"I think you've lost your mind," he said through the application of his hot wet washcloth. His dark eyes, over the wet green-blue cloth, were wounded.

"This is nothing new." She sounded mysterious now. "When I was younger I planned to run away."

He was startled and dropped the washcloth to the bowl. "Since we've been married?"

"No. No, it was before that." No need to tell him it had been when she was eight.

"Alone?"

"Of course not." She smiled to herself at the clearness of the picture she had of Tom O'Shea's blue eyes and his bewitching punch for trolley transfers.

Laurence smote one hand down on the rim of the washbowl, helplessly. "Lost your mind, but if you won't be happy till you've tried, go ahead and try. If I didn't know you'd come back in ten days like a homing pigeon *and* a bat out of hell, I wouldn't let you go. But then," he added, opening the mirrored door before him and bringing out the bay rum bottle and splashing some on his smug yet sorry face, "I never *have* refused you anything."

"Darling!" she cried. "And when have I ever asked you for anything?"

"What's got into Mother, do you think?" Clare had asked Laurence privately as they walked downstairs for breakfast. "She's embarrassing my friends." Laurence thought a minute, appeared to be about to speak, and then decided not to answer at all, his banker's instincts having descended on him early that day. An automatic professional loyalty to wives and clients, however whimsical they might be, though so often overlaid with exasperation, was coupled in this instance with a nineteen-year-old habit of considering that Clare was a child and should not be concerned with adult matters. Clare, rounding the newel post, glancing at him so uncommunicative and handsome, thought to herself: I'll never let Jo get away with any of this not-answering. "I'd make her go to Vermont," she said aloud, less from conviction that Vermont was the place for her mother than because she disliked not being replied to. "You could go up together and visit Aunt Sadie and Aunt Effie, some week end."

Hennie stood, late that afternoon, with the porter who had her luggage, in a white-painted bedroom in a guest cottage of the Seagull Inn. Curiously virginal, seaside bedrooms always are, even in inns, even in boarding houses in sandy side streets where it must surely be that all too many people have slept; the bedrooms of actual virgins are far less chaste than these pure, wooden-walled rooms. The salt airs moving freely, night and day, through rented rooms near beaches keep these painted chambers innocent or soon return innocence to them, between occupants. This room was very small, with white board walls and a thin mauve cotton rug, and, once committed by the rug, someone had tied lavender ribbon to make low waistlines on the thin white curtains. Hennie walked over and removed the ribbons and put them in a bureau drawer; she gently shook the restrained curtains so that they fell straight and then lifting a little into the room on the tide of salt air began breathing in and out. A mauve-decorated Woolworth lampshade over a bulb swung above the bed that, high, humped, immaculate, and solitary, filled half the room. "I wonder if this place is what I mean," she speculated aloud, turning on a heel, inspecting. The porter pouted with surprise, swung her suitcase on the only chair and left, and she set her dressing case on the white bureau.

"It isn't that I don't love you all madly, as usual," she had said that morning as she kissed Laurence good-by. "It's that I want to get away and be alone for a few days. I've been so odd lately, you know." But this was the moment she reaped the reward of having brought them up to be polite. "You must have noticed." She had spoken rather fast, being uncertain if they understood a word she said, and had looked, but in vain, for comprehension on the three faces of her loved ones, so she had hurried on, "For instance, if only I were a fashionable Frenchwoman I'd go to a nunnery, make a retreat; that's what they do, they pace up and down cloisters for a week, in solitude. Lovely. And then come bursting back out and have a wonderful time; I'm rather planning to do both at once."

Will, still behind a bowl of shredded wheat, said, "Cripes," but mildly. If he had tried his best he couldn't have thought of a less agreeable way to occupy himself, but he was very fond of his mother, nearly as much as he was of his cat, and said no more, except that she seemed to be turning into a Frenchwoman, and she asked him if he had started his letter to the little French boy yet, and he said no, he hadn't had time.

The Seagull bore no resemblance to the sort of place a fashionable Parisian might retreat to—there were no gray towers, no pleached walks, no oratory garden—but the small white room was cool and quiet, empty and free. "Here I shall begin a new life; here I shall come to terms with myself and stop trembling. Oh, heavens, for the first time in twenty years I am alone! Now I must make things happen to me!"

Outside the window a concrete path ran through fog to the inn and beyond it a rising slope of sand and harsh grass hid the beach and the Atlantic Ocean; she could hear the hidden waves crashing up, snoring back, and was pleased to remember that only moving water stretched between herself and the coasts of Spain.

She undid her dressing case and began laying out the contents. The manager of the Seagull, a plump, pallid Mr. Fletcher, who looked as though it had never occurred to him to set foot on his own beach, had told her there were several other empty bedrooms and cottages; it was so late in the fall almost everyone had left; the inn would soon be closing, and such few people as they had staying on would be gone in another ten days. She told herself she was glad of that; it narrowed her choice of companions in adventure. She aligned the enameled comb with the brush, and then laid out a diminuendo of nail files and scissors and orange sticks, ending with the forever unused shoehorn. A cool salt breath from Spain poured in the window, stirring the released curtains and pouring a moving coolness over her face that felt so hot and tight from the tiresome train ride along the length of Long Island. "Alone, for a week, or ten days," she said aloud, but softly. "On my own."

Most of the chairs in the dining room were empty; all the tables had silver and glass on them and white cloths with four points hanging down, but not more than half a dozen were occupied. A couple sat by the front window, and a solitary woman in the center of the room; single men here and there looked up from their plates as Hennie came in, and then down again, politely, and she ignored them for the time being. As Mr. Fletcher had said, it was nearing the end of the season now and this scattered few must mean summer was over. Mr. Fletcher issued from behind a screen, swallowing, put her at a small table, and though all summer long, with the place full, the rolls and biscuits must have been served piping hot, Hennie's roll broke with a dull cold snap that told of relaxed vigilance and a late-September *laissez-faire*. She began to wonder whether the man of the couple by the front window was aware how surprisingly he resembled Robert Louis Stevenson, and whether any or several of the three or four men so quietly eating were in love with the lone woman, and if so, how much. She began on another roll; fog must have been one of its ingredients. At home Laurence would have picked up such a roll and then put it right back on his plate, with an elegant meaningful gesture of rejection, and looked down the table at her and said, not in the least reproachfully but as though it merely must be she didn't know it, "Stone cold," and her foot would start probing about for the bell under the rug.

But here—here it didn't matter at all, and sitting by herself she experienced an uprush of undedicated extra strength that at home would have been expended over the temperature of rolls and Will's haircuts and Clare's clothes, and a multitude of errands up and down the house. Here at the inn this strength remained untapped and went sliding and slipping around inside her, extra and free, waiting for a prey. She could feel it rising in the column of her throat. She tried to frown it down, and Mr. Fletcher, peeping at this moment from his cage down the hall, asked himself what was making Mrs. Stacpole look so grim all at once; if it was too much salt on the flounder he was sorry, but what did she expect, coming so late in the season?

After dinner Hennie sat in the lounge, expectant; other guests might come through who had not dined there, other and possibly more romantic than the occupants of the dining room. Double doors were thrown open at one side of the room to reveal a gift shop, but no one was in there except one woman, and the fact she remained there, taking short steps this way and that, occasionally touching the wares, adjusting them, making infinitesimal changes in their position on shelves and tables, led Hennie to see she was the shop proprietor. The contents of that gift shop must be a very, very old story by now to everyone staying at the inn, and Hennie made herself the easy promise never to set foot within its doors. She turned over the much worn pages of a magazine dedicated, so its subtitle declared, to the pursuit of gracious living, and she half-read the answers to questions troubled subscribers, terrified they weren't living graciously, had sent to the editor. "What do I give my mother-in-law for Easter?" "What does the gracious hostess do when she wins the bridge prize?" Maybe I should write a letter, too. "Dear Editor, What do you do for a normal woman of almost forty-four who has begun to feel she's floating?" Turning a page she glanced up and there was the man who resembled Stevenson tacking resolutely toward her with his wife, through a sea of maple furniture. With determination they caught and held her eye.

They sat down and told her she was new there. They were very friendly and questioning, and soon Hennie heard herself beginning to gabble with the extravagant affability, somehow shy but unbuttoned too, rooted in social difference, that so lamentably overcame her when she was with strangers she would never have spoken to first. At such times a senseless humility caught her in its grip; unreasonably, she would feel she must somehow at once justify herself to them. No doubt they were perfectly happy people, but because she could not think well of the woman's shoes and earrings she felt a deep subterranean guilt at her own possessions, not least her intangible ones, and she started in to gabble to prove she was a friend. "It's absolutely delightful here, isn't it? So restful," she said, "and *quiet!*" on a rather high note. She hoped they would say no, the place was really the haunt of the eminent, the handsome, and the gay, all of whom had happened to dine elsewhere that evening.

"All these antiques and all," the wife said, tossing her chin over her shoulder toward the maple, the Currier and Ives prints, and the ranks of sulky pewter along the walls. "Atmosphere. The people here though, I don't suppose you've had time to notice, they're kind of funny, because I mean we've been here three weeks now and all they say is 'Good morning' in the dining room, when you come in, and not another word all day. Meet you face to face in the village and they stalk by. And no games room, which I think is a shame because of the lovely people you always meet in games rooms, full of fun, often," she finished, coming to the end of her breath if not of her grievance. Hennie was swept back years to her first day at a new school when, like long-fasting beasts of prey, certain members of her class had come gamboling around her— the fat, the spotted, the rejected, the ones she soon enough was to learn to call the "unat*tractiv*e." Wiser now, much warier and much kinder, knowing she was leaving in a week, she smiled on these two.

"You been here before?" asked Stevenson.

She shook her head. What had brought these two to the Seagull in the first place? "But it's delightful, isn't it?" she was sorry to hear herself reiterate; it wasn't essential to sound half-witted to keep them happy. "And so restful."

"Yeh, it is; almost too much so, we think. It wouldn't hurt to have an orchestra, except there's no place to dance." The bright-eyed wife looked her over. "You need a rest? You don't look as if you did." You are one of the waited-on, her glance said; it is impossible to be mistaken about that.

"Oh, not a rest exactly." These were not the strangers to whom she could explain the exact, the delicate, peculiar nature of her trouble. "Not but what I'm a hard-working woman," she said, though she should have crossed her fingers at the words. The wife angled around for what work she meant and then for her name, and when she got it said, "I seem to have heard that before someplace. Do you write or something?" and was at once reproved by her husband, who asked, playfully, how many times had he told her not to ask that question?

"You know how angry it makes *me* when people ask *me* that," he reminded her, throwing up his profile to show how much it resembled Robert Louis Stevenson's, and then turning quickly to flash dark eyes on them both, and a forgiving smile. Hennie supposed he had been forced to take up some form of literature for his life work only because of the arrangement of his features; it had been unavoidable, though in his soul, perhaps, he had yearned to be an orthodontist, but the mystery of who he was was not enough to keep her and presently, pleading her long train ride from Connecticut and the soporific effect of the air blowing over the Seagull, she escaped down the foggy path to her cottage.

"You see the pin she's got on?" the wife breathed, watching Hennie's retreating back. "I swear that suit is three years old though, the way the skirt was cut."

"Diamonds? Rubies? I can't say I noticed. Phony."

"Not a phony size, if you know what I mean."

But he insisted, perverse from boredom. He had seen what his wife had not, that this woman would never become their playmate. "She's too long in the shank for my taste," he said, and his low-slung wife eagerly agreed, though they both stared after the last of her as though she were candied fruit someone was taking away.

"She don't have much to say for herself," the wife said. "She don't sound like she looks, if you know what I mean. Shy, maybe," but at that Stevenson snorted and asked what she had to be shy about, anybody like her.

They departed. The next moment Hennie reappeared, hopeful, coming back from her cottage which she had found lonely. "I'm wide-awake as a hawk," she had said, applied a fresh sweep of lipstick and returned the way she had come. She settled herself gracefully by the fire, linked her fingers with a pretty negligence, and, indeed, in less than five minutes was talking with a sandy-haired man in brown; sandy or gray? Hard to tell, in this low-ceilinged room.

"Charming place," this Englishman said. "Your first visit here? M'wife and I have been here the whole summer, and we've found it delightful." He rocked himself back and forth before the fire, glancing downward; when he rocked back he must be almost able to see, beyond the periphery of his brown waistline, the tips of his well-polished brown shoes. "M'wife is back in town now, but I stayed on for a bit of golf and so on. Roughing it," was his explanation of tweed at nine in the evening. "Care to take a walk tomorrow morning?"

One must not be an easy mark; there would still be ten days; Hennie said how nice but what about another time because she was afraid she would have letters to write, and as soon as uttered, the lie sounded perfectly plausible; she looked gravely up at him to see if he thought so too and he must have as he gave an acquiescent "Ah." He strolled away, and she went to the inn desk to buy stamps to give body to her falsehood, but she had to wait; the clerk, holding the office telephone to her neck and staring into dark foggy space through the window paid her no attention, presently saying, reproachfully, into the receiver, "*Hello.* Hello!—Hello, is iss th' night clerk at th' laun'ry? Well then, where's Judge Larmer's pajamas?—Eh-yuh, well, lass night he hadda sleep 'n his drawers 'n thass not comfor'ble y'know!" She slammed down the instrument and confided to Hennie, "Yah. Laun'ries!"

"Yah," Hennie agreed. With a fog-curled strip of stamps she had no use for she started back for her cottage by way of the lounge, but lurking just outside the double doors was the mistress of the gift shop, and Hennie was drawn, helpless as a webbed fly, into its complicated interior.

"I have everything," the owner said. "Only exclusive lines. I'm Miss Price so I call my shops Price-less Presents."

"Charming." Oh, you poor soul, thought Hennie. There were bayberry candles with verses where *candles* rhymed with *rambles* and frilled glass vases too small for anything but chickweed and cocktail napkins cross-stitched within an inch of their lives. She looked down with compassion and dislike into the small features turned up to her and knew in a flash what kind of underwear the little woman was wearing, always wore—pink rayon with a shallow scooped neckline; she knew exactly.

Why does a woman run a little shop? Because of the interior certainty that one day a stranger, dark and of course tall, will stalk silently in at the door and laying his long hand on the top of a pile of chintz pot lifters he will ask her to be his own and this belief sustains her through inventory time and Indian summer. Every time the door opens, she looks up, not to welcome the woman shopper with the suède handbag—sometimes the Misses Price cannot restrain a *moue* of disappointment—but to encounter the face of the stranger. If not today, then tomorrow, or next week. And then off they two will go at once, arms entwined, leaving the door open for the wind to rush in and toss all the racked greeting cards into the air.

Hennie opened her mouth to say she would buy the candles, when Miss Price, who must, thus, have missed many a sale in her long life, darted across the shop.

"But this is nice." She indicated a threatening tall shell-work jar. "This was a great deal of trouble and I made it myself so I ought to know. Not Northern shells though, *oh* no; these are all Florida shells because I pack up here and go there when the season's over here." Her glance went seeking some other lure. Hennie asked when the season was considered to be over at the Seagull, and then Miss Price couldn't help directing a glum discouraged stare deep down into her shell-work jar where cobwebs and dry spiders had been safe so unaccountably long. "That's what I was beginning to wonder myself. Not till later usually, but nobody's bought a thing off me for a week." She turned and picked up a sachet of the palest green. "This one is extremely dainty," she said, sadly. "And I have others."

"If I were you I'd close up right now and take a few days' vacation before you go to Florida; why not?"

"Oh?" Miss Price's mouth worked as she took in and began to digest this revolutionary suggestion. "Reelly?" she murmured politely, to gain time. "You would?" There was no question in her mind that this tall woman in pink tweed must be a walking monument of worldly information. She would have disbelieved anyone who said —even Hennie herself if she said it—"But this Mrs. Stacpole is actually a very simple soul beneath the fine pink surface and her knowledge is limited; if she is kind it's because she has always been happy, a Puritan by inheritance, pretty by luck; she understands other women in imported tweed and can talk with them by the hour and she knows what to say to chambermaids with appendicitis pains, but there is a vast body of human beings in between whom she has never even encountered." Miss Price would have looked askance and unbelieving. She would have replied if she dared that she knew for a fact that this Mrs. Stacpole, and all such, have no problems at all, none whatever, and bottomless checkbooks and they dress for dinner every night in long black velvet even when there is no one at home but their husbands. Such people live a foot off the ground and are somewhat larger than life, Miss Price believed, and for those reasons she reverenced and hated them. "You reelly would?" she asked. "But what would Mr. Fletcher say?"

"Who?"

Miss Price gasped, flung up a furtive paw to cover her mouth and devoutly hoped the great man wasn't lurking outside the double doors. "The proprietor of this hotel. But I could close up and go visit my married sister in Newark; she's always after me to."

"Do." To Miss Price's further amazement Mrs. Stacpole then bought not only the pale green sachet which Miss Price hadn't realized she admired at all, but a lilac one as well and a box of bayberry candles. When she left the shop carrying these treasures Miss Price gazed for a long, thoughtful moment at her narrow back, through the gap of the double doors she was, even at the same time, closing, closing.

Hennie yawned and yawned and stumbled out of her clothes. Any intention she may have had of lying sharp awake for a short bout of schemes for a richer life was abandoned without a fight. She gave a hoot of laughter that became strangled in yawns when she caught sight of her pile of books, crowned pretentiously by Shakespeare's sonnets in red leather, and pulling out the light, she toppled into bed. Tomorrow was time enough to begin living; there was the whole week ahead. In mid-yawn she dispatched a good-night blessing in the direction she believed Connecticut to be, comfortably sure that whatever emergency or accident she was likely to think up would never happen, simply because she had; for this was the form of insurance she lived by. Two minutes she lay with her eyes wide in the dark, lapped in impersonal hotel sheets, imagining disasters—a maniac burglar creeping into Will's room; impossible for it to happen because she had thought of it first—a car mounting the sidewalk and mowing Laurence down on his way home from the bank; no; tended to—Clare committing suicide because Jo said he really loved the only girl in his Torts class; no; never Jo—dear Stockinette trapped all night by her paw at some unusually tight mousehole; thought of; hence disposed of. Agnes's canniness was almost a form of insurance all by itself, and very likely the oil burner wouldn't blow up tonight because it wasn't cold enough yet to have started it. She closed her eyes, maternal duty done. She stretched, and pulled her thin nightgown down her long legs, rolled on her side and stretched again. Through the fog, quite near, the unseen waves fell and drew back, fell heavily and drew back, and fell again—

The bastion of fog stood only along the South Shore of Long Island and back at the Stacpoles' a flood of September moonlight came through the window of the upper hall, lay over Stockinette in her oval wicker basket and cast on the wall close behind her shadows of a line of interlacing scallops, the osier rim of her accustomed bed. Her eyes closed, and opened; it was too light in the hall; if Hennie had been at home the curtains would have been drawn, providing the darkness so necessary for quiet sleep. One lovely blunt fur paw held down a lemon-colored rubber duck which long ago when she had been a new, supposedly lonely, kitten, had nightly been put into her bed for company but for which she had from the first entertained a scornful loathing, so that ever since, every night at intervals, could be heard the sounds of her battle with it—pounces, the strain and creak of osier, and a shrill mechanical protesting whiffling from the duck. Every battle subdued it, as Stockinette supposed, forever.

In their beds the Stacpoles might smile, and murmur, "She's playing." She would have been wild if she had known they believed any such thing.

Tonight there was too much moonlight. The window loomed above her, bombarding her with horrid radiance. She lay tense, her paw unrelaxed on the idiot duck, her topaz eyes wide and watchful. At moments sleep welling irresistibly up inside her caused the fur lids to come slowly together, but every time they slowly opened again; too much light. The tallest woman wasn't in the house, that was why. Then the middle-sized woman should have pulled the curtains, or the other one, but she always moved so quickly she never stopped to think what might be essential for a cat's comfort. Stockinette glanced sharply down at the duck and gave it a blip.

The door to Will's room opened, and he slipped into the hall, holding up with one hand the pajama trousers which were forever sliding down his thin hips. With the other hand he tried to gather up Stockinette, had to use both, she was such a stretchable cat, snatched at the pajama trousers, and staggered back to bed. "Ah, there," he said, drowsy with the time of night it was, and love. "Angel puss. Heavenly body." His narrow hand, grimy because Hennie was in Long Island, passed delicately along the furry slope. Her built-in purr started for him immediately. In the Stacpole household there was a rule against Will's having Stockinette with him at night, because the doctor had said perhaps the reason Will snuffled at breakfast, calling down cries of "Handkerchief, for heaven's sake!" was an allergy to cats. Whether this was the cause or not was a matter of indifference to Will and presumably to Stockinette. They managed to pass a part of most nights together. "Darling," he whispered into an attentive, triangular, furred ear.

Soon he slept, but she couldn't; she was restless. Even in this darkened room odd streaks and spears of moonlight lay on the floor and the furniture, and she hated to think how it was brimming her basket out in the hall. Presently she rose up from under Will's sleep-stilled hand and thumped off the bed and out the door. Climbing slowly back into her own bed her glance encountered the ever-open detestable eye of her duck; it was beaming forgivingly up at her, welcoming her back, and she gave it a blip, subduing it yet once again and—or so she supposed —forever.

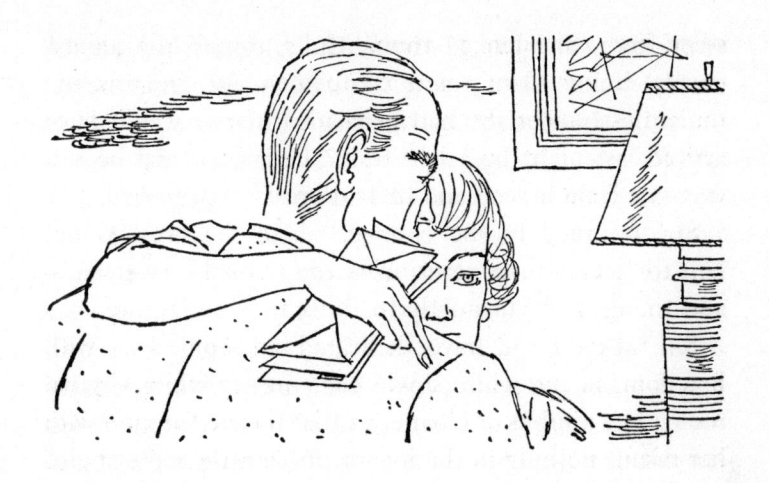

CHAPTER FOUR

Having slept late, Hennie found even fewer people in the dining room than had been there the evening before. She crossed to her table with that peculiarly elated-looking walk of all who traverse summer hotel dining rooms in sneakers. Orange juice away from home tastes as though splinters of straw and ice were melting in it; coffee, away from home, is an entirely different drink, sometimes better. From her table she had a fog-softened view of her cottage and presently she saw a colored maid thrashing about in it. The window flew up and a mop head came out and was furiously shaken, fluffs and curls of dust refusing to rise, drifting down the heavy, humid air; the mop withdrew. Now the bedroom would be a monastic cell for Hennie to spend her morning in, in contemplation, or perhaps better—a monastic cell to stay away from. She looked thoughtfully around the almost empty dining room for a companion. Where was the romantic stranger she had persuaded herself would have arrived last night by a late train? Perhaps it had been a very late train indeed and he had breakfasted in bed.

She returned to the cottage, where she brushed her hair for a long time, scrutinized the enamel on her nails, and then sat down quietly to think over her future.

She sat erect and grave, dedicated but soon a-sway with boredom, in the white single chair in her white virginal room. The nimbus of Chanel 22 that traveled around with her meant nothing in the incorruptible little white-angled cube of space. There was no sound except the faraway lisp of waves in fog. She sat looking down at her hands which she had folded to resemble as much as possible the hands of a Chinese sage, and so they did, except for diamonds, sapphires, and the pink nail polish. Quiet; quiet; let her now face it. "The root of my trouble," she began aloud, in a low, reasonable voice, the voice of a woman putting something up to herself in the plainest terms without fear or favor, "is that all of a sudden I am suffering, no, enjoying, no, no, I am *taken with*, that's it, this completely internal gaiety." The limp curtains furled in at her on a breeze. She looked at them. "I know," she said, and they drifted out.

She undid her carefully sagelike hands and laced the fingers together in a more negligent and worldly pose, and then quickly changed them again into a game of "Here is the church and here is the steeple. Open the door and see all the people," and then, ashamed, sat upon them. "I have a need to scour away ordinariness. This deep need will not let me rest and there's nothing for it but simply to start leading a double life; just one doesn't begin to be enough. Laurence doesn't understand me, that's clear. How do women manage to lead two lives?" Perhaps she would have to leave home altogether, but not go far. She would not be able to walk past the house because she would be seen from the windows, and pounced on, but surely it would be unreasonable not to check up somehow on her loved ones. No one could expect her not to do that! Perhaps once a week she would hire a cab to carry her in short dashes past the house. Tears rose into her throat at the picture of herself, crouched, peering from the window of a yellow taxi. "Not quite so fast, *please*," she would say to the driver. What would she do if she observed in the course of this reconnoitering that Gino had not polished the door knocker? She bit her upper lip, considering. Perhaps she could keep in touch with the family through a series of anonymous post cards. After this she heard for the first time the foghorn blowing from the point.

She stared over the white sill earnestly into the white outdoors but at the same time and for all her earnestness she felt laughter boiling within. Her thoughts set themselves on this roll of fog, hemming in the coast, hiding the multitudinous affairs of the peopled coast line, because it was idle to pretend that she had come to a desert for a retreat; the South Shore teems. Days and days of fog there had been. How far out did the layer extend, out over the sea and all its millions of jeweled fish? Did it taper off out there somewhere into sunlight, and was there then sun all the way to Spain? "Ah—easy as anything I could whizz out over the water and see." It took an effort to remain seated when it would have been so very easy to rise up and fly, horizontal through the window and then swoop, up and off. Rows of passengers on ships at sea would look up from the Book-of-the-Month and see her, an angel in pink tweed, soaring along over the blue water. "Look," they would say to each other, pointing her out, "who do you suppose *she* is, flying so fast and so well?"

By ten o'clock that morning she was sitting in a wooden chair made to fit people who had been born V-shaped, on the lawn, under the low-hanging ceiling, the suspension of gray vapor; a constant damp breeze came trickling from over the slope of coarse beach grass to curl her short ash-blond hair and wet her lashes. She read from her red leather book, timing the intake of the long plangent lines to the slow swishing approach and withdrawal of the unseen salt waves, themselves moving in iambic pentameter the other side of the slope.

> When forty winters shall besiege thy brow
> And dig deep trenches in thy beauty's field—

Times have changed somewhat, what with modern medicine and cold cream, and Shakespeare would be surprised. She lay thinking of the streams of women one can see any day along the avenues of big cities, shoppers on Fifth Avenue, for instance, their shoulders shrugging their selves forward, their legs like scissor blades cutting ahead, ahead—forty-year-old American women with their bright mouths and anxious faces.

> How much more praise deserved thy beauty's use,
> If thou couldst answer "This fair child of mine
> Shall sum my count and make my old excuse,"
> Proving his beauty by succession thine!

She skipped, reading here and there. The small square page fell open and lay flat; someone, not herself, must once have been accustomed to read here.

> But were some child of yours alive that time
> You should live twice, in it and in my rhyme.

Such a lot of that. What pretty arguments against birth control the sonnets made. They slid in and out of her mind, iridescent, slipping up the shell-strewn shore of her consciousness, slipping back down. Then all at once she knew she was being looked at, and there, a few feet away, sat the woman who ate alone in the center of the dining room.

Some minutes previous this single woman, Mrs. De-Lancey Watson, had come out of the inn and, taking a V-shaped chair nearby, had fixed her eyes on her fellow guest, concentrating on waking her up. Perhaps because Hennie hadn't really been asleep, or not more than half so, success crowning this friendly attempt, now she smiled and said, "I'm Helen Watson," and edged a bit forward up the sloping seat of the grim chair. "You're Mrs. Laurence Stacpole, aren't you? I saw it on the register so I thought you must be Henrietta Clayton because my sister

Sallie—Tilberry she was then, was at St. Tim's with you ages ago and I remember—well, wasn't your husband the Stacpole who was at Westminster with Arthur Andrews? I *knew* it!" she cried in triumph, needing for corroboration only the beginning of a hunted look in Hennie's eyes. "Isn't that wonderful!" She did believe, always, in putting things on a familiar footing at once with anyone her practiced scrutiny approved, and via boarding schools it was almost always possible. "I do love everything cozy, and schools are such a help when you're off somewhere, aren't they? Except not when you're too far off, like traveling in England for instance, which we do—Standard Oil, DeLancey is—because I never can remember one from another there or which is which, and get them mixed up with names of well-known prisons. Except Eton, of course." She smiled at the woman in the other chair who smiled back and said how nice, though she did not, Helen Watson noticed, say she recalled Sallie Tilberry or that Arthur Andrews was anything like a household word in the Stacpole family. Shy, perhaps; or with a wretchedly poor memory—that the more likely, as she didn't look shy.

"*How*ever—" Mrs. Watson said. "This is an awfully pleasant little inn, on the whole, though you'll find some rather gruesome types do manage to stray in from time to time; I mean that dark man and his wife with the blouse, if she is. They're the end, absolutely, and I make sure to avoid them like the plague, not but what I envy anybody who writes," she went on, not afraid to sound as broad-minded as she knew herself to be. "I only wish I had the time for it because it must be such a relaxation, but would you have the time for it?" Mrs. Stacpole said she mislaid at least three months out of every year as it was, and most of every morning. With a sweet, shared resignation they shook their heads over the multitudinous hardships of the well-to-do.

"And anyway, I haven't anything to write about," Hennie said, sounding pleased. "Tell me, are there any interesting people staying here?"

Helen Watson gave a little laugh she hoped was not too abrupt or deprecatory or patronizing in any way, and said heavens but she had enough to write about, all too much, oh Lord yes, but not the time; no, never the time. "Oh, I have done one or two little things; they're nothing too wonderful, but one did come out." She screwed up her eyes as though she couldn't quite recall when or where this little thing had seen the light of day, or as though sun instead of a steady press of fog lay on her lids. "About seven years ago."

"In the *Junior League Magazine?*"

"You saw it! Or no; no." Why that inexplicable guilty look in Mrs. Stacpole's eyes? "But a very good guess. Not a story exactly; it was more like a character sketch, about this cute old woman in Scarsdale." Mrs. Stacpole encouraged her to tell more, saying it sounded very interesting. Why then did she look as though she might be going to sleep again, Mrs. Watson naturally wondered. Sea air, presumably; not used to it yet; it takes a day or two. "I thought you just might have seen it. I sign my own name, Helen Watson, Scarsdale, though of course I had transferred from Rochester at one time, as you know, as you know Sallie, and of course I was Helen Tilberry then which I should have used *if* they had published anything of mine then, but they didn't. Well, I wrote up this cute old lady who makes afghans out of old stockings and then I also have in mind a novel, more or less novel length though possibly a little shorter like *Ethan Frome*, all about this set of friends all shut up by a bad snowstorm way off in this Adirondack cabin, my dear!" Perfectly safe, obviously so, to tell Mrs. Stacpole this long-cherished plot; she didn't look as though she'd have the energy to steal it. She kept stretching her arms out in front of her, the insides of the elbows of her orange wool jacket uppermost, linking her little fingers and stretching, and almost yawning, and Mrs. Watson could see it was perfectly safe to tell her anything. "So there they stay for ten chapters absolutely snowbound with all their reactions, I mean their reactions to each other."

"It sounds absolutely fascinating," Mrs. Stacpole said in a voice holding more interest than Mrs. Watson had supposed might be forthcoming. "I'm going to read it; it sounds terribly good. Why don't you begin working on it right away?"

"Well, but how can I?"

"Couldn't you?"

"But here I am for the rest of the week and DeLancey driving down to get me and then the children will come back to Scarsdale from a ranch out West and there's the blood bank I work for and the first meeting of the Thursday Sewing-Reading at my house, what's more. Oh, and the start of that awful round of dentistry and dancing school! I have no time to myself," she finished, trying not to sound complacent. Never should it be said in Scarsdale that Helen Watson had won literary fame and fortune at the expense of her children's teeth. She decided Mrs. Stacpole must have the unpleasant type of mind that can't stick to any one thing for any length of time at all because of the next thing she said, stretching her arms again—"I know a man who is quite a good landscape painter but all last winter he didn't lift a brush because he said he was waiting to be called for jury duty." Mrs. Watson replied, gently reproving this unnecessary change of subject, but willing to shift her mind, that as it happened she had never served on a jury but if she ever did she was certain it would be very, very interesting from the human angle. All at once she found herself enveloped in a blue mesmeric stare from the large eyes across and heard Mrs. Stacpole saying "If I were you I'd go home this afternoon and start your book right after breakfast tomorrow morning. Stacks of fresh paper, and notebooks, and sharp pencils!"

"But good heavens, I have my room here till Wednesday. Mr. Fletcher expects—"

Mrs. Stacpole smiled a warm smile, and Mrs. Watson wondered how she could have thought for a moment the woman was absent-minded. "Innkeepers constantly have people go off at the drop of a hat; they expect it. It's part of their business," she said earnestly, and Mrs. Watson received the impression innkeepers would be somehow disappointed if this were not so, and then she found herself hoping Mrs. Stacpole might not consider the Watsons lived stultified lives and didn't get up once in a while and go, when least expected to. "You could get the whole plot down in new notebooks before the children come back, and after that it would simply tear along, a chapter a day, I shouldn't wonder. Are there any fascinating people here at the inn, did you say?"

Mrs. Watson, perched now on the very lip of the sloping seat, drawn up there by the intensity of her feelings, slowly said, calculating, "I suppose I could. It would, wouldn't it?"

Presently, in a town suit and a town hat she came to her bedroom window, high above the lawn, and communicated with Hennie in a strident whisper. She held her handbag and gloves, symbols of a happy martyrdom to her art, over the sill so Hennie could see them. "I'm leaving before lunch and Mr. Fletcher is fee-ourious!" she hissed. Hennie beamed at her, and held up a single finger as though she meant "Come-down-and-tell-me-all," but it couldn't have been that because by the time she got down the two flights the V-shaped chair was empty and Mrs. Watson couldn't even be sure the whisk of orange-pink around the corner of the inn was a shoulder, disappearing. "Never mind," she thought, and began working her gloves on her fingers; "I'll just catch the 11·13 as it is, and I *must* remember to send her a copy the minute the book comes out."

Hennie went walking with the pear-shaped Englishman. She hadn't actually planned to quite yet but as she was lurking for sanctuary in her cottage her glance had strayed through the window and come to rest upon his hopeful figure, and a minute later when she came out buttoning a long red coat against the cold fog, there he was, wandering ever nearer, at the corner of her cottage, elaborately casual, hands in pockets, gently blowing fog beads off his sandy, or gray, mustache. "Oh, ha! Why, there you are!" he had said. He had added, "I have a nice little fire going in my cottage."

Hennie smiled at him over the knot she was making in her scarf. "But you English," she said, "you simply love to be out in all kinds of weather, the worse the better; or is that one of those transatlantic illusions?"

"M'hm, yes," he agreed with regret and fell into step beside her. "Yes, we do, of course. There's nothing like a good blow, we say." They ground along the beach for a time until the fog began lifting and a sharp new wind blew them inland, along a gray road to the village. Hennie felt she could walk twenty miles; she skimmed along; her short hair blew back and cold salt air scoured her skin. "I came to the Seagull to be alone!" She shouted the lie through the wind to her companion, a mercury of laughter rising in her throat and she laughed out loud when he shouted back, taking her arm in his, "Oh, absolutely! Best place in the world for that!" and all too soon they were facing each other across the plastic top of a table in a coffee shop.

"Play golf?" he inquired, staring lovingly into her eyes.

Hennie made a face and said no; she didn't play anything if she could help it. "I hate all games; I just like to sit; I specially hate to watch them," she said and saw a look of withdrawal come over his nice round features. "I haven't any competitive spirit whatsoever, but I do realize that's a terrible thing to admit to an Englishman, but I can't help it and I don't try to because if there is one thing I dislike it's *striving*. Cream?" I hope this won't discourage him, she thought; I'm perfectly sure he was going to ask me to play golf with him in the morning; maybe I shouldn't be so fierce.

"Sorry to hear you say so," he said. "I was just going to suggest golf in the morning. I'd be awfully glad to give you a lesson." Their minds' eye pictures of his hands guiding hers were identical.

"Sugar?" she asked, smiling on him over the softly concave toast. Did her hope of learning to live sideways include Mr. Batten? He was so easy. He was no feather in her cap. Silly to have come all this way if adventure in any large sense became impossible because she knew such a nice man as Mr. Batten to be lurking, waiting, watching for her, like a great fond cat at a mousehole for her to come out to him. His very presence at the Seagull might jeopardize acquaintance with the stranger who had, or would, or might, come by the late train. Somehow must she induce him to make his departure from the Seagull? But Mr. Batten was looking the very picture of solidity, sitting there, one splendid red fist on the edge of the table. Let me see; let me see; there must be some way to shake him off as he is so terribly not what I mean by living a double life, oh, absolutely not.

"Three spoonfuls, please," he said. "Oh, thanks very

much," he said, accepting his cup, not looking at her, but, dear me, could that be his sturdy knee she felt beneath the table? And a minute later, was that his well-shod foot? She redisposed her long legs without ceasing to beam on him, and when, presently, she inquired, "More coffee?," lifting the pot with its ingrowing lid, it was with every indication of solicitude although she had by then decided that at luncheon she would prop Shakespeare against the water pitcher and right after dessert at dinner speed to her room by the side door, and in the long trance of a hot tub some way would occur to her for getting rid of him forever. She had frequently noticed, and indeed pointed it out to Laurence more than once though each time she felt she hadn't his entire agreement, if any, that if she did not actually think out a problem but simply let her mind go limp then perfect solutions materialized out of nothing at all, out of the air, out of the swaying, warm-scented atmosphere over a tub for instance, or from the cube of cool darkness of one's own room, at night. "It's much the best way, darling," she had said, but he would only give his head a little shake and appear to be consciously and with difficulty refraining from speech. Surely to goodness if Mr. Batten had been hanging around the Seagull all summer was there any reason why he shouldn't go along home now, to his wife and family, and leave her free to seek adventure? He must not be allowed to become attached to her.

"Such a nice walk, and elevenses," she said on the inn lawn. If we never meet again, what of it? inquired her charming look, and she gave him her hand and a final-parting kind of smile, warm yet receding. But though he grasped her fingers and said good-by for now, he was as full as she was of schemes.

"Tell you what," he said, holding her fingers. "I'd ordered myself a two-inch *filet mignon* at the bar and grill in the village for luncheon—Fletcher's chef is at a complete loss about beef—and I'd be delighted if I might ring them up now and say two."

She had never seen a kinder face, a rosier, more hopeful face than Mr. Batten's. She looked away from it murmuring *oh*; she looked everywhere, down at the grass, at the horizon, at the sky. "Oh, I am so sorry but I had planned, had promised, to lunch at the table of, well, what *is* their name!—stupid of me—that interesting-looking couple, you must know—he looks like Robert Louis Stevenson."

Mr. Batten shook his head, let go her hand, and scuffed his brown shoe at a late dandelion and said he hadn't the remotest idea whom she could mean. He advised putting them off; why not dine with them tonight instead; but she demurred; she didn't want to be rude, she said; they had seemed particularly eager to have her, she went on, unable to refrain from widening her eyes at hearing this lie, which elicited a gallant but sorrowful "Of course, of course" from Mr. Batten. She said he must know who they were because they had been at the Seagull for three weeks past. He shook his head again, said he hadn't seen them at all, but then he brightened and said well, if that was the way it was he'd eat his way through his lonely *filet* and be back at the Seagull by the time she was through being nice to this couple she spoke of—he couldn't possibly think who they might be—in plenty of time for tea or an early highball with her in the living room of his cottage, before the fire. Now that, she cried, was brilliant, and beamed on him, confident of finding in the interval some way to avoid it. She went hurrying off to find the Stevensons and invite herself to lunch with them, not that it was necessary if Mr. Batten were to be away in the village, but having dreamed up the luncheon party she felt it would somehow be unfair to the Stevensons if it did not take place.

Luncheon with the Stevensons was very late. "Thank you so much but I can't have another," she was still saying after one-thirty. The more I don't care for them the politer I get, she noticed. "Two such wonderful Martinis after a morning in this sea air and I never drink in the middle of the day anyway, and I'd be too sleepy to sit up, even."

"Ah-*ha*," said Mr. Stevenson, in a tone he may have believed to be full of the most merry implications, and he lifted a dark commanding finger at the hovering waiter. She had to cover up annoyance with a smile because after all she had sought sanctuary with them. "Thank you very much," she said meekly, furious at heart. Undoubtedly Mr. Batten would have ordered a great many cocktails too. At last they went into the dining room. It's just simple snobbery, she told herself, making me regret that wonderfully acquiescent shade of pink Mrs. Stevenson's blouse is. Pink? It's a sly cerise. But probably if the truth were known I'd love to wear that color myself and don't dare, and how can I possibly be presumptuous enough to apply social yardsticks to a color God must be quite partial to, seeing how much of it there is around. And what if Mr. Stevenson leans a little low over his soup plate? About twice as low as I ever let Will—more like Stockinette over cream he looks—then no doubt it may simply mean the poor man needs glasses and can't bring himself to wear them because of what it would do to his profile. All this is far preferable to fending off Mr. Batten on a long, late afternoon walk home from the village after a stimulating steak luncheon; linking arms would be only the beginning; there would be a loving, nudging hip in no time, surely—and happening to glance up she found herself staring directly into the very eyes of Mr. Batten himself, eyes calf-sad and reproachful, blue as sapphires in his red face, gazing across knives and forks at her from his accustomed table.

What could she do then but devote herself to Mr. Stevenson? And what she was rewarded with was a long account, half-bravado, half-forlorn, of why the Stevensons were spending their vacation at the Seagull. "But it's too ritzy for us," he said in a loud voice. "That's what I say and so does she." He waved his spoon toward his wife, proud of her loyalty, and she laughed her quick, loyal laugh, at once embarrassed for him and delighted with his daring. "Too God-damned ritzy," he said a bit louder, and then his wife whispered, "Oh, sweetie, hush," and tucked her chin into the big bow of her blouse. "Been here three weeks," he went on, for all the echoing dining room to hear, "and haven't got to know a single living soul, except *you*." He bowed gracefully to Hennie. "How we happened to come in the first place was, when I was a boy my family used to take their two weeks another part of the island, you wouldn't know the name in fact, and those days we always thought the Seagull was the last word, so when I got financially so I could manage it we—but now, three solid weeks!" All at once listless, the noon cocktails gone out of him, fingering the tines of his fork, he said heavily, without rancor, "Now I say the hell with it."

"Oh, I do see." Hennie's voice was soft, the voice of an understanding pigeon. "Horrid. Absolutely horrid for you because it's a stupid place really, and you know what I'd do if I were you? I'd go back to the place you used to go to and have some real fun for the last week of your vacation." She leaned forward in her eagerness to have them made happy, ignoring the automatic, periscope-like flicker in Mr. Stevenson's eyes automatically directed at once into the neckline of her sweater—longing to smooth and soothe away their silly disappointment. "You bet I would; tomorrow morning, first thing!"

The man who didn't, after all, resemble Stevenson so very closely, asked, dubious, "But Mr. Fletcher?"

"To hell with him," said Hennie, and sat back. Like everyone living she longed to be thought wonderful and when a few did she felt for them an incorrigible scorn. "I don't see why you *don't* go," she said, and now her voice was very little like a pigeon's; more like a jay's.

As soon as it was decent, she escaped—perhaps even a little sooner than then. She sped along the path to her small white room free at last from both the painful confidences of her host and the injured stare of Mr. Batten, who had with such mad, unreasoning quixotism forgone a *filet mignon* for her sake, though when she had shut her door, chancing to glance through her window she saw, floating reproachfully nearer in the fog, a pear-shaped figure. She ran down her white shade with a whizz.

Hennie had the lounge to herself for tea. She had waked from a Martini-induced nap to find the sun shining and beyond the crouching mastadon dunes the booming sea was blue. The doors to the gift shop were closed, until next June she realized with a slight start at her own doing, and there was no sign of the Stevensons, who must have gone while she slept. She found she was remembering Mrs. Stevenson's loud giggle with a maternal kind of affection and she hoped, and sent such a wish after them, that they would have a high old time at the place they were going. Mr. Batten was nowhere to be seen; presumably he had stalked off alone to the links, round-faced, solitary, and offended, breathing in large gulps of sea air as he strode in order to breathe out reproaches at woman's perfidy.

She carried her tea tray out to the lawn.

She hadn't been long in a warm sunny angle when he drifted around the near corner of the inn and fitted himself into one of the V-shaped chairs with a dexterity betokening a summer of practice. His expression was extremely bland.

"Not playing golf?" she asked. "I thought that was what you are staying on at the Seagull for."

"M'mn, yes; it is. Well, as a matter of fact, I stayed on because m'wife and I had a, well, a bit of a tiff last week, what you might call a tiff I suppose, so she went off to New York and I stayed behind, to teach her a lesson. Care to have what you people call a highball with me before dinner? I keep a supply of everything in my little cottage."

"But I'm rather sorry for her, aren't you? Thank you so much, but I had so many Martinis with those charming Stevensons that I have vowed myself to milk for the rest of the week. But terribly kind of you. She's probably feeling terribly lonely, and sorry she—tiffed with you."

"Oh, no. No; I shouldn't think so. Buying herself one hell of a lot of new hats more likely. It's what she always does when we have a bit of a—what shall I call 'em—a tiff, and then," he finished gloomily, remembering, "I get these monstrous great bills from all these hat women."

Hennie laughed. "Wars are expensive. But I'm glad a few hats, in your case, mean peace again."

"So far yes, or an armistice, rather." He was cautious. "This time, I'm not so sure." He stared solemnly up at a sunstruck cornice, snow-white against the deep blue sky. "There are limits to a man's patience, aren't there?" he asked somewhat vaguely, as though he had not yet fully established once and for all what those limits might be. "Matter of fact," he confessed, "I can't for the life of me remember what it was this time we couldn't agree about, so how do I know what I might be letting myself in for if I apologized and said she was right; damn it, maybe *I'm* right! See my difficulty? Annoying, the whole thing, and I can't seem to concentrate on anything and sometimes I wonder if she understands me. *That*," he said, only too obviously just seized with the inspiration, and turning round full eyes upon her, "was what I wanted to talk to you about at luncheon. Your advice, I wanted."

"Oh, I am so sorry. The sea air and our lovely long walk together this morning *crept up on me* and after luncheon I went right to bed." Alone, she nearly added. "But now it's lovely and invigorating, isn't it? Though the chambermaid tells me the radio says fog again before night and, of course, winter's not far off."

He answered, "Mh'hmn, yes," politely, but it was clear he wasn't entirely mollified, even by her romantic implication that it had been he who could take the tender blame for having tired her out. They sat on, silent, soaking up the sun. Hennie dreamed: I could telephone his wife in New York and I'd say, "Dear Mrs. Batten, though I am but a stranger to you and shall ever remain so, may I tell you your husband is lonesome and sorry too, even if he doesn't know for what, and he would love to be invited home now. He isn't the stuff heroes and romantic strangers are made of; by no means is he. So, furthermore, Mrs. Batten, this would be a kindness not only to him but to me as well because I have left my home and am here at the seaside seeking—but so far I—" But the haughty matron Hennie could so vividly see in her mind's eye said, only, "*Oh*, really?" into the telephone, from under a perched, a terribly expensive hat of unforgiving arcs of stiff veiling and high bows of the most relentless satin—a hat that could have been bought only out of revenge.

"So if I were you," Hennie said aloud to Mr. Batten, stifling a jet of laughter at this phrase so recurrent with her of late, "if I were you I'd pack and go up to town without the least bit of warning, and surprise her. You could tell her you had been having a wonderful time down here and then she'd wonder what you had been up to." Here Hennie saw fit to widen her eyes at him, and to lean the upper part of herself toward him over the arm of her chair, hoping he would be ultimately left with the impression that they had indeed had an illicit interval together in his cottage. "And take her an enormous box of flowers too," she suggested unselfishly, warming to her work. "Wouldn't she be surprised?"

"Jove." A faint and faraway but perceptible and growing glint appeared on Mr. Batten's face. "She would, wouldn't she! Ha! Yes, she would. Baffled's no word for it." He thrust his hands deep into his pockets and his happiness began spreading over him, warmer than the sunshine. "Clever, m'dear, you're very clever. Don't know as I'd have thought of it myself. Teach her a lesson, wouldn't it? Just toss everything into the motor and I'd be home in time for dinner. M'hm—dinner at home." Deep emotion flooded his voice. "Dinner—at—home." He struggled up out of the dreadful chair and beamed down at her, stretched in the sun. "And you, you look me up some time when you get to town for a day's shopping. You do go to New York to shop?"

"Constantly."

"Good. Good; we'll have tea together, shall we?"

"Yes, let's. Some day during the winter I'll call you, indeed I will." They squinted lovingly at one another in the strong sun and then, even before he had quite gone, closing her eyes she had forgotten what he looked like.

"Gone away, gone away, gone away," she sang, the sun on her lids, and warming the length of her. "Every damned last one of them gone now and here I am, alone at last, in the blessed sun. *Now* let's see who turns up by the evening train. Hear the waves, tumbling up and falling back, and the wind, looking for something all over the place, the low accompaniment to solitude. Did I make that up? The low accompaniment to solitude, by H. Stacpole, her only poem. Ah, this is peace. Surely in seven or eight more days someone, some stranger—"

All at once she rose up and walked lightly in at the inn door and up to Mr. Fletcher at his office window. "I find it somewhat too quiet here," she said severely to this astonished man, "so I am afraid I must change my plans and I shall have to leave tomorrow morning—no, today, in fact, by the 5:10."

The poor bewildered manager opened his hands. "But madam, I thought—" Here he remembered to bow, but when he came up from the curtest in his repertory Hennie was walking lightly away, saying, "I am very sorry." From the doorway she glanced back at him over her shoulder, in a way appearing just as surprised as he; she smiled at him, and nodded, and said, "Very sorry" again, while he continued to stand there, confounded, shaking his head, his eyes popping and his mouth ajar.

Passing through the Stacpoles' pantry at the end of the afternoon on his way to the back hall to get his leather jacket and go home for the night, Gino touched the handle of a water faucet just enough to set the water dribbling. The drumming of this thin but persistent stream into the sink might in time penetrate through to Agnes's attention and she would have to come in from the kitchen and turn it off. He also, with practiced deft silent foot, moved the pantry scrap basket somewhat away from its accustomed place though not much, and if she didn't notice this when she came in to turn off the water, and if she put the light out and then, perhaps, tossed something toward it, a crumpled-up orange paper, a used paper towel, an empty Huntley and Palmer biscuit tin, who knows what?—whatever it might be would fall on the floor and she would have to bend over and pick it up again. He smiled, there by himself, visualizing this large-hipped stooping and simultaneous grunting.

In the Stacpole living room Clare sent glance after glance of love and admiration, waves of them, over her brother's head to Joseph Wood, believing, although she was a girl of over-average intelligence and had done very well at junior college, that only they two were aware of these bright fluctuations. The narrow dark rough head between them she supposed to be filled with thoughts of model airplanes. "Done your homework for Monday?" she inquired, in an elder-sisterly way.

"Nope."

"Well, it's getting late and you know the law about no homework after dinner, so you—"

"And I amn't going to do it."

"Will!" She tossed an appealing glance, though actually she could not have cared less if her brother went ignorant as a savage back to school Monday morning, over his head to the man at the other end of the sofa. Normally, neither would Joseph Wood have had any concern for Will's long division or his spelling, but he strongly felt the pull of Clare's appealing eyes.

"Old man, how will you ever—" he reasonably began, but Will threw himself to the floor and rapidly somersaulted across the rug to the door.

"There wasn't any!" he shouted, collided with a chair, righted himself, and disappeared into the hall, over and over. He returned at once, demurely, on his two feet, and beamed at them from the doorway. "Nut tests, all Friday morning," he explained. "Anyway, tomorrow's all Sunday."

Clare shook her head after his sneakered feet had thundered up the stairs. "I hate to think what *he* got. Barely passed, probably."

"Oh, I don't know." Jo attempted to sound tolerant; after all, he planned to make the child his brother-in-law. "Seems bright enough."

"He is and he isn't, if you know what I mean. I mean sometimes he's imbeciliac and then other times rather horribly clever. He's such a mixture. I like people to be just like themselves all the time, don't you? Sometimes

I've wondered," said she, to whom the idea had only that minute providentially presented itself, "if Mummy weren't too old when she had him."

"Oh? How old was she, then?"

Clare had to calculate, tapping her fingers on a pillow. "Thirty-three, if I'm nineteen and he's ten."

"That doesn't seem so very old," he began, but at a warning look appearing on her face, "well, pretty old at that. It wouldn't be for a man, though," he stoutly averred.

"What? Oh, yes, well, don't gloat."

After a little silence he inquired, rather too casually, "Where was it you said your mother had gone?"

"Mummy? Oh, she's just gone off to an inn on Long Island."

"She has? What for? With a group of her friends, do you mean?"

"Why shouldn't she?" Her voice was sharp, but he was not enough used to it yet to know the sharpness had fear in it. "I'm sure I don't know any reason she shouldn't go away for a while alone if she wants to. Why shouldn't women lead their own lives?" she asked, and laid her hand across her abdomen to warm away the quaking there. "It's a free country."

His crew cut stood up straight with surprise. "But *you* wouldn't—" he began, but she cut him short by saying she couldn't think of a single reason in the world why her mother should stay home every minute.

There was another silence. Jo appeared to be turning

over something in his mind. After a while his brow cleared, he stretched, recrossed his legs and took out his pipe. "Oh, well," he said, his voice overflowing with tolerance. "They haven't got much to occupy them at that age. Have to keep going somehow, I suppose, or they'd stiffen in their tracks." He scratched a match along the underside of Hennie's prettiest table, and Clare rounded on him.

"If you knew what it's like here without her, all day! Will behaves like a fiend and those two in the kitchen are beyond all. I have to tell them and tell them things and *then* they don't do them."

"You'll be all the gladder when she gets back."

"Yah," she said inelegantly, and added in a gloomy voice, "if she ever does."

He retired into silence. Will could be heard thundering about upstairs. From the kitchen came a waft of roasting meat. Actually, perhaps the house was not too different from its accustomed self. "Are you happy?" she murmured. She leaned her head back against the chintz and leaving his pipe behind him he came along the sofa to her like a spider down a thread. They murmured and kissed. "You are happy?" she whispered after a time. "I have to know."

"You know, Clare, Clare darling, I've said I've been happy before, other times in my life, but now I can't remember what about and I see I never was!"

"I'm so sorry for *other people*," she burst out, and he agreed with fervor. She lay and watched his love for her dilating the black pupils in his nearby eyes, and the smile she caused folding back his cheeks. "It'll be wonderful," she said. "But we don't want to wait too long, do we? We don't want to be old when we have our family. I mean, as we just said, look at Will. It simply isn't safe, that's all I mean."

He stirred and shifted and glanced away from her. "The minute I pass my bar exams," he promised, but she sighed, and took his hand and played with his signet ring. "M'hmn?" he asked.

"I didn't say anything," she said softly. There was a considerable pause; then she said, "As a matter of fact I've always felt, all my life that is, I've always felt June weddings were terribly conventional somehow, haven't you, and white velvet is so becoming, after all. It gets sometimes so I can hardly bring myself to *go* to a June wedding with all that syringa I know there'll be. Or whatever it is."

"Velvet?" cried the poor bewildered boy, and taking back his hand he moved one space down the sofa.

Clare was speaking out loud but not to anyone. Or perhaps it was to herself she pointed out, in a thoughtful kind of voice, "Though I suppose in spring vacation even, though it's often still cold then, velvet would look funny."

The only thing Jo was able to contribute to this conversation, and Clare didn't seem to hear it, was the observation, delivered with dignity into the black charred empty bowl of the pipe he had taken up again to arm himself with, that probably there were worse things in this world than being conventional.

Laurence's back was disappointingly better now while his chief audience and sympathizer was not at home. "Gone visiting," he said to inquiries; even to himself he would not say "gone away" because of the way it sounded, and certainly she would come home in a week, in a week or ten days. There was a song she sometimes sang about the house about Malbrouck, who had gone to the wars. *"Il reviendra-z-à Pâques, ou à la Trinité—la Trinité se passe—la Trinité se passe—"* He wished he had not remembered it.

He was walking home to dinner through the misty late afternoon, having hung around in his office all Saturday, making up work for himself after everyone else had left. He paced along the pavement of the wet colorless avenue, with the stems of its oaks soaked and dripping faraway up among gauze veils. From time to time, by the giving of a delayed jerk to himself, he managed to summon up in his back satisfactory twinges, but they would be in a manner of speaking wasted, without anyone to describe them to; just as it is said that the falling of great trees in a forest makes no sound unless someone is there to hear, so was it with Laurence's sacroiliac joint—the pains were nothing without Hennie to commiserate. He was not likely to tell her this fact about himself. He might, some day, for her enlightenment, tell her about the falling of trees in forests, but then she would say she didn't believe it. "Squirrels," she would point out.

"And damned little commiseration I've had out of her lately," he said to himself, going down one curbstone and up the next, "only a lot of high-powered nonsense."

He had lain a long time awake in the dark, late Thursday night. He had heard her, after all her talk, soon drop easily into sleep-breathing. He had waited a few moments and then roused up on an elbow, leaned across the unseen, sometimes limitlessly wide, dark alley between their beds and waked her with a mournful "Have I *done* anything you don't like?"

Slowly she had swum awake, murmuring, her arms coming out to push back the sheet that, like a shallow wave, had lapped over her shoulders. He could tell that the whole recent, undesirable scene had gone completely out of her mind, and he waited, most patient, most uncomfortable on his fast-numbing elbow while, across there in the dark, she began collecting her scattered wits.

"Not a thing," she finally assured him, "but in a way what I mean is, it would be better if you had. See what I mean? If I only had something to struggle against!"

He had thumped backward. "Good God Almighty," he had grumbled.

Now, tires of homebound passing cars swished past him, a hushed recurrent whoosh-whoosh on the wet asphalt; they passed and passed in two streams, with white-faced identical anonymous occupants staring out from under the wet glistening turtle tops. This mist in the air would string out into rain before night. "Damned twingey weather," he said and waited for corroboration from his lumbar region, but none came. It must be very gloomy and gray on Long Island he thought, and whereas twenty years back he would have been genuinely concerned at having his love spend a miserable wet week at the sea, concerned but simultaneously satisfied because of the pleasure he would take in telling her how sorry he was, now, although he loved her far, far more than he had at that twenty-years-ago time, he was able to regard her probable disappointment with a bland equanimity. "We all told her not to go to the sea, anyway," he remarked to a dun leaf which had been interrupted in its slow spiraling to the wet walk by the eddy of the slow slipstream of his walking to slide over the brown sharkskin shoulders and fall behind him to the wet pavement. "And what the hell she thinks she's doing there *I* don't know."

He would have been glad to consult some good friend about her behavior, but each good friend he called to mind he rejected, for one reason or another. The truth was, he was embarrassed by Hennie's high spirits, and hoped no one would get to know about them. He didn't for a minute believe she wanted to be away from home for any length of time, but for occasional half-minutes he did, and these suspicions, mingling gastrically with a faint dyspepsia, caused him a melancholy.

Edward Latham was coming to dinner with him. Many a time lately he had reminded Hennie they ought to ask Edward Latham, the new trust officer at the bank; he had come from Cleveland and maintained a bachelor's apartment downtown. "I'm keeping him up my sleeve," she had told Laurence. "A perfectly good bachelor is too good to use up all of a sudden, without a reason. It's like having money in the bank," and Laurence knew what that phrase meant to her—large neat piles of stacked coins, mostly shiny fifty-cent pieces or ten-dollar gold pieces, to be drawn on when necessity occurred, but he was not willing to regard Edward Latham in this way; his social conscience revolted and he had, a trifle treacherously, asked him to dinner in her absence. If she had bewildered him by dashing to Long Island for no reason she could scarcely object to his asking Edward Latham to dinner behind her back.

Laurence was tall and thin, with a long face and thoughtful eyes. "In a way," Hennie had once said, scrutinizing him minutely, "you remind me of Abraham Lincoln."

"Rugged?" he had asked, pleased. He had been much younger then.

"Oh, no, not rugged at all, thank goodness. Nice smooth hair."

"No beard either, or hadn't you noticed. If I keep my clothes pressed it's only to please the crass depositors."

Hennie said did he think he ought to derogate the father of his country like that, and Laurence had replied he should have supposed that even way back in kindergarten someone would have told her that—but she had interrupted with a bright smile.

"My mother never let me go to kindergarten. She'd rather have me playing out in the sun and fresh air in the back yard. I've told you! That's why I'm so healthy."

"And ignorant," he had added, smoothing a lock of her hair back over her ear.

She had told him then she couldn't imagine how she had ever thought for a minute he looked like Lincoln because as a matter of fact there wasn't the faintest resemblance. "I see *you* splitting rails!" she had scoffed.

"Not cutting down cherry trees?" he had asked meekly.

He stalked his quiet way home up the avenue and turned off it toward his own house. Even as he crossed the street, diagonally, looking at its white clapboard front, glistening white, formal, and one would suppose uncommunicative of everything except the assurance of comfort and ease within, he knew she was home. He swung open the door and there in the hall stood her suitcase and dressing case.

"I knew it!" he called at large, delighted.

She appeared around the library door. "How could you have? I scarcely knew it myself." Her arm with a handful of mail went around the back of his neck. "You mustn't have known! I meant to surprise you!"

"I am. I am flabbergasted. Did they throw you out?"

"I just came away," she replied airily. "It was an awfully nice place. What would you say to a gin and tonic while I look over this lovely big pile of mail? But Agnes says you have a man coming to dinner so maybe we'd better wait. Who?"

Will came bounding down the stairs in pursuit of a wayward tennis ball, and Laurence said to him, "Look, Mummy's come home!" Hennie, slitting open the tops of envelopes, said, "We've met."

Will gave them a fleeting, loving smile. "I know. It's suave," he agreed, and disappeared.

Comfortably seated at either end of the sofa, each with a ghostly pale drink because they had decided why on earth wait for Edward Latham, each with a pile of mail, Laurence said, "Well, tell me about it. Nice place? Good food? High spirits all settled down now?"

"An awfully nice place but I just thought I'd leave and anyway I hadn't gone for the food. It didn't suit my purposes, somehow."

He looked up from a colored advertisement for a ten-dollar gift box of Wisconsin cheeses, then threw it toward the heap of discarded mail growing on the floor. "Purposes?" he asked with discomfort.

"You know the way I've felt lately—well actually you don't and neither do I, but I thought if I went away for a change—"

"Yes."

"Well, there's no such thing," she told him mysteriously.

Will and his tennis ball came into the room, and she called him over. "Darling, do you know what *mort dans la Résistance* means?" French? Will inquired; no; he didn't at all; they hadn't *had* that. *"Mort pour la patrie,* then?" enunciating with clarity, but Will, escaping to the hall after a ball he must have been in league with, called back it sounded kind of familiar but not very.

Hennie explained to Laurence about the family setup of the Mésuriers. "So I asked for another boy too, for Will to write to. That makes two monthly packages, but

I couldn't bear to—bear not to—it's awful and unforgivable to disappoint children, don't you think so? So here's the card for another one as well."

"My God, I'm glad you're back," he said laughing, leaning over to kiss her just as in at the doorway, long-legged, long-armed, came Edward Latham, smiling, smoothing back his hair along one side of his head.

Laurence got up and introduced him to Hennie. "She returned to me unexpectedly," he said. "I don't know why, but back she came, bag and baggage."

"But that has a rude sound, somehow," Hennie murmured.

Edward Latham had a memorable handshake, with lingering qualities, overtones, which left his partner in this gentlest of indoor sports wondering, with pleasure: Now how could I have made such a good impression *so soon?*

Before he would sit down their guest said perhaps in this case they would rather he just ran along and came another night—his man could always produce cold meat and a salad at no notice—but simultaneously his other hand was out for the long glass, and Hennie leaning from the depths of the sofa was offering him potato chips.

"Laurence is always so terribly gay when I'm away," she said, "dinner parties every night, but when he goes away, I simply mope. Is there a Mrs. Latham who mopes for you?" She eyed him over the rim of her glass, knowing for a fact there wasn't. It seemed she had pressed the exact button to start him off, and he presented them with a pocket version of his life then and there.

"As a matter of fact, no, there isn't." He had a charming slow voice, rather as though he were feeling his way in a not entirely familiar language, so that it was less of a surprise than it might have been when in the course of his life's history it came out he had spent most of his childhood in Paris while his father pursued a minor diplomatic career.

"How delightful. So you must have worn black smocks."

"Like peasant children? Why should I? Oh no; I played in the Parc Monceau in a long succession of sailor suits and then went out of them into plus fours and Hotchkiss. And then Yale. I've always thought how fortunate I was to have been spared the *brou-ha-ha* of Paris with the Americans in it in the twenties."

They all agreed his parents couldn't have done a wiser thing than send him to Hotchkiss at that juncture in our civilization, but Hennie spared a kindly reminiscent moment, remembering as though it were yesterday her friends and herself buying detachable rhinestone heels in the Rue de Rivoli in 1928, and very short jackets of some dubious white fur which they kept assuring each other couldn't possibly be rabbit, and dresses with beaded panels, none of which had after all proved so very useful back in Connecticut, and in fact her shoe repair man had refused even to try to attach the glittering heels to her best evening slippers. "A real frog scheme," he had said discouragingly.

"And then," Hennie prompted Mr. Latham, who scarcely needed it.

"You will be bored with me by now. Did you have a pleasant change on Long Island, Mrs. Stacpole? Must I really? Well, then, I'm a banker with leisure, maybe more leisure than is good for me; I don't know." His large, light blue eyes roved slowly around the room as he spoke, pausing with appreciation, here and there, on a Lowestoft bowl and an old silver tea caddy. "Sometimes I think so," he slowly said.

"That's where a wife comes in handy," Laurence said, but Hennie had leaned forward and was speaking too.

"I beg your pardon?" he inquired, the light blue headlights turning back her way.

"I was only saying, asking, do you really feel that way, that maybe—that you have more strength than you know what to do with, and you must go out of your way to make things happen?"

"As a matter of fact no, Mrs. Stacpole, no, not that. I've suffered from a child with low blood pressure, and it's been a great drawback to me. I don't know if you know anything about low blood pressure." He looked from one to the other but Hennie had lapsed against the sofa back again, and Laurence said he wondered if that wouldn't be another condition a wife would be useful for.

If Mr. Latham stayed rather longer after dinner than the Stacpoles might have expected, he was not a dull companion. They learned that another reason for his slowness of speech was in the fastidious, to him pleasurable, search, the selection, rejection, and eventual choice, of *mots justes*. He had the further gift of recounting anecdotes of such a civilized calm nature that it wasn't always clear when the point had been reached, and Hennie decided this was extremely worldly and attractive. "—and that day as I was standing at the exhibition before a truly vast painting called 'The Battle of Santiago,' up drifted an elderly and charming man, a stranger to me as it happened, a man both spare and courtly, and I could not resist approaching and saying to him of the painting, 'Very fine, isn't it?' Because it was, in fact, a tour de force, impressive if not entirely admirable. And do you know what he replied?" Edward Latham drew his cigarette case forth and slowly made a selection, concealed the case again, and smiled into the turned attentive faces of his hosts. "He said, 'I can't say. I wasn't there.'"

Before he left he stood for a considerable time, still talking. With never a lapse in practiced ease and fluency he balanced, tall, in the center of the room, moving back and forth a little, and all at once, an extension without pause in his account of a boat trip along the Loire in 1948, a long hand swerved down toward Hennie, was shaken, he was beamed up at, he was gone.

CHAPTER FIVE

Next morning Laurence, all traces of his backache gone and forgotten, stood, eyes shut, in the dim shower, with his face raised to the beneficent fierce hot white spray, and rubbed himself down, slowly. So she had come back. He risked the future of his soul by saying to himself he wasn't in the least surprised. He soaped his long thighs. Nice chap, Latham; a good trust officer, very prepossessing, making a good impression on the bank's clients, but he'd stayed too damn long last night, though; ought to have had sense to go home before eleven-thirty with his hostess just back from a train trip and presumably tired out, though to be sure she hadn't looked it; she had looked wonderful, and here he leaned and rapidly manipulated the handles until jets of pure cold sluiced violently down him.

He had meant to be especially quiet that morning, subduing the usual clinkings and cluckings of dressing, the snap of buckles, the clatter of shoe trees, so she could continue to sleep, there in her warm bed. One look over at her and into that warm bed he slid, scarcely dry.

"Oh, you feel like a lizard," she murmured, waking, putting her arms around his cold shoulders to warm him. "A great big lovely cold wet lizard."

He laughed into her hair. "I'll go."

"Yes, do," she whispered, wrapping him tighter.

Later, brisk and businesslike, Laurence stood before his mirror, flipping into the accepted twentieth-century shape his conservatively brown banker's tie; even on a Sunday he was not one to wear bright patterns. "Our friend Joseph has been around a good deal while you have been away," he said.

Hennie lay watching him, the sheet and silk cover under her chin. "I had an admirer at the Seagull, too. I needn't have come home to you at all, if I hadn't wanted to; not for a while, anyway. If Mr. Fletcher had looked the other way for a minute I could have moved right into his, my admirer's, cottage, at the drop of a hat. Are you listening?" Laurence gave a slight snort, and she at once rebuked him, not for doubting her power to charm but because of the kind of sound snorting is, and then lay thinking back to Long Island and the utter unlikelihood that she could ever, even under his utmost pressure, have succumbed to Mr. Batten's sturdy wiles; disappointing; but there it was. Then memory, a drifting unsteered ship, sailed up closer to the present moment, and she recalled last evening and Edward Latham and how his large pale blue eyes had rested on her with pleasure; but hadn't he gazed on the Lowestoft bowl much the same? What if *he* had been at the Seagull, in Mr. Batten's cottage, in Mr. Batten's shoes? How strange that he had never married; rather, that no woman had ever married him. "He must have a secret sorrow," she said.

"Joseph? Oh, I shouldn't think so." Laurence was bestowing about his person, sliding off the chest of drawers and into his pockets, the varied objects without which he would not have felt himself fully dressed, the notebook here, the billfold there, a shoal of change somewhere else; something in each pocket, like Will. "He's getting very good marks in law school, Clare tells me, and he certainly seems to have her just about where he wants her. She's too young, though."

"Of course; much. Not really though, do you think?"

"I suppose not. Hard to believe." He looked down and sighed, but she knew him well enough to know the sigh might as likely come from thinking he had meant to shine his shoes but hadn't and wasn't going to as at the fleet passage of the years. She sat up and threw the covers down the bed.

"What do you say we take him for luncheon with us to the Old Mill today? Because if he's going to be a Stacpole, you know what I mean, we might as well get used to having him around constantly. Anyway I have to get up to start packing parcels for that miserable little French boy. *Two* boys."

The Stacpoles and Jo drove west and then south through a clear warm Sunday morning, and leaving the station wagon parked on a village street, walked down a lane, over a bridge, to an inn they had discovered some years back. Others had discovered it too, and afternoons during the week coveys of well-dressed stout women between the ages of fifty-five and senility descended on it to lay waste large plates of *pâté* sandwiches, cress sandwiches, cucumber sandwiches, and *langues de chat*. "Unspoiled," they often pointed out to each other, "quaint," but then couldn't restrain a gasp and a blink when the bill came. Quaintness comes high, they decided, unlatching their afternoon handbags; it costs a lot to remain unspoiled, they then reminded each other.

Today being Sunday there were no tea-party women driving down the lane, and Laurence was relieved they had the place to themselves. A hundred years ago this inn had been a mill but the dusty men in aprons and the machinery and the loaded sacks had vanished, and now on an irregular triangle of flagstoned terrace still thrusting out, like a low prow into the brown moving water, only potted oleanders stood, and four or five unoccupied round tables laid with yellow and white cross-barred tablecloths and elegantly peaked napkins. The stream, overhung everywhere by drooping branches, parted at this stone prow and flowed away back on both sides, almost level with the terrace floor. Trailing tips of trees leaned into it, the leaves scraps of always-wet green silk, just under the surface of the water, sliding, sliding downstream but never letting go.

The Stacpoles chose the table nearest to the prow. Laurence established his presumptive son-in-law across from him, where he could observe him. I scarcely know him at all, he thought, in spite of his being around all the time; but then, of course, I'm not; that's not right.

"Now eat slowly," Hennie said, while a maid in full, colored skirts and a coif like the white sail of a ship, came around with a deep dish. "The French don't gobble the way we do."

"Why French again?" asked Will. "You're always talking about the French, it seems to me."

"Don't you see? She's wearing a French costume."

How quiet it was. The only sound was the sliding of the small brown river and, presently, the lisp of the felt soles of the maid retreating with her dish over the flagstones toward the inn kitchen. Pools of the sunlight that dropped down among the trees lay trembling here and there—on a tablecloth, on a stone bench, on the brown smooth hair of a Stacpole child, on a pot of geraniums in late-summer exuberant flower.

"Those are truffles," Hennie said to Will, who had leaned toward his plate and was eyeing suspiciously the slice of foreign food lying there. "Those little black things. Isn't it heavenly here? Probably by next week it will be too cold to eat out."

"Are *those* truffles?"

"What did you think truffles were?" asked Laurence.

"Well, but in Ancient History class," Will murmured doubtfully, and at once, complacent, Laurence and Hennie smiled over his head at each other signaling, they couldn't help it, how right they had been in the face of family objection to send the children to a progressive school. "There was this old Roman guy," Will was saying, poking at the gray-tan slice on his plate, "and he had truffles."

"Which old Roman guy?" Clare, very good and gay and pretty, obligingly tried to cast back some eight or nine years over her crowded recollections to the time when she had been ten and had studied the same Ancient History book as her brother. "I don't remember anything about truffles, do you, Jo?" Jo, prompt and loyal, said certainly not; nothing whatever. Laurence hoped he wouldn't always be so prompt, so loyal; it would become boring for Clare. And he thought it ill-advised of Hennie to reach over and pat Jo's hand. Jo didn't seem to care for it either, and sat back.

"Oh, yes, he had them. But I didn't know this was what they were!" Will glanced up sharply at his mother, as though he had not been entirely without experience of her occasionally being wrong about something. "Are you sure? I thought—" Fork dangling, his gaze wandered away, up into the blue sky above the treetops. "I thought they were something bad he had in his throat."

"Snuffles," Clare suggested, the *u* meticulously pointed.

"Quinsy?" asked Hennie, who could well remember her own mother's accounts of racking attacks she had suffered at the turn of the century.

"Tonsils," Laurence said in spite of himself and glanced apologetically over at Jo, who frowned and refrained from speech; right away Laurence thought the better of him for this; maybe Clare was a very lucky girl; no nonsense about Jo; Laurence must warn Hennie not to be so whimsical when he was around; it bothered the boy.

"No, no." A finger traced the yellow pattern of the tablecloth. "I don't know if it was a disease, exactly. It was because he was bad, I think," Will added, making matters no clearer. Laurence, though as nicely as he could, said perhaps it wasn't essential that they pursue this matter to an utter finish, and turning to the young man he had every reason to suppose would eventually though not yet be a member of his family, and whom he knew to be of a serious disposition, asked him how he thought Yale Law School compared with Harvard Law School, and Jo gladly opened his mouth to reply to this good question, but Hennie leaned over the table, looked reproachful and said she'd like to know what use was an expensive private-school education if parents let interesting subjects of conversation just dwindle away, just die, without running them to earth? Clare asked if other people, other Romans, had suffered too from whatever it was, in those remote days, and further, if people still had them, but Will didn't know; he said he supposed so, but then his sister quickly pointed out that he had little enough ground for assuming any such thing. "No evidence," said she, with a loving softening to her voice and a glance over at Jo, whom she knew would one day twist juries and slippery witnesses around his little finger. The Stacpoles forgot to enjoy the *pâté* while they pondered; to be sure they went on eating, but in a lamentably un-French, un-epicurean way, and Will did not eat at all.

Laurence forgot his own recent advice. "Rome was not so long ago, as the crow flies, and this Roman who was troubled with truffles, he must have had a name, so then we'd know, perhaps, what actually was the matter with him. Now think back. Cicero? Caesar? Catiline?"

"Are you quite sure they were in his throat?" his mother asked.

"I thought so."

"False teeth!" Laurence said without knowing he was going to speak a word. Let Joseph think him a silly old man of forty-five; he was on a holiday; Hennie had come back to him like a lamb to the fold; he felt released, expansive, and called the maid and ordered a California Sauterne. Probably it wasn't necessary to tell Hennie to be careful with Jo. What a good place for luncheon. What a fine family he—

"Maybe he wasn't sick, exactly," Will said, "but there was *some*thing bad about him."

"Never mind, never mind." Hennie appeared all at once disenchanted with learning. "And eat your luncheon. Tell me all about your childhood in Dayton, Jo." But Clare appeared to have yet another suggestion trembling on the tip of her tongue; Laurence recognized that accompanying look in the eye and forestalled her, saying, "Let's all forget it." It would be too bad to let Jo come to the conclusion they were *all* foolish.

"Well!" Will flew onto the defensive. "It's in history! And Miss Walters said—" But Clare, with the raised eyebrows of one who has the prospect of a maternal life of her own not too far in the future, interrupted. "Good *heav*ens! Is she still a*live?* Old Falters Walters."

Laurence said the whole subject was now definitely closed, and asked Jo how much time the law students gave to the study of present-day banking methods, but Hennie briefly betrayed him a little by murmuring, "Well, I don't know, I'm sure, but it seems as though we ought to—" and sighing, but Laurence knew it must have been the falsest sigh imaginable, because she looked perfectly happy, glowing, and at peace; whatever nameless excitement she had been troubled by earlier in the week had slipped off her; all that emotional flurry and scurry seemed over. She gazed about their water-bound little world. "How still it is here. You'd never know we were in Connecticut at all. I believe we're going to have salmon for the next course. Do you fish, Jo?"

"He—" Will began again, but they turned on him. "Oh, all right, all right!" Offended to the quick, he flung from his chair and stretched out on his empty stomach on the farthest point of the gray stone prow. This brought his face about a foot above the moving brown water, which sent up dappling lights and gleams, gold refractions to move over his throat and the underside of his chin. His veiled eyes gazed downward. He reached his fingers into the water; ice-cold it was in spite of all the golden lights and the golden sandy bottom. The sun from high above the trees sent floods of light hurrying down to strike through the water on the golden sand, and they came glimmering up again, it seemed more slowly, to the green undersides of the tented, overhanging leaves. "Truffles," he was whispering, rebellious, over and over. But back at the table the rest of the family, with one accord, had decided the whole subject was too boring for anything, and except for him they were eating salmon now, and so very slowly and appreciatively that the most captious Frenchman would have approved.

"You look so shiny, darling," her mother whispered to Clare.

"I what?" But the girl's attention, like a good pointer's, was elsewhere fixed and she did not hear a word.

"Will," Laurence called. "Come on back, Will, and eat your fish." He did not stir; his hand trailed downstream like a leaf in the water. "I said, come now." A reluctant inchworm, Will slowly humped himself upward once in the middle, stood up, and returned.

"It wasn't a disease," he said. "I remember now, and I don't think they were in his throat either, but they were because he was bad."

"Oh, forget it," advised Clare, full of tolerance and the mild California grape.

"I can't, but I do remember now, I'm beginning to remember anyway, it was a thing Miss Walters said he didn't have enough of. That was it—*he didn't have enough of—of—*"

Clare permitted herself a groan, and Laurence smote down his hand, once on the table, and fixed his son with a stern eye and opened his mouth to say that *once and for all*—but Will got ahead of him.

"*Scruples!*" he yelled, radiant. His lashes flew wide, his

eyes danced and he threw back his head. "Yea!" He caught up his fork and gaily pierced his fish. "What do you know!" he cried. Beginning rapidly to eat, his glance leaped from face to face of his family, and between swallows he repeated in a voice of wonder at himself, "What do you know!" He was so relieved he believed they must be so too. "What do you know—but the guy didn't live lately," he added, gratuitously, for their further enlightenment.

"Good God! We never supposed he did!" Laurence burst out, but just then Hennie caught sight of the starched white sail advancing from the kitchen through sun and shadow; it veered around an intervening potted oleander and bore down upon them; there was the whisper of felt shoes on stone.

"Hurry up, Will," she said. "Everybody stop talking to him so he can catch up. Here comes a fruit tart as big as a cart wheel."

A thick sheet of late Sunday afternoon sunshine fell through the library window. Hennie was at her desk slitting open dividend envelopes like a clever monkey; these she had hoarded the evening before; the kernels she neatly abstracted and she consigned to the scrap basket the husks, the slips of paper bearing urgent advice from the boards of directors to invest in government bonds and words of adjuration from a lower level not to dare to change residence without filling out on dotted line.

Clare came in, perched on a chair arm near the desk,

and demanded without preamble, "Don't you disapprove terribly of late marriages?"

"Forty or fifty-ish, do you mean, or those old souls in the evening paper who finally make up their minds at eighty? Have you ever noticed how many of them have lived right next door to each other since their school days?"

Clare took a quavering breath and her eyes begged at her. "Mummy! You *know* I don't take teasing nicely, which is a subject I've thought about quite a lot actually and I believe it's because people only tease me about the things I care about."

"Darling, I'm a fiend. But, lamb, you're only nineteen. Standard Oil of New Jersey, Du Pont, *and* the Texas Company."

"I'll *be* twenty."

"You know something? Probably you think I don't discuss you and Jo enough, with you, but it's only because I'm so absolutely contented about the whole thing. Look how well he fitted in at luncheon."

"I see. Did you think he did really, Mummy? I had a feeling once in a while he was nervous, sort of. I mean, we are rather silly, don't you think we are, a little bit?"

Hennie laid down envelopes with their pleasant kernels still unharvested, and her paper cutter, and appeared to consider. "Have you thought how there's such a long, long time to live after twenty? Ages and ages, though not that it feels like that." The sunlight lay warm about her. Time was not long enough, no matter what people said, what Laurence had said, and she herself just now to her child. All horizons bent their dark lines around too close. Last year was gone, gone, and next year would fly by. But then her mind, that ever-darting fish, floated easily back up to the surface, up to cliché level. "A thing you have to wait and work for seems nicer in the end. Haste makes waste," she added.

"Oh—words!" cried the desperate child.

"That's all very well to say, but how else can people communicate?"

"We aren't communicating."

"Tell me, then, darling. You're afraid of something. What is it?"

Clare's head bent, carrying the soft dark curtains of hair forward beside her cheeks. "What if he gets away?" she muttered.

Then Hennie put her papers and cutter right away in a drawer and came to perch beside her child and encompass her with her arms. She put her mouth against the soft hair that always smelled a little of shampoo powder because Clare never quite got it rinsed out, or was it simply the child herself, smelling delicious? She whispered, "Darling, he never, never will. You don't begin to know your own strength. Probably he sometimes doesn't answer when you speak to him and you think that means something? No, no. I'm an old middle-aged woman now and I *know*, I can tell, he's yours for life, whether you want him or not; he's that kind of man. Do you always remember to use a lot of hot water when you rinse your hair?"

"Mummy!" A smile began to break through. "You're so

good! But you will kind of help me with him, and not discourage him, not scare him? I get him screwed up to a point, and then he slides down again, and it doesn't help any when we, or any one of us, sounds witless."

"Why, of course it wouldn't—though who of us does? When do you actually think you want to be married?"

"Quite soon."

"M'hm, I don't know as I think too well of that."

"Very soon. I think in vacation, but sometimes he says yes and then other times—"

"Spring vacation, you mean; you don't mean Christmas?"

"Well." A becoming, mutinous pink began mounting over her face. "I just think it must be lovely to be all married and safe, so I want— It must be lots of fun, I mean?"

"Oh, it is, it's absolutely the only thing. But Christmas would be too soon, much too soon. This is the only wedding I'll ever be able to give and let's make it something absolutely beautiful, *not* like other weddings; airier!"

"Not fanciful, Mummy!"

Hennie's hand dropped from her child's waist and she dreamed and brooded. "Why not? Why must every great occasion be exactly like every other? We're all such sheep. And why don't American men wear their hair that romantic half-inch longer like Englishmen? But maybe that's beside the point. But with your wedding we'll have the chance to do something bright and gay, but do we? No. Just tramp, tramp up the aisle in ten yards of white satin like every bride since Eve—" Clare turned away her head from her mother; she had indeed seen herself flowing altarward with a white train—"and a round half-dozen healthy bridesmaids in Bendel taffeta galloping on ahead. How can you bear to!"

"Well! And what was your's and Daddy's wedding like, if I may ask?" She went to sit on a chair across the room.

"My darling, haven't I just been describing it? And pewsful of spinsters, all drinking rather warm champagne —later—; just a huge holy cocktail party." Clare's face was as tight shut as a clam. "Let's wait and have it in the spring on a great green lawn somewhere, with violinists hidden behind trees. And a flowering arch."

"I suppose," Clare said thoughtfully, bitterly, "you'd plan to have me come running lightly over a hill onto this lawn you speak of, barefoot."

"*Primavera!*"

"That's what I thought you meant, but I guess for one thing you've forgotten just how pregnant *Primavera* is."

Her mother murmured, "That's not only coarse but beside the point. Now I'm thinking about Jo."

"He would have to be there, I suppose," came a cold voice. "Somehow I can't quite see him prancing on strewn rose petals, not with *his* big feet."

"They aren't so big."

"They're enormous!" the poor girl cried, pride and outrage in her voice. "They're twice the size of mine. They're twelves! Mummy, why do you always try to minimize him?"

But Hennie was floating, rocked in a dream. "Maypoles," she said, "and gauzy temples and ribbons whipping in the breeze. There's no law against a clergyman wearing blue, is there; or crimson?"

"Now listen to me." Clare smoothed her skirt, folded her hands and fixed her mother with her dark eyes. "Enough's enough. This is *my* wedding and please stop looking like that and be some help to me."

Hennie's dream came tumbling down. "Mercy on us," she said, eyeing her daughter. Clare stayed silent, and presently Hennie said, "But even if you could find an apartment and so on, which I doubt, it wouldn't be awfully romantic to sit and watch a man do homework almost a whole year, do you think?"

"*Yes.*"

"I see. How fierce you are! Then I'll make a compact with you: If you promise to stop worrying I'll join forces with you." Then she remembered to give her child a large, sad look. "But you don't consider a bit how lonesome Daddy and I are going to be."

"Oh, I do," Clare replied in exactly the right tones without any corresponding interior emotion whatsoever. "I don't want to leave home for a minute, it's just that— Big or little then?" she asked with interest, and her mother understood her at once.

"Not too big, wouldn't you say? We could get about eighty in the living room if we opened up the big doors to the dining room too. Champagne and tiny sandwiches. Nobody wants to eat if there's enough champagne. And we mustn't forget the old aunts," she said. Clare came back and perched on Hennie's chair arm. Like two pretty witches they leaned toward each other, weaving for each other a spell of words, weaving thoughts and words and smiles together in a fabric, a gold tissue wafting between them, merging at its edges with the gold of the sunlight around their shoulders, and lying in their laps in heaps, a growing tissue of schemes. "And a great big very expensive cake," one of them promised the other, softly.

The grandfather clock in the hall boomed out a slow seven. "Time to see about supper. Tell you what," Hennie said, getting up. "Let's celebrate our collaboration tomorrow; let's go buy you something absolutely unessential, and don't say you'd rather have the money for a pressure cooker because I won't stand for it. Something with a frill, greeny-blue."

"Pink," said Clare firmly. She too got to her feet. "I accept the frill if I must, but it must be pink. I know exactly what I want," she unnecessarily added.

They went out arm in arm, Hennie observing the girl from close to, with a laughing, sideways glancing. "Darling," she said, amused, impressed, her disappointment at so much matter-of-factness only feather-light, "he hasn't a *chance!*"

The object of the Stacpole women's pretty scheming, Mr. Joseph Wood, sat in his room in the law school and glowered. He had taken off his coat and tie, and Moore's *Federal Practice* lay open in his lap but he was not reading. He said out loud that of course he had the greatest respect for Mr. Stacpole, and he loved Clare deeply, deeply, but when it came to Mrs. Stacpole, and Will—

"When I have children," he announced to his room, to the goose-necked lamp and the India print curtains and the rug, so much too blue, that his mother had so kindly sent him from Denver, "by God they're going to stay sitting down at the table!"

He slammed shut *Federal Practice* and opened Pomeroy's *Equity*. "She's ruined him, that's all. The boy's not fit to grow up." A cold trickle of suspicion snaked across his heart. Had she ruined Clare too, in some way he couldn't see? Under that charming soft-brown exterior could there be something of her mother in her? "*Any-thing* of her would be too much!" the poor boy said and he knew for a fact he didn't want to be married, not to Clare or anyone; especially not to Clare, a Stacpole.

CHAPTER SIX

A seven-thirty factory whistle slid into Hennie's sleep, a thin boomerang of a wail flinging up into the early air and returning to ground. She rolled on her side, stretched, and slept again.

"Laundry day, madam," Agnes said soon after. She was on a journey up and down the house, collecting rumpled heaps. "Pearl came early today."

After breakfast Hennie encountered Mr. Tuthill, descending from upstairs. He bent the worn blue of his blue jeans and, slowly kneeling, partly disappeared into a hall cupboard. He's so old, she thought with remorse; I shouldn't let him kneel. Aloud she said, "Just the new shelf in my bathroom, and to fix those two shelves that are wobbly. I don't know why they should be, do you, when nothing else in the house is?"

This he quite properly made no reply to. "M'hm'mn." From the rear view of him the aged man appeared to be giving the matter of shelves his entire, seasoned attention, but when he withdrew his head from the depths he said, "I'm out to Treadway's, Branford way, putting up a pre-fabri-cated cottage." Back in her kitchen Agnes was singing with great good cheer, "Blest be-e the ty-ee that binds, Our heart's inhuman love—"

"Just a little straightening and stiffening, somehow, if you could? We keep flowerpots on them, you see. Maybe that's it, that they're too heavy? It wouldn't take you long, I should think and *also*" she went on quickly, "there's a place in my bathroom—"

"Comes on a truck in twenty-seven bundills, and we had 'em all unloaded afore noon. You know Treadway's?" He sat back on his heels, his long, long feet in rubbers, demurely side by side. He made no move to employ the folding rule sticking out of his pocket, nor the pencil between ear and cap.

"No, I don't believe I do." Mr. Tuthill *m'hm'mn'd* again, more than ready to enlighten her but she pulled her subject to the fore by force. "Do you think angle irons would help?"

"Not so far from Lester's place, where his house is." His voice was gentle, ruminative, his heart away with the prefabricated cottage. "Past Lester's, a way, to be sure, but not so terrible far."

Who in God's name is Lester? Hennie cried within. "Because we're planning to paint the woodwork in this hall," she said. "Gino's going to and we thought if we could get you to fix the shelves first, at the same time you make me the new one in my bathroom it would be— it would be—"

"He don't own, I don't mean. He rents."

"Is that so?"

"Mm'hmn. But I hear he might buy, possibly."

"Do you think you could?" She bent over and put a hand on a shelf, moving it. "You see, just a little wobbly."

Mr. Tuthill shook his head, not hard, not in refusal, but as though any instantaneous decision, pro or con, would be too much to expect of him. He creaked up, strayed out through the pantry, out across the kitchen floor in his big rubbers, toward the back door, saying slowly over his shoulder, "Doubt it. Doubt if I can find the time— Such a rush, ever'thing, these days." His look over his blue shoulder was gentle; she must know, everyone knows, how time behaves. The back door opened just enough to let his thin body through sideways and softly clicked and he was gone, escaped, vanished as if he had never come at all.

He had won again. He always won, that man. Even when she managed to catch and pin him down to using his worn cherished tools on her behalf, then too he was the victor and she the victim, the captive, because part of the price he claimed was that she must stand on one foot and then the other, sometimes in desperation sitting down on the edge of a tub, while he murmured on and on. "I did surely think my number two bit would do it but see here—see here? I have to use my number three; reminds me of a job I had, well, some time back now, nineteen-fourteen, nineteen-thirteen maybe, along about there; just such a situation as you have here; they was this tile wall, very similar to this I'd say." Kneeling, he would peer up into a corner, and feel up there, with his dry old hand. But if she so much as shifted her feet he slowly withdrew from the corner, gazed up at her from under the gray cap she had never seen off, and slowly say, "Come right in the end, however, don't you fear, because what I did then was, I *took* my number three bit, yes, and I give her a terrible poke," he breathed in a voice so fading-soft it would not have stirred the silver fluff on a dandelion head gone to seed. And she would listen, and say, "Ah," with her mind off somewhere else entirely, say, "Yes, ah yes, I see," in admiring tones, because if she didn't listen to him he would go away, to kneel in some other woman's house.

This morning she went back into the living room and found Clare reading in a corner.

"In a bad light," she said.

Clare quickly put down her magazine, not in obedience to her mother's observation, but because she hadn't really been reading but lying in ambush. "I know. Are you doing anything just this minute? Could we have a little dis*cuss*ion about something?"

Hennie said she'd love to; she had expected to have to spend half the morning cheering on Mr. Tuthill while he made a few essential repairs here and there about the house. "But he leaked away out the back door," she complained. "He's positively gifted that way, so nine times out of ten he escapes and you have to telephone for weeks before you get him back. Did you want to discuss a new fur jacket? Because I've been wondering, what would you say about beaver? Oh, did I tell you what happened the morning I was trying to talk to Daddy about a jacket for you?" She recounted her encounter with Gino, how he had looked, appalled, and how she still averted her face so she wouldn't laugh when she met him about the house, but Clare gave a quick tremor of reserve, perhaps of distaste, and Hennie thought: How sad is virginity; the best thing about it being mostly it doesn't last. "Well, darling, that's perhaps not what's on your mind. With beaver, though, you get a good, strong, pretty fur." She was feeling very gay this morning. She was going off with Kitty for the middle of the day. "And beaver *goes* with everything, seems to me."

"Mummy!" Clare was full of daughterly affection; she now smiled at her mother, thinking how pretty she was, and kind, if a bit boringly inclined to ramble on about trivia. In the night she had come to the filial conclusion that she must give her the pleasure of pretending to consult her about herself and Jo; probably some of her recent distraction was really hurt feelings at being left out; and they hadn't been able to avoid noticing that for a grown woman she had unnaturally few problems. "Not nearly problems enough," Clare had once informed him, and then regretted saying so, as it sounded disloyal. It would be a benefit they could well afford to confer on her to let her think she was having a hand in their affairs, if they were careful to keep the upper hand. "Doesn't your mother ever get tired?" he had asked his beloved as yesterday afternoon's luncheon party had straggled away from the mill.

She had given the matter thought and then slowly shaken her head much as Mr. Tuthill did, from side to side several times. "No, I can't say she does, as a matter of fact. When Will and I were younger maybe she did, but the last few days, not at all! It's kind of embarrassing, almost, though I don't like to say it of my own mother."

"Does she like me?"

"She'd better."

"Find out sometime," he had said, and a momentary coldness in his voice had startled her.

So now she beamed on this same problem mother and came forward to sit down, neat as a brown elf, on the sofa, where Hennie joined her. Clare cocked her head in an uncharacteristically coy pose and began without quite enough breath to see her through, "I've been wanting to ask you, oh, for ages, what you really think of Jo, irrespective of any wedding plans or anything, but what you *really* think of him as a man. This is *nothing* about weddings. But *as a person*. I want your serious opinion." She smiled warmly at her mother, thinking: It doesn't matter, just this once, this lie, because my intentions are so praiseworthy; my intentions sterilize it; kindness cancels out mendacity, like problems in fractions. "You *and* Daddy," she added. "Do you think I'm right to be so attached to him?" She looked brightly at her parent, hoping hard for a little opposition, all prepared for it, her hazel eyes beautiful with guile. "What do you think?" she inquired softly, falsely, ready to pounce.

Hennie slowly chose herself a cigarette and lighted it. "My darling, if you really love each other it shouldn't matter what we thought, should it?"

"Well, but!" Clare drew back. Heavens, she wasn't going to be modern, was she? That would be a fine way to behave all of a sudden, after perfectly routine years of perfectly normal parental tyranny, years of "Don't do this and yet you must do that." Only last week had occurred a stimulating clash of wills over a mere umbrella. Could it possibly be that her own mother was one to care more deeply about a possible case of wet hair and snuffles than the choice of a lover? For an instant Clare was visited by that long-outgrown suspicion: Is my mother really my mother or am I a changeling? She sat back and fixed her eyes on her parent. She couldn't help feeling blank and empty at all the sudden, new *laissez faire* about the house. She watched earnestly, not blinking, and longed for some sign of dictatorship. Oh, if her mother only knew how reassuring it would feel to be balked, even if only a little. "I thought you might have some objections," she said, trying not to sound disappointed; it was impossible not to feel defrauded. "You *or* Daddy?"

"My darling!" Hennie leaned toward her daughter, and now Clare was much relieved to see tears trembling, shimmering crystal puddles in the large blue eyes. "You will never know how much I'll miss you, never till you have a daughter of your own, but the last thing I'd ever do would be interfere between you and the—the man of your choice. How stuffy that sounds, and I know you wouldn't want me to be stuffy. But I wouldn't interfere, not if he were a Fiji; nobody has the right to interfere at a time like this, and you're old enough to know what you want out of life." She beamed, and the tears sparkled. "And I think Jo is divine, and Daddy does too; does think so, darling. And furthermore we've arrived at a really delightful time of life we didn't even know was coming, so we hadn't any warning—surely we never expected any such thing—when we realize that *children know best.*"

Oh, for heaven's sake, thought Clare, and sighed to hear her mother so unbecomingly making to her all those points she had expected, indeed had anticipated, having to make for herself. How was it this talk was not going at all as she had planned? In a way, it seemed to be reversed, and moving too fast for her, and downhill. Jo was going to be much amazed when she told him, and chagrined too, she hoped, believing as she did that men like to struggle for their loves. "Then you don't think I'm making any mistake." Her voice was dejected. "But Mummy, I'd thought, we had thought—but the way you put it makes everything seem to be the wrong way around."

But if she had supposed her mother would now say, "What *do* you mean?" she was again disappointed; a bright light appeared on the woman's face. "Clare! Do you feel that way too! But sideways, darling, sideways, not the wrong way around," she gently chided. "Life going sideways." She blew smoke out over the sofa arm. "I've realized it so strongly lately, so strongly, but I didn't know you did too." She stretched out her arms along the sofa and took a deep breath, and smiled at the seriousness of her child. "Why didn't you ever tell me?" she demanded, affectionate and peremptory. "Here I've been supposing it was only me. Such a relief."

"I don't know *what* you're talking about. I have to go now." She came to perch on the sofa edge to make one last try to induce her mother to behave. "So you've *no* objection?"

"Nary one. I think he's heaven. Tell him he really ought to come talk to Daddy some time though, only because of *les convenances,* and he won't mind because he must know only the brave deserve the fair." She looked up at her daughter and gave her a wide smile.

"Oh, I don't know about that," Clare countered instantly; must her mother have everything her own way, always? "I sometimes think the timid ought to have something, to make up for their being timid, you know, because they must know they are and be miserable about it. But Jo isn't; not at all!"

"I know he isn't. It's very obvious he's full to the brim with courage and brains. I see him on the bench, thundering—well, maybe not actually thundering. Shall we go buy your frilly thing now, before I have to meet Kitty?"

Clare said thank you but not today, wondered why she had, and departed the house.

Before she left to pick up Kitty in the car, Hennie reread the reply to her letter to the *Amis de la France;* it said that if she felt that way about it, though more than likely it was merely some clerical mistake, enclosed as an alternative she would find the dossier of André Leclerc of Neuilly-sur-Seine (Seine) whose father had indubitably died fighting in 1943 and would she please return Paul Mésurier, St. Martin des Champs (Finisterre) immediately. The letter bristled like a porcupine with implication of Mrs. Stacpole's narrow-mindedness, and Hennie hooted gently while she read.

She got out two sheets of her best letter paper and drew on the fruits of God knows how many boarding school hours—long, long hours in a cream-paneled room where hairy Mademoiselle with a chalk and pointer led twenty girls through a synopsis of the second act of *Le Bourgeois Gentilhomme* or the review at a brisk canter of the verb *s'asseoir,* while outside the classroom windows snow had lain on lawns and gardens or May breezes had strolled through the treetops. As she wrote to André Leclerc and Paul Mésurier the recollected tedium of those morning hours lay around her shoulders in a heavy shawl. French class had been the last before luncheon, and only the girls who were without boys for friends piped up to say they found *Le Bourgeois Gentilhomme très amusant;* the rest, the pretty ones, the gay ones, were fiercely employing the best part of their minds willing that letters with Princeton or New Haven postmarks would be in the man rack for them. All through *Le Bourgeois Gentilhomme* and indeed through *Zaïre* and *Hernani,* Hennie's prayer had been, "Heaven, let it be from Bruce, let it be from Bruce, *make* it be from Bruce and not just one-from-the-family. I promise to write to Granny and Grandpa every week the rest of the year if you do. And I'll send the family those snapshots they've been after me for," all the while drawing great sultry-looking B's down the margins of her verb notebook. She hadn't even heard of Laurence Stacpole in those faraway days; she might just as well, might better indeed, have put her mind on irregular verbs after all, and it was with painful slowness that she wrote to both Paul and André, "*Mon fils et moi nous sommes très contents si vous serez content avec les bonbons et le tricot et le boeuf en cannes que nous allons vous envoyer.*" She had said in her first letter, some days ago, to Paul, "*Dîtes à votre soeur Geneviève de m'envoyer ses mesures et je l'enverrai une robe chaude pour l'hiver prochain,*" and now she repeated the kind suggestion.

She mailed these letters and did the shopping necessary to fill the gaps in two parcels before she swung the station wagon uptown to pick up Kitty; they were to go off on a jaunt to the remnant room of a silk mill some fifty miles away.

"I'm sorry I'm late," she said, as Kitty settled herself in the front seat, "but it's really not even ten-thirty yet. Writing letters in French to two perfectly strange French children I used my entire vocabulary up the first time, then and there, and have very little left to go on with. Of course, I expect Will to take over any day now." Kitty turned an alert, kind face, bird-neat under upswept hair and small hat, and offered to drive. "Oh, no," Hennie replied, "thank you, because I'm really not tired at all, actually. It's getting to be a kind of *thing* in this country, to say we're exhausted all the time, haven't you noticed?" Kitty said so much of the time it was true.

The hard white road slid away back under the station wagon. Like a clasp on an endless tape the car raced along the road, zooming up the gentle rises of hills that were no longer real hills but only parkway slopes graded for efficiency, sliding down into impersonal valleys no longer part of nature but only gradients under the watchful eye of the highway commission. Ornamental stands of dogwood planted by men in red caps at the behest of this commission were no sooner glimpsed than passed. "California," Kitty said, as a car sped past them on their left. "Heavens, and Texas. Poor Gracie," she went on without a pause, "she's mad for some silk, and I tried to persuade her to come with us but she couldn't. You know Gracie; always some committee."

"Couldn't possibly?" Hennie's sympathy was aroused; zooming along like this through the early fall sunshine was so exactly the right thing to be doing that day.

"Well, there was some meeting, poor dear."

"Oh, poor dear, then let's get her some. I simply adore buying silk, but as a matter of fact I haven't a thing in the world I need any for at this particular juncture. Velvet and jersey's what I really think about this time of year."

Kitty said cheerfully but wasn't it delightful how, the minute they saw the lovely stuff, all spread out and shimmering before their eyes, they weren't going to be able to resist buying probably quite a good deal of it, and Hennie pressed the accelerator deeper at the very thought.

They were pleased at their shared weakness, which they thought to be rather adorable and feminine of themselves, and Kitty, turning to Hennie, confided, "I have a horrid jealous nature. Do, do make me get Gracie the best piece we see. I mean I could scarcely bear to look at that dress Olivia wore at the last Assembly, it was so *beautiful!*"

"I have one too."

"That dress? Oh, you shouldn't have. Oh, what will Olivia—"

"No, no, no. A horrid jealous nature, I have." Kitty interrupted Hennie to declare she didn't believe a word of it. "Oh, yes, I have. Sometimes I can hardly bear to tell people they've got pretty things on, and, in a way, I like them to worry if I think so or not; for a little while, anyway. Then I love to dazzle them with my approval. *You*'d never do that." Kitty said with a touch of pride that she often did. Then Hennie, wanting to be strictly fair to herself, said perhaps such behavior was balanced in heaven against the other times when she went out of her way to say something nice and flattering about some people's awful hats and dresses. "Sometimes I'm very surprised at what I hear myself saying." Kitty said that was only natural, and nodded too, when Hennie finished, "So I may be really kind at heart after all."

"Though I don't know as *that* proves it," Kitty suggested in a *volte-face*. She turned her erect head and gazed out at the fleeting fields. "I wonder if those remarks aren't startled out of us sometimes by the sheer horror of the garment itself. Take Mrs. Hendrickson's skunk coat for an example."

"Dear God, yes; I couldn't agree more." As she said this Hennie felt a twinge because once, when Clare had had whooping cough, Mrs. Hendrickson had walked through a snowstorm to bring a book of paper dolls. "Old Mrs. Comfir's beaded jacket, Olivia's velvet raincoat, if we come right down to it."

Kitty agreed such a coat had to be seen to be believed.

Some power superior to better judgment, a force there is no use trying to struggle against, some magnetic force peculiar perhaps to Route 5 that pulls inhibitions clear out over the open tops of car windows, now began acting on these two. There is no sense in pretending there is no such power. Hennie was exhilarated by the way the miles looped by under her, the free day unshackled, no keeping account of the hours; it had been decided not to pay any attention at all to what time it was that morning; if they got home by luncheon time, all right; if not they would stop for a hamburger and coffee on the way back. A crown of black birds rose from the head of a high tree and moved off, changing shape, ovaling away. The easy confidences of her companion surprised and pleased her and twinges of regret at what she heard herself confessing were quickly overlain with gaiety. Inhibitions, one by one and in handfuls, slipped away from both of them and were sucked, like lengths of blue and cherry-red ribbon, right over the glass top of the lowered windows; if they fluttered and planed a moment in the air, in the slipstream of the station wagon, neither woman looked back to see or to deplore. Kitty even told Hennie how she truly felt about her brother-in-law, the one in Montreal, so that Hennie said she thought it was only honest to unburden herself then and there about Hennie's sister, the one with the Chow dog and perhaps a lover, but that she instantly regretted. "But that I *shouldn't* say; probably it isn't even true. In fact, I don't believe it is or could be, with those legs. She lives in Boston. Promise me you'll forget it."

"You're shocked? But lots of people, people we least suspect—"

"Not shocked at all. I merely mean it seems so unlikely, with those huge legs. Promise me you'll forget I even mentioned her."

"My dear, absolutely! It is forgotten." But Hennie, stealing a look, knew that the bird profile against the window, against the flying background of grass and trees and sky, was never going to forget anything; no; never; one never does. "South Dakota," Kitty mentioned, as though to soothe Hennie's repentance, of which she was as aware as Hennie herself, and Hennie knew she was aware —but how charming Kitty looked, there in the other seat, so chic and so really deeply understanding. Hennie told herself she had never realized how fond of her she was; the rather brittle exterior had put her off. The *thrumming-thrumming-thrumming* of the tires on the pavement anesthetized her. She sank deeper into warmth and companionship.

"But nobody knows anybody else," she said in a low voice.

"I know. Hennie, it's because we have these hedges around us, each one of us has, great thick yew hedges."

"Glass, I think. Because we can see each other, but we don't communicate."

Kitty interrupted. "Yes, glass! You're absolutely right. Beautiful splintery glass hedges, with all the leaves and berries and twigs glass, all as high as—as high as one's hat!" She laughed, apologetic.

"Don't laugh," Hennie said sharply. "It's true. And one can see through it all right, as you say, and wave and smile, only one can't hear what the other is saying. Lip reading might help. Do we turn off here for the factory, or beyond?"

"Beyond."

Hennie was happy about Kitty. All these years of friendship and she had never suspected her real nature; she forgot that her own sensitiveness was recent. "Do you ever think everything is made too easy for women like us?" she asked. "That there's some kind of conspiracy, perhaps? When we were young we supposed the future would be *harder*, but it hasn't been. Do I sound like a fool?" As she thought back her eyes glazed, but not dangerously, not enough to prevent her from giving plenty of leeway to Massachusetts drivers. "What I've just recently decided is that we are capable of living two lives at once, which would perhaps entail being two people, simultaneously, and I've told Laurence, but he can't see it. I believe the reason so few of us is a whole round one is because we have so many opposite, opposing, oblique instincts pulling us every which way and if we could just sort them out into two separate sets we'd be all right; or in any case, better than before. I've always felt this way." She narrowed her eyes and thought back. "Maybe not. But now, everything looks so bright and promising I go around *squinting*."

Kitty looked grave. "You mean you think it would be more logical and practical to exist on two planes, if quite convenient materially, than try to cram everything onto one?"

"Yes, I do. Don't you?"

"Few of us would have the courage, or the energy, but maybe that's just because we haven't tried."

"Maybe it would take *less* energy. All the dissatisfactions in life A, we could fix up in life B. Kitty, did you ever think maybe the world wasn't so blinding bright as we remember it to have been when we were young? It was, though, wasn't it?"

"Oh, yes," Kitty said, sadly and at once, her eyes and mouth regretful under the looped ribbon that was her hat. "It was, all right. But now what's become of all that narrow headlong bright shiny stream, almost a waterfall, wasn't it, of being young?"

"I never knew you felt this way!" The car swerved.

"Look out! You never asked me. Nobody ever does ask any real thing, anyway."

"And so that bright stream thins out and thins out and fans out, into deltas, shallow, fit for paddling in, only. Marshy. Very level, wherever you look, for people like us." And Hennie took a deep breath of comfort, having found a friend. She was not alone any more and never would be because here was just such another as herself. "What should we do," she asked, "to make life more the way we want it?"

"What shall we?"

"I don't know. We must think." She breathed deeply again to give herself courage, and leaned to the woman beside her. "Do you feel as if life could go sideways as well as—" she started, but Kitty sat up straighter and peered through the windshield.

"Here's the turn!" she cried. "Sooner than we thought! Careful—ah, you made it." She sank back. "Absolutely," she said with conviction if not clarity; then, "And if I see a really pretty light print I'm going to get it and put it aside for spring. Don't you think that's wise? Mélisse can make it up for me. Only if it's irresistible, though, because I don't believe in buying what's only a *little* pretty; do you?"

"No. No," Hennie replied, sighing, and unable to refrain from adding aloud, "We're trapped, that's what we are; we're captives of comfort," and Kitty, searching in her handbag for her powder, agreed.

They left the parkway, drove the car up beside the long, old-fashioned, red brick factory, and entered eagerly, eyes darting every which way, under the unexpectedly pure white springing portico. The remnant room was gigantic, very long and very high; rising up behind the strewn counters were immense, curly-mullioned windows alternating with vast mirrors for the indecisive to peer into, to hold up pieces of colored silk to their chins to see if the effect was becoming—becoming or intolerable. Only the lowest fraction of these huge mirrors mirrored the frieze of questioning women, the greater part of the glass rising high, aloof and cold, impersonal and quite untenanted; perhaps up there it reflected the colored counters far across the room; no one was up there to see or know if it did. Some women were not to be reassured by seeing themselves reflected in possible navy blue or green or ocher and in that echoing hall some of them were always to be observed, hands holding the variegated folds high, faces tipped, waiting, their own taste in abeyance, for decision to descend mercifully on them from heaven. Bored, indulgent clerks rested the small of their backs against the laden shelves behind these counters, watching the straying, darting customers, the undecided, the ever-hopeful whose eager ranks Hennie and Kitty now joined and like early robins fell upon folded lengths concealed beneath other lengths and pulled them out to the light of day and their own pretty scrutiny. They folded these remnants over their arms, unable yet to make final choices. Kitty, after ten minutes of a love affair with a piece of pink printed with white birds, all at once had had quite enough of it, knew she had got it out of her system forever, and coolly laid it back on the counter in favor of a length of two shades of swirling yellow.

"And this one!" she exclaimed after fifteen minutes of culling, to a flowery green and blue drift of something very thin and airy. "Look at this!" She floated a length of it out before her.

"But you saw that earlier, when we first came in; you

had it over your arm for a while, and I wondered at the time—"

"I couldn't have. It's the most beautiful piece I ever saw in my life. I am struck all of a heap with it— Did I? Then I don't see why I ever put it down even for a minute. What if somebody else had bought it!" She tucked it between self and arm. "And we mustn't forget Gracie."

"No; such a good idea. Let's separate and each search."

They met again ten minutes later, each triumphant. "This *is* Gracie," Hennie said, unfurling blue smartly cross-hatched.

But Kitty's brows were questioning. "You think?"

"Well, I definitely do, don't you? With her eyes?"

Then Kitty shook out a soft rustle of pink and green. "Unusual? I mean, Gracie's really the smartest of us all, isn't she? And I think she'd adore this."

However, Hennie couldn't honestly agree. "You think?" she inquired. "I picked up another for her, just in case. What do you think of this?"

Kitty gave a cry of quick concern. "I don't want to be discouraging, but Gracie wouldn't be seen dead in it, I know that. All those practically phallic-looking little squiggles!"

"Are they? I don't think they are. I mean, are they really?"

"Oh, my dear!" And Hennie was left, not for the first time, with the sad conviction that there was much, so much, of which she probably stood in far greater ignorance than any other living woman; whose fault? Then Laurence's!

"I think she'd love it," she said stubbornly, and returned it at once to the counter. She moved off, and browsed, slowly. The first rapture of bargain finding was over. The huge high room was an aquarium, and she only one slow-floating, straying fish in its many-colored depths. She gathered up a sweet quiet dotted length for a dressing gown for Clare, a piece of pale apricot for herself, for something, someday.

"May I get these?" she said to a clerk. "And I'm looking for a piece for a friend, something very smart." But she didn't sound so very interested in this project and the clerk pushed open her charge book with long manicured fingertips. Hennie leaned against the counter, entranced, drugged with colors. She rested one gloved hand on the counter and stared down into the hair of the girl bent over the charge book. She could see only the rich brown hair, very fine and thick, shiny, brownish-black, with a rich slow wave in it; it had been born straight, no doubt, but now a single wide wave went through it; thick, fragrant hair; Hennie lost herself in the probable smell of it, in the wide wave, and for the time it took to write "7½ yds @ 2.95"—over went the bottom of the pad, and the pencil quickly did arithmetic all by itself—and then "22.13 and tax"—Hennie *was* that girl and knew everything about her, saw her home, saw her mother and father and brothers, knew her evenings—washing underwear in a small porcelain bathroom bowl with not enough rim—but what pretty underwear!—so that the rinsed clothes dripped over the edge—partook of her early mornings at the kitchen table with coffee, a cigarette, a mother rebuking, "You don't eat enough to keep a bird alive," her father's fond, impatient, "Come along if you're coming. Where I work we got to be on time." And there would be evenings Hennie wondered about and longed to know. The pencil point trailed swiftly down a list giving tax information; very brisk, the pencil was. That slow sly wave in the hair was for evenings in boys' borrowed cars, for dancing at red and green neon-lighted roadhouses and for the rides home, with pauses. "Twenty-two thirteen, tax sixteen cents, twenty-two twenty-nine," said a stranger-girl, looking up, as brisk as though her head had never, never been altogether too heavy to lift from Bob's or Wally's or Roy's shoulders. "With tax," she said again. She smiled frankly at Hennie. "And here is the slip; you pay over there at the cashier's, please." To a fellow clerk when Hennie was out of earshot she announced, "A pin like that, if it was mine, I shouldn't wear it under the edge of my collar. Me, I'd plant it right out on the bust where it would do the most good."

When next Hennie and Kitty met it was at the cashier's counter where a great deal of folding and wrapping and mathematical checking took place as well as some lending back and forth of five-dollar bills and pennies. They left, happily burdened. "I don't know what I'm going to do with it all," Hennie said, "and I'm only afraid I shan't have any excuse to come up again in the spring."

"I know. It'll melt away though, one way and another. How I do love that place! Everything there is so divinely unnecessary."

They drove home more slowly, more soberly. Once in a while Kitty reached into the back seat and pulling over to herself one of the rustling parcels, tweaked open a small tear in the paper and peered in. "Yes," she would then say, "I'm really glad I got that one. I wasn't so sure at the time but I am now. The thing is, years ago I once didn't get some divine stuff, dark brown with aquamarine cats' eyes on it, and I've never forgiven myself, so now I simply don't dare take any chances." Hennie at the wheel agreed it was much safer to get it for the very good reason that then you had it. She must restrain her natural curiosity as to what she had actually bought until she got home, but she had an agreeable, miserly yet lavish impression that there was a great deal that was hers in back there.

"But you know what!" she exclaimed as she let Kitty out at her front door. "Gracie!"

"Oh, my goodness, so we didn't." Kitty gathered up her bundles. "This, and this, and this. All the others are yours. So we never did; how terribly stupid of us. Still," she said, giving the matter a judicious-sounding if lightning solution, "I shouldn't wonder if she really wants any she'll go herself."

"I suppose so. And probably be better satisfied." Hennie leaned toward her friend. "Kitty, let's not forget what we talked about on the way up. Let's live strangely!" The bright face under the looped hat looked back in at her, alert and agreeable. "Our years are going by so fast."

"Yes." The bird profile turned. Above the large armful of paper bundles it appeared to brood unseeing up the street. Then Kitty turned a brilliant smile on her friend. "*We* won't forget," she promised. "It may not be easy, but it won't be too hard for us."

"No, no. Not us! We will live sideways just as hard as we can."

"We will," Kitty promised again. "We absolutely will. If I didn't have my arms full of all this perfectly beautiful junk, we'd shake hands on it."

Meanwhile Clare had walked to the cafeteria, her head bent in confused thought.

Jo was there, balancing two antiseptic-looking aluminum trays with an assortment of cutlery and two paper napkins; cloth napkins were charged for, a penny each, and although his father was vice president of a flourishing tool factory in Colorado, and Mrs. Wood, too, had never felt the pang of penury, being descended from a long line of affluent Westerners, nor were the Stacpoles destitute, the young pair were earnest about not falling into extravagant ways.

"I talked to Mummy about you this morning."

"What did she say?" he inquired, bending his crew cut over a short length of some nameless fish.

Clare sighed. "Women of her age," she said regretfully, "they're so self-centered. I gave her every opportunity to pretend to object, which it seems she almost ought to if she takes being a mother seriously, but she didn't at all. I mean, if anything, she seems pleased."

"That's wonderful." He had recovered from his tremors of the previous evening and now trembled that he had been so weak as to give in to them.

"She didn't object at *all!*"

"Wonderful!" He put down the battered fork and took her hand, a smile spreading all over his serious face.

"No, it isn't. She's changed, in some ominous way. Why, I believe that only last week she would have acted more like a normally cautious mother, but this week—everything's gone to the winds. I can't explain it, but I think it's very strange that *you* should stand up for her!"

"But why, Clare, why isn't it wonderful? *I* think it is," he stoutly said. "No matter what she's like, we want her on our side, don't we?"

"Oh, don't tell me you don't understand either," she wailed, and looked about ten years old, her face lifted, her soft dark hair falling on either side. A little doubt crept into his mind; perhaps she was somewhat young for him after all?

"Tell me," he said gently. "I'm sorry if I'm dense, but I don't see what's so terrible about your family being willing to give you up, and have me in it. But your father needs a haircut," he added. "I saw him on the street today. Don't tell him I said so."

"It's Mummy I'm concerned about." She put down her spoon, leaving half a tinned peach to founder in its own dreadful juice. "She goes roaming around the house like a bird of prey, thinking up things for people to do they don't want to. She says she's fit to fly, and we don't know what she means, Daddy and I don't. I know he's worried, but he doesn't confide in me because the fact is, he thinks I'm a child! There's only one good thing, though, she and her friends have enrolled themselves in a tile-making class for the next few days, she and a lot of her friends, and maybe that'll tire her out. I have *some* hopes."

"Now what would she do with a lot of tiles," he wanted to know, genuinely interested at last. "Your house is all done, isn't it; that's one of the things I like about it, it's so comfortable and settled but not at all shabby, if you see what I mean. And why would you want her to be tired?"

Clare patiently explained. Was she always going to have to be patient, the rest of her whole life, explaining things to the very people who ought to have known them anyway? "It merely would be more normal in a woman of her age to *be* tired once in a while. Other girls' mothers are always saying how exhausted they are. Oh, I want to grow up and be married and everything; I look forward to it, but I don't know—sometimes I wonder, is it that thirty per cent of anticipation is despair? *Oh*," she finished angrily, but carefully folding her paper napkin into a triangle, "I'm afraid you'll never understand women."

But now she had gone too far; there were limits. With the gesture he had so much admired in his future father-in-law at the luncheon at the mill but not yet had an opportunity to employ in public, he slapped his hand down once on the edge of the table. She jumped. "So you think that, do you?" he inquired coldly. His eyebrows climbed his candid brow toward his crew cut. "I'm afraid, actually, you don't yet know everything about me.

After all, you've only known me since last June." He narrowed his eyes slightly, as though he couldn't recall all the many and varied and surprising experiences of his past that began crowding on him whenever he gave them a chance; his regard went, unseeing, out over the cafeteria while his thoughts visibly roamed backward, but her eyes over the rim of her coffee cup were fixed unblinking on his face. She hadn't so far given such a matter thought— other girls, other loves— A sickly flicker, a yawning little ripple of jealousy, shot across her stomach, warred with the cafeteria fish and the tinned peach, coiled up and settled in, just under her ribs.

But Joseph Wood appeared more and more pleased and satisfied; smug almost. "Finished?" he asked, without bothering to look and see. "We'd better be off then, because I've got a beast of an assignment due in tomorrow. Sorry if it hurries you. Maybe you'd rather stay and finish your peach?"

"Why would I?" cried the poor distracted maiden, casting down her spoon. "It tastes like a piece of soap!"

That afternoon, passing a doorway, Hennie saw Pearl looking down at the board, slapping the iron back and forth over a defenseless doily. "This tormented ahn," she was saying aloud to herself.

Hennie paused and turned in at the door. "Pearl, how are you today? Something the matter with the iron?"

"Afternoon, Mrs. Stacpole. Nothing's the matter with the ahn." She loomed fat and black above the frail board. She removed the doily to a pile and flipped a damp napkin over on its back on a square of bath toweling. Hennie asked why and Pearl's vast brown face glistened with surprise and amusement. "Only way to fatten up a monogram; you didn't know? Mercy, everybody's known that, for generations and generations. It's one of them true things like true love never do run smooth." She was delighted to find Hennie so ignorant, but then a recent grievance came floating back up to the top of her mind. "But ah sure hates big tablecloths," she burst out. "Ah merely can't stand 'em."

"But we never use big tablecloths; we haven't for years; nobody does any more, but I can remember when I was a little girl we always had them *and—*" she went on for the benefit of Agnes who came in just then with a box of Sudzem, "—only one maid who did everything, old Annie Carlson. Heavens, great dripping tablecloths and counterpanes and the irons heated on a coal stove, and bread baked twice a week. I can remember the big aluminum hand kneader thing." The two women listened respectfully, and murmured in their throats in a polite way. "So," finished Hennie, "things are better nowadays, some things are. Why, we haven't had a big tablecloth out since I can remember." *You better not,* said Pearl's look. "No. Doilies are plenty good enough for these times."

Pearl was not placated. "Over to Mrs. Comfit's, Tuesday, great big tormented things, they puckle in the centah, every time."

In one of her very rare moments of relaxation Agnes stood, swayed back tall onto her heels, one wrist folded over the other at her waistline. Hennie could see, as though she were seeing double, the countrywoman Agnes might have been, the woman she would have been if she had stayed home in Perth and had stood often in just this way in the road outside her cottage door or talking across her garden wall, gossiping with her neighbor—the easy, settled, backward stance, the slight gesturing with the hand lifted not far from the waist. "So I said— So then he said—" But Perth was a long way off, and a long time ago. She must have been staring at Agnes, who all at once cocked her head sideways and a pretended look of listening came into her eyes. "The bell, madam, I think. I think I hear the front door," and away she went in a scurry of dishonest tact.

"Nobody, madam," she was prepared to say if she encountered Hennie on her way back, "I must have been mistaken." But it was not necessary because when she returned to the warm ironing room Hennie had gone.

Pearl produced another perfectly plumped monogram. "Look what I can do even with this miserable ahn. Imagine not knowing," she said to Agnes, and Agnes resenting faintly, faintly jealous of Mrs. Stacpole's resuscitation from the past of that universal old genius Annie Carlson, said, Ah, what they knew and what they didn't know, it would fill a book, reelly it would.

"Anyway," Pearl said, "Ah didn't expect to see her here today. Ah thought she'd went away, Mrs. Comfit's Nellie said."

"She went. She came back. There's things going on these days," she added, and lifted meager eyebrows up to her candid bulging brow. "I wouldn't want to say."

"Oh dear me," Pearl cried. "Oh don't tell me another word about it," she said in a relishing voice, putting down her iron and clicking off the switch.

Agnes's blue-button eyes slid toward the door; then she went over and closed it softly, and tiptoed back.

It was nearly closing time at the supermarket. Bright lights were turned on. The butcher's assistant, thought Hennie as she contentedly roamed the aisles, resembled Mr. Batten. She guided along ahead of her a large wire basket on wheels, a contraption strong enough to restrain small wild animals and wasted on paper boxes, little bottles, paper bags of tea and coffee. From time to time she consulted a long narrow curled slip of paper from the fixture on the kitchen wall, whereon Agnes had written a dozen items essential to the continued well-being of the Stacpole household. Gino was supposed to shop for groceries; today he had escaped by taking the lawn mower to the repairer while Hennie was away, and Agnes had not been able, under the rules of their game, to do anything about her desperate need for salt until Hennie had returned from the silk mill. "But send Gino," she had said. "Where is he?" Agnes, who knew exactly where he was, back at the repair shop to collect the mower, had implied God alone knew where he had gone.

"Brillo," Hennie said, and her eyes searched the loaded shelves.

In her thin hard pink tweed from Princes Street, slipping and sliding over silk from France, in shoes from

Florence and stockings from Wilmington, Delaware, the scent floating around her that had been created by Frenchmen who would possibly have thought her too tall for beauty, she had left her house, stuffing the long curled list into her London handbag and announcing to an empty hall, "Off to the A and P," and now she leaned, hanging over the open, chilled, and lighted meat counter, and said, "Bacon." Sidelong she watched other women pluck cellophane-wrapped pieces of meat out of the cool depths, hold them long before their eyes, scrutinizing, calculating, turning them over in doubt; would they be enough for tonight and some left over? Hennie while admiring their knowledge didn't want it for herself. For down the line of the counter she caught a glimpse of a profile, and a hat she knew.

"*Kitty!*" she called, and steered out and around rapidly in the direction of her one true friend. Fate was with them, that they should meet again so soon after plighting their troth, as it were. "How wonderful!" Kitty was her confederate, her accomplice. "How *are* you?" she demanded, as solicitous as though Kitty's health were uncertain, as though they had not passed the better part of the day in each other's company.

"Look." Kitty held up two murdered hens. "Which do I get for chicken pie? This, or this? I was hardly home before I was sent out for chicken, for pies," she said, "in all my ignorance."

The man who resembled Mr. Batten said, "Help you ladies?" Kitty frankly told him her dilemma and suggested searching out the head butcher of all and asking him. "Nah, dear," said the man in the white coat. "Little as I know, he knows less." He went away. Kitty, pursing her lips, read the crayoned slips of paper pasted on each bird, and said *really* she didn't know which, but as one was heavier that was the one she would take.

Hennie, her hands on the handlebar, her face glowing, an admonishing angel in a well-cut suit, stood over her friend. "You haven't forgotten," she said, "all those things we said, said and vowed?"

"Mercy, no," Kitty lied briskly. Or was she lying? Hennie couldn't tell. She couldn't be; how could she have forgotten so soon?

But then Kitty smiled on her brilliantly, lovingly, absent-mindedly, and said as a matter of fact she would take both chickens and that ought to satisfy Bertha, if the woman was emotionally capable of *being* satisfied ever, which she, Kitty, seriously doubted. She laid both in her basket, veered it expertly away, smiled again at Hennie with her head on one side, lifted a beige-gloved hand in farewell. Mournfully Hennie watched her stepping away, back into her wonted groove with her two cellophaned hens; perfectly content, and blind. Kitty hadn't really become detached from her usual self and life; some membrane held her and she had been tweaked back by it, and been glad to go. Hennie watched her stop and buy endive, giving her whole attention to the discovery of the fairest.

"Betrayed, betrayed." Hennie started up her wagon with her knee. "Pepper. Salt. Raisins. Bread sticks— Betrayed, that's all!" she said, her throat aching.

CHAPTER SEVEN

Bending over a lump of wet gray clay on a table, closing her eyes, Hennie received her whole childhood in a blast up her nose. Nothing else in the world smells the same as wet gray pungent entirely unique and unforgettable plasticene. When she was ten, snippets of it could always have been found in her bedroom, minute flakes of austere gray-blue, sullen rust, yellow that so quickly turned to gray with use; she remembered how dust and the delicate grime from fingers mixed into the yellow quickly and permanently. Always in those days there had been clay particles flattened into her rug.

"Ah-h," she breathed. "What a delicious smell." On her left Kitty, who had once taken a world tour and not forgotten a single thing she saw in India or Egypt or the Pacific Islands, struck her lump a professional-looking blow and flattened it. Seeing this, the other women in the tile-making class all did the same and then looked hopefully along the long zinc-covered table to their instructor, who smiled a qualified smile back, tossed her long straight greenish-orange hair, and said, "Well now, class."

Whose idea had it been in the first place to persuade Adolf Domenico to lend them his pizzeria mornings and, when their tiles were finished and ready to be baked, to harden them in his burning white furnace? Kitty's, most likely. She was the most likely to have ideas. She it was who had once organized the fantastically successful outgrown mitten-and-ice-skate shop at the school and, as though it had not been enough to relieve the mothers of a problem inherent in bringing up children, with the proceeds she had instantly bought a really comfortable sofa where the teachers, though only one at a time to be sure, could stretch out for a respite when these same children had become intolerable. "It's the reverse of a vicious circle," she had pointed out at the time, with pride. So probably to make tiles had been Kitty's idea. The instructor passed out small tools, sticklike blades and spatulas. "Today," she disappointed them by saying, "we won't actually start seriously but we will just play around and get the feel of the clay. Tomorrow we'll really get to work." She bunched her stubby fingers together and held them up and rubbed them against each other. She had almost no fingernails, but the tips of all the restless fingers up and down the table were red as begonia petals. "We have to get the feel of our material," the instructor said while everyone's face fell. Everyone had supposed trays of tiles would have been ready to slide into Adolf Domenico's furnace by the end of that morning, each woman's vivid square so much, so noticeably more remarkable than her neighbor's. Jars and bottles of enamel were ranged down the center of the zinc table. The women longed to get their hands on the rich smooth colors.

This combined kitchen and restaurant was an entirely white room and probably had once been a stable. All the brick walls had been whitewashed a hundred times; soft fat sacks of flour to make a thousand *appizze* slumped in corners, softly sighing, and giving off a gentle white exhalation if they were touched. Beyond a dropped barrier like the bar at a railway crossing two of Adolf Domenico's helpers, two pale dark boys in white cotton pants, singlets, and long aprons, moved about at their work, sliding Italian glances at these incredible women seated at a table like children, or like a double row of large tropical birds, so bright, so brisk. The Italian boys whispered to each other. The whole back wall of the room was the front of the stove—a white brick wall with a square soot-black door, which a worker occasionally opened to check the fire and there, except for the morning's interlopers, flamed the only color in the whole room —a secret blazing spread of violet and rose coals shimmering and softly flashing like a small view of hell, a framed vista, or like a bed of orange roses. When this happened the tile-making class, as if mesmerized, slowly turned their feathered heads to stare into the burning depths, stare and stare until the heavy soot-colored door was clanged shut again and then it was hard for them to drag their bemused eyes away. Only then did they turn back, slowly, to the chill gray heaps on the zinc.

Olivia, thin and crisp as a piece of celery, sat erect at one end of the table, making geometrically perfect corners on her practice lump. The instructor called down a kindly suggestion that she take off her jacket because she might be getting the edges of her cuffs in the clay. "I'm not," she replied, imperturbable and amiable, and she wasn't. "I only want one tile anyway," she said. "For under iced tea, summers."

Hennie couldn't decide. Last evening she had loitered long before the living-room fireplace, playing with the yardstick. With her mind's eye she saw, instead of the painted wood molding, a triple row of incandescently beautiful tiles. She warmly assured Laurence, placidly reading a letter, that here at last and quite by good luck only was a project to expend her vigor on; her new-peeled perceptions were about to be put to use. "You won't need to worry about me any more." He had *h'hmn'd*, started a new page, and she had turned her back on him. What if no great artist had ever employed tiles for his medium; she would be the first. "Good God, it's a Henrietta Stacpole!" future generations of museum directors would cry, receiving into reverent hands some square fragment flashing green and blue. Every one of her tiles would be a masterpiece, like tapestries from Angers. She had indeed recently—yesterday in fact—considered devoting herself for the rest of her life to some vast, secret tapestry with cascades of flowers and wreaths of animals against a deep blue background—no, deep green— "Oh, but the hell with it," she had decided at last, sweetly reasonable; "where would *I* conceal a loom!"

"Forty-eight inches by thirty-six," she had then said, manipulating the pliant stick. "Shall we keep the mantelpiece or not?" she had inquired, turning to Laurence reading his letter from his aunts in Center Sandwich, who said they wondered why they hadn't heard from him for such a long time and was anything the matter? "Perhaps it would be wisest to wait about asking Mr. Tuthill to come and rip out the molding till after I get the tiles all made and finished." Getting no answer she turned back to the mirror above the mantel, and lingered, coming closer to the smiling glass, experimenting down herself in the exact middle with a forefinger. Should she tell Mélisse to cut the new jersey lower; why not? Edward Latham would love it; the lower the prettier. "And some day I shall be too old to," she had said aloud but not believing, and Laurence, flipping over a page which inquired if with them the leaves had started changing yet and starting in on the next, which dealt with the harvest from their quince tree, said, "What?"

"And they will become immensely valuable and priceless—oh, not in *our* lifetime, of course," she said, dashing a look of incipient interest from his face.

"I see."

"Yes." She stood with one hand along her cheek. "I think I shall have a rather intricate vine running all through them all as my hallmark."

"You want future biographers of the great Henrietta Stacpole to draw the conclusion you were a dipso?"

"It needn't be grape. It could be clematis."

Laurence shook his head, advised against it; not safe, he said; posterity was usually a traitor.

She contemplated his long dark figure stretched in the light of the lamp. "No, no. I'm not going to worry about that. Can't you just see old experts peering at them with magnifying glasses?"

"Yes, indeed," he said politely, but returned to his letter.

"I need to know something. Tell me what you think. Would it be a mistake to have them attached here with cement? Maybe some day they'll want to be in a museum, and then, too, before that, if they're fastened here forever, what if we move to a smaller house when the children marry?"

"Grandchildren, grandchildren," Laurence had murmured, not raising his eyes from the elegant small handwriting of his Aunt Effie.

"Of course! Stupid of me. The house full of them. Well, that's good," she had said earnestly, "I'd hate it if I had to stand by and watch somebody trying to pry them off, and perhaps chipping."

"You know, we really ought to go up to Center Sandwich for a visit."

"Yes indeed. When, I wonder?"

Now, at Adolf Domenico's, she picked up a tool and drew a dragon on her flattened clay. "What does the end of a dragon's tail look like?" she asked her neighbor, who cast a look on Hennie's handiwork and said oh, she had supposed it to be a cat. "But forked, I believe."

"Free hand, free hand," sang the orange-haired instructress, as if to her whole class but really because of Olivia, whom she had caught using the side of her engagement pad to make a straight line.

"I haven't heard that phrase since kindergarten," Kitty said, and Hennie experienced a pleasant interior jolt and then a corresponding sinking as she recalled how marvelously understanding Kitty had been on the ride to the silk mill and how she had let her down at the grocery. But there was still a bond between them, stronger than the cord between herself and any other. Even so, it should have been stronger than it was, more like the certain comfort in holding a love letter in one's lap, warming one right through the skirt—and she ventured a conspiratorial glance toward Kitty, but Kitty's pointed profile was bent above the sharp leaf she was incising on her practice tile and she did not look up. No matter, as Hennie's grandmother had been wont to say when disposing of some trifling obstacle to complete contentment; no matter; she *knows*; and I'll pin her to the wall one of these days; she knows what I mean and we don't have to keep talking of it all the time; I'll just have to keep at her. She's my one hope, except, perhaps— A picture of Edward Latham, seven feet tall and deeply sympathetic, floated into her mind. She enveloped with a large, loving, amused look, her unconscious friend across the table. She then smoothed away the dragon's pickle fork tail and now it did most surprisingly resemble Stockinette.

Olivia and Kitty went to have luncheon in the Dark Bar. They had invited Hennie to join them there but she had said she didn't know, maybe. She had an appointment with Mélisse for twelve, but that could mean anything. If some old dowager had the eleven-thirty one then there might still be an endless discussion going on of fullness here and here and the virtues of the surplice neckline; bits of lace and fur would still litter the fitting-room floor and what was left of her own morning after the tile-making class would be in ruins. "And dowagers always turn back at the door and talk some more," she pointed out. "You know how they do; we must remember to, when we're them; but I'll come if I can. The Dark Bar? Good. But don't wait for me."

"I don't believe she's going to." Olivia held the menu far off, the infinitesimal, beautiful lines at the outer corners of her eyes a fan, while she debated within herself: chicken salad sandwich or tongue. "Two Martinis, anyway, John, while I decide," she said to the attendant waiter. "Dry for you? Dry. No olive. What's she having made at Mélisse now, do you suppose?"

"Another velvet skirt for the evening. You know, that big kind she wears every night; very pretty."

"Aren't they? Awfully becoming to her," Olivia agreed. "They must be warm and cozy."

"Yes. You know, I've been wondering if I ought not to have one of them too. Do you think Hennie would mind if I—well, actually, it wouldn't be copying at all because anybody might have a long velvet skirt, mightn't they? But they do look, as you say, so warm and cozy and I mind the cold so; I mean I mind the discomfort. I mind discomfort more than most people do."

"How do you know you do? I mean, other people mind it too but perhaps they—"

"I mind much more," Kitty said calmly. "I always have," she said, to clinch the matter.

Olivia wondered, "What does she want another one for, she's *got* two."

"Well." Kitty squinted at her menu and then scrabbled apologetically in her handbag for glasses. "Isn't it terrible? I'm blind as a bat. Chicken on whole wheat, I think. No mayonnaise. Not for you either, I suppose?"

"Middle age suits her, I think. She looks awfully well this fall, but I can't think what she needs another velvet skirt for, can you?"

"No, I can't," Kitty said frankly. "She's getting so vague lately she's probably forgotten she has the blue one and the black one. D'you think she honestly is so vague, or just pretending? *I* don't think really vague people say they are. I don't believe they even know it."

"What would anyone pretend to be vague for? No," decided Olivia with that candor so admirable her friends sometimes wondered if it didn't border on naïveté. "I believe she really is."

They sipped at their Martinis, their eyes reflective, the eyes of dryads in that almost-deserted cave of a black bar. A large hotel rose above this quiet retreat but none of its noises penetrated the seclusion; sometimes the one waiter coming through the swinging door from the kitchen let in a little clatter, of cutlery, chefs' voices, or the syrup stream of a radio tenor, but all these sounds were absorbed at once, sopped up by the heavy black woodwork, and silence flowed back like deep water or shade under forest trees.

"I'm devoted to Hennie," Olivia said, and Kitty agreed.

"Do you want another Martini?" she asked.

"Well, I could." They summoned the waiter.

Kitty ran her jade bracelet around on her wrist so she could see and admire the clasp. "Would you say she was putting on a little weight?" she inquired, in the kindest voice. "Just the inkling of hips?"

But Olivia's extreme candor forced her, it might seem with a trifle of regret, to deny this. "*Not* really," she said. "She's more, I think, mellowing."

"Mellowing." Kitty considered the word, lightly touching the jade and diamond clasp beneath her cuff. "That may be it. I wonder if mellowing, though, doesn't lead straight to hips, in time? I rather hope myself to be a lean, pointed old woman, in a rather French way."

"Oh, you will be, no doubt at all! I can see it, perfectly; very smart," Olivia said, but at that Kitty didn't look too pleased after all.

"Not scrawny!" she warned, her voice sharp.

"Oh, no, no," Olivia soothed, but in the momentary pause that followed did they both rather vividly see Kitty at sixty—erect, distinguished-looking, but quite a little like a dry old heron?

"Waiter," she called plaintively, and over sidled the man who had no other function in life but to care for their wants. "I think I've changed my mind and I *will* have a little mayonnaise after all."

Olivia declined to change her order. "But I wonder what color this time," she speculated.

"A warm apricot, she told me," Kitty was able to inform her, and Olivia said, judicially, that that ought to be very becoming indeed.

Edward Latham, whom nobody had ever, even when he was a boy, called Ed, sat in the Stacpole living room swinging one foot above the other and smiling. Edward Latham was lazy, and kind, and aware of both these facts and sometimes congratulated himself thinking how satisfactory it was when one led to the other, as indeed it had in the present instance, he having earlier that afternoon, rounding the windy corner of the tall bank, nearly run down Hennie, and when she had said, somewhat breathless from the gusty wind beating her face pink, would he come in later for tea, he had not bothered to think up a reason for not going. Kindness had flowered out of this indolence; anyone could see with half an eye she loved having him. He went a step further and admitted to himself he much enjoyed being there.

He swung one foot above the other and smiled. "What a charming dress," he said.

Hennie said, "Thank you. You look just like Stockinette when in one of her good moods."

"Who?"

"Surely you've met her? She's around."

"I didn't get the name."

"Just someone we know. Very delightful. Not married. You'll meet her one of these days; *of course* you can't be expected to know everybody in town yet, just living here a matter of months. More tea?"

But he had not yet begun to drink from his cup; he would have preferred to find her dispensing cocktails but the preference was a mild one, and presently he took a sip. "No solid food, thank you," he said to the approaching plate and its overlapping shingles of bread and butter. "My waistline hasn't changed in twenty-five years. It's my chief treasure, the way some men feel about their Renoir or their Cézanne."

"Wonderful; would that I could say the same." She gave a false sigh, gazing downward, and then they both laughed, but he teased her by saying nothing.

"Exercises?" she inquired, when the compliment she had every right to expect was not forthcoming. "Do you beat yourself around the waist with dumbbells, or whatever it is men do with them, or waste yourself away in Turkish baths?"

"No, no. I don't seem to need to. No, I have only my low blood pressure to contend with. I'm very lucky." That wasn't boasting, he hoped, but it was the truth that his long flat body to which he never denied anything went about the world in its fine British shoes, its fine wool and cotton coverings, with no change at all in weight and outline from one year to the next. He had been amused to observe an infinitesimal convexity showing on Laurence—really only the suspicion, a suggestion of convexity. "Married men," he said, sounding very kind indeed, "they lead such an absorbing life, getting more tired than us bachelors by the nature of things—" Hennie here batted her lashes at him but he appeared to pay no heed and went blandly on "—worrying over sick children and money and all those constant domestic occurrences." He had always been sure the problems of the married state were very real, very tiring. "I mean to say, they can't help it, can they, if they tend to slump a bit with relief when the crises, if that's not too strong a word, are over? That's my theory, anyway," he said, and took another sip.

"How terribly clever; I'd never thought of all that." She leaned toward him. "Tell me, then— Oh, here's Clare." She had seemed to be about to ask him something or to confide in him. Slowly she subsided backward against the sofa, though enveloping him still with her wide gaze, and he had a twinge of regret, at something lost. She turned her head and called into the hall, "Tea, darling?"

Clare came in, windblown and sparkling. He had never seen her so pretty; she had seemed to him a brown, quiet little thing, more crisp and sensible than her mother. Now he was pleasantly impressed when she included him in her smile, a smile carved and folded back in her cold, glowing cheeks, and forgave her for interrupting what Hennie had perhaps been about to say to him. "Hello, Mr. Latham— I met a friend unexpectedly, after his class. We've been running!" she said to her mother. "Tea must be clammy by now, isn't it?" Her white, girl's hand that had never yet scrubbed nor weeded crab grass nor washed a child's knees nor held an icy flashlight while on a dark night a sulky husband changed a tire, these pretty fine-skinned hands lifted to the collar of her red coat and sweetly undid the single big button.

"Stone cold," Hennie admitted, "but have some bread and butter? Mr. Latham has just been expounding to me a fascinating theory, and I must say I believe every word of it." She went on to give her version of his theory of waist expansion in the married man, but to his surprise Clare's dark eyes took alarm, she darted an inimical glance right into his face as he lay in the large chair and, turning, she cried to her mother, "But it doesn't *have* to be that way, does it? Oh, I hate fatness! Mummy, it *can* be avoided, can't it?"

He wondered at her, that a mere young girl should appear to mind so much what was a silly theory only, and in fact one he had only just made up to amuse Hennie. Clare was too serious; she needed teasing. He started to nod at her and assure her that statistics could be found to support him, and was going to add sad and inevitable and ridiculous embellishments, but Hennie shot a fiercely mother-hen look at him, a Hecuba look, biting him, in a brief moment when Clare turned her head away. It utterly silenced him, and then she said to her child, most earnestly, that of course, of course it could be avoided, fatness could; nobody *had* to get fat; every young man could stay slim if he wanted to. "Marriage has *nothing* to do with it!" Then the two unaccountable creatures burst out laughing, and Clare kissed her mother just beyond the corner of her mouth in a delicious curved area Mr. Latham had already observed, gave a hugely fantastic false sigh and cried, "Mummy! You do relieve me!"

Hennie went on to remind them that as a matter of fact the average American male aged twenty-two to fifty-two was much too busy to put on weight, too busy for any use actually, and Clare, grave again, nodded and said yes of course that must be so; a pity really that men's lives were so drab; and she added, "And furthermore, another thing I've noticed, when men get tired they become kind of, you know, *skeptical!* It's sad, I think." He said he had observed for himself that this was true, and he must try and fight against it in future.

Then Clare suddenly sprang up and ran off upstairs, calling back "Good-by, Mr. Latham. Excuse me!" When she got nearly to the top she whirled around in her great red capelike coat and came partway down, leaned both hands on the banister and called, "But maybe you're staying for dinner?" The heavy red folds fell softly down around her.

"As a matter of fact, yes," her mother answered for him. "That is, he's coming back to dinner and take me to a concert this evening."

"Not Daddy?"

"No. He'll be in, but I'll be going out."

"So am I," Clare sang, and floated up and away.

He couldn't ask outright. He felt he didn't know the family that well, not yet; he hadn't lived in town long enough either. But he was curious.

"I'm just a curious old bachelor," he said, and waited.

"How old? I can never tell, about men; women, of course, I know to the minute. I can't tell about colored people, either." She beamed on him from beyond the teapot. So she wasn't going to answer his unasked question; how unfair pretty women were. He put down the cold cup at last.

"Forty-four," he said.

"Me too. Well, not till next year."

"You don't look any older than Clare."

"And often feel far younger," she informed him. "And behave so too, I greatly fear. Though in a way I've reached a plateau in living, if you know what I mean. I can stand in the middle and look all around; revolve; yet I feel trapped. I am captured, by something that won't let me head anywhere, any more. Oh, I *have* everything, I know that. But there's something more I want, if I only knew what it is." Her large eyes wandered to the corners of the room, to the windows, and happened back to him, and she was a little startled to see an almost smug look on his face. "Probably I'll never get it," she said hastily, but the pleased, conspiratorial expression continued to glimmer in his eyes, and he laughed, pulled one side of his open jacket up and around from between him and the chair arm, settled the small of his back lower into the chintz cushion, laced his fingers together in anticipation. She was such a pretty woman. "Tell me," he suggested. "It won't take me long to go home and dress. Tell me. I'm an accomplished listener."

✦

Hennie idled up the stairs Clare had so recently run up. She must dress; Laurence would be home any minute. She wandered about the upper hall and then, rather more quickly, turned in at their door and went to scrutinize herself in the glass-flower framed mirror. She leaned on the dressing table and, with the greatest pleasure, looked at all of herself that was reflected. Her cheeks were bright, her hair stood out; she solemnly directed a deep look down past the opening of her dress and what she saw there must have pleased her for she smiled, but then, right away, "Poor Edward," she said, sincerely. Though there were moments when she was not as good-looking as she believed herself to be, this was not one of them.

She had just spent a very enjoyable hour, for what is pleasanter than to encounter the blue gaze of admiration and have it all to oneself, pouring over oneself? Like a flower expanding, she had told him simply and fully just how she had been this week past, how exuberant and hopeful and unfulfilled, and the acquiescent sounds he made deep in his throat had been the greatest comfort to her. They grew deeper, actually, as the tea hour lengthened, the dark came down the street, up to the house and pressed against the windows, and she had to reach up and turn on the lamp over her head. When she had looked down from this gesture she had encountered a steady stare from him that had made her color come warmer. Right after that, even though he had to hurry home to dress and return, they stood a long time by the front door.

Now by the dressing table she took up her comb and ran it upward through her hair. Laurence appeared in the room reflected behind her. "I didn't hear you come in! It must be later than I thought. I'm changing. Edward Latham's coming to dinner."

"*Again?*" Laurence said. "Why is this? Did we ask him?"

"I suppose I must have," Hennie agreed. "He's a nice change, and then too I've always found I pay more attention to how I look for dinner if anyone is coming in; you know I do; so you're the one to benefit in the long run." Laurence hung up his jacket in his closet, and yawned. "It's a little something semifestive to look forward to, at the end of my long housewifely day, to have someone to dinner. Oh, I do look forward to *your* coming home, madly, the way I look forward all day to my lovely hot bath before bed."

"I've no objection to him, not what you could call an objection. He's a good talker and a good listener, I'll say that for him, keeps quiet and submerged while listening. But then, do you notice, however long he stays under eventually he has to come up with a *bon mot* in his teeth." He yawned again but managed to inquire between spasms, "If I'm a hot bath, what's he?"

"Oh, I d'know. Nothing." He's an unexpected flick of expensive scent in my ordinary life, that's what Edward Latham is; and something to think about. She pulled a long velvet skirt from its hanger, a fur-collared and cuffed sweater from its drawer, made the deep obeisance of women correctly putting themselves into brassières, straightened up and ran a comb vigorously again and again through her ash-blond upstanding hair. "He's got two tickets for tonight's concert."

"I see."

Over the dinner table Edward Latham's slow, considered, fastidious, uncontroversial, often gallant, sometimes whimsical speech flowed equably like clear shallow waves across a beach at the turning of the tide. Hennie didn't know, couldn't be sure, whether it was Agnes's lamb with garlic that was so noticeably contenting him or the pretty contrast of herself rising out of colored wool and a circlet of narrow dark fur; she was aware of his appreciating both, but Laurence sent Will upstairs for his soda tablets.

"Oh, I'm sorry, darling. Garlic. I forgot." Her eyes were contrite on him, her fork suspended in sympathy. The ungrateful owner of a flawless digestion, she sometimes failed to remember what a doctor had gaily diagnosed as Laurence's "typically twentieth-century hair-trigger gut." "I'm terribly sorry, I did forget about you and garlic."

"It's all right," Laurence said, patient, his fork at rest.

Will returned with a small bottle and a phrase he had acquired from reading advertisements. "Hurry-worry stomach," he said, handing his father the bottle.

"Please, Will."

Later, when dessert proved to be *crême brûlée*, Laurence informed their guest, in a voice lightly laced with malice, that it was wonderful to have a wife with the digestion of a sea gull.

Because a guest had come to dinner Will did his homework in his bedroom, and Clare, too, after a polite interval in the living room, rose up in the lamplight and said, "If I'm ever going to get some letters written before I go out, I'd better go do them. Good night, Mr. Latham." And she kissed her father and mother good night, though was there a trace, a wisp of disapproval in her kiss to her mother, and a questing, backward glance at the three grownups grouped around the fire?

"Ah-h-h," Hennie said, and stretched her long arms, her hands coming out like pointed white tulips from their dark fur circlets. "We don't need to hurry, do we? This is the best moment of the day."

"Yes," the men said, "yes."

"Probably you never have a chance to sit down all day, until after dinner; so busy," Edward Latham suggested.

"I? Oh, no. No, I don't have such a fearful lot going on all the time." She couldn't help being honest, though Kitty had once told her how boring it can be. "No. It's just that now, sitting here for a little doing nothing, one is more aware that though time is always passing and leaking away too fast, just sitting still, with friends, seems to trap it somehow, for a few minutes anyway. Do you know what I mean?"

Edward Latham nodded. Laurence filled his pipe and put it between his teeth. The fire flapped. Upstairs began the loud, irregular, irrational thuds and thumpings that accompanied the doing of Will's homework.

"We believe he drops dictionaries," Laurence explained. "We aren't sure. Usually he studies down here after dinner—" He rolled an eye toward his wife, but she was dreaming into the fire, "—and then he manages to keep hold of his books, but once upstairs— I don't know, it may not be dictionaries. Perhaps he's playing with something and not getting his work done." He yawned, and tried to pretend not. "Fact is, there's a family rule he doesn't work after dinner anyway, for what it's worth."

"The thing about women," Hennie said as though to herself, "is that so often we persuade ourselves we have to pretend we're simply exhausted all the time. 'My dear, I'm ex*haust*ed,' we say—you know the way we do!—but actually that's sometimes only because we're afraid somebody will think we aren't, or am I betraying my kind?"

"My dear Mrs. Stacpole," Edward Latham said, "or Hennie if I may, women are no different from men in that respect. We all pretend to be pushed to the limit every moment of our waking hours."

"Edward, I believe you're right," she said, and rising with a smile and a swirl of the velvet skirt for him, she went to find the Cointreau decanter and three small glasses.

Later, sitting beside him in the auditorium—they had missed the whole of Debussy—Hennie speculated: Would she prefer to have Edward Latham become the kind of family friend the children would call Uncle Edward, the kind of friend who would bring Will foreign stamps that came on letters to the bank and give bath salts to Clare at Christmas, or would she keep him all to herself, a secret? Would it not be flying in the face of Providence if she treated him as just another friend when, with his deep sympathy and admiration, he had perhaps been sent to her in her hour of need? Or could he serve in both capacities?

"Not both," she said.

He leaned. "I beg your pardon?"

"Nothing."

The conductor raised his arms, shook them, and a torrent of sound burst from his men. When the concerto was over the sound of clapping was like a heavy summer rainstorm on the leaves of a forest.

"Is it that low blood pressure you keep talking of that makes you so peaceful to be with?" she asked him, as the lights went on. Some men would have pretended affront at being labeled peaceful-to-be-with, but his slow blue gaze came smiling around on her.

"That might be so."

"But haven't I always heard low blood pressure makes a person low-spirited and gloomy?" Up past his neat head, far, far up against a skyey ceiling, swam gold plaster cupids in high relief, painted clouds billowed, miles of gold molding ran around and around. He replied, calm and reasonable, that he had nothing to be gloomy about. But she wondered about him; it seemed odd and unusual, and hardly even credible. She had many friends and most of them had plenty of what they needed and indeed far too much, yet they kept on reaching out, avid. They weren't restless, she considered, merely avid, their faces turned sharp toward the next hour while their present occupations, whatever they might be, lay still uncompleted between their hands. It must be that Edward alone of all the people she knew had some secret, because he had himself, without mentioning it to anyone—so like him!—mastered that technique she longed for. And the swift corollary to this was: Then she must spend as much time with him as she could. She reflected on the hours and hours and hours, and even whole days, in the lives of people we know well, and we don't know what they are up to. She smoothed the velvet of her lap, reflecting. She might happen to know So-and-so's dentist appointment was for ten o'clock yesterday but what she didn't know and never would was what he may have been doing the hour before it, or the hour after it, and he may very well have been up to something merry and wonderful.

If this was so, and she was easily able to persuade herself it was, then the safest thing to do would be to attach Edward to herself. Anyone who had the secret of living sideways was too valuable to let go. She would become very fond of him, very fond. Tears rose into her large eyes as she put it to herself she might even have to run away with him. One can't run away by oneself, as she had discovered; it is surprisingly lonely. So it must be with Edward, *faute de mieux*. He's charming, she thought, and I could learn to love him. But then, practical despite all, she wondered if for convenience's sake alone it would not be better to stay at home while leading the double life she felt herself so well fitted for.

The lights went down, the conductor came striding fast like a man setting off for a long brisk walk by himself and was surprised to find all those people there, halted, resigned himself, and bowed to the accompaniment of the clapping that always hurt Hennie's ears. The violinists preened their necks for the last time, the lights sank further and Edward leaned two inches nearer Hennie.

She sank into a deep bath of sound. She was happy, aware of the near shoulder but not thinking about him any more. The waves of music rose. In the seat ahead of her a very young girl was sitting and Hennie's bemused eyes watched the child's fingertips unconsciously trifling at the thick dark ends of her short hair, slowly, voluptuously, feeling away at the very tips of the thick dark feathers of hair, mesmerizing herself, mesmerizing Hennie. The gold and crystal waves of the concerto reared higher. Light and music were crashing together on the lighted stage, and Hennie pulled away her gaze from the child ahead to watch the frenzy. In the midst of all that leaping light and sound the concert grand stood, a huge black butterfly with one shiny lifted wing. A vast exulting humming and glupping beat out from the tulip-topped gold harps, their strings curtains of gold falling rain.

Laurence was reading in bed when she got home.

"It's getting colder," she said brightly, coming in. "Winter's just around the corner, I suppose."

"I suppose."

"I thought you'd be asleep." She took off her bracelet and hung it on a little Venetian glass tree. He watched from over the top of his book.

"I stayed awake to tell you some news. This afternoon

when I got home I came on Gino and Agnes in the kitchen talking to each other."

"Laurence!" She turned from her dressing table and stared at him. "It's not possible! The end of the world is coming! Why didn't you tell me that instant minute?"

He had, of course, intended to; he had hurried upstairs with the surprise for her, but then she had at once told him of her evening's plans and he had been pulled up short. As he watched her now he saw her recall that moment and turn away from him back to her table. He saw her whom he knew so well thinking: Perhaps it is because of me, my changed self, that those two spoke to each other at last; what were they saying? He knew her very well. Often he watched the passage through her of what with her passed for thought—the long trances and daydreams irradiated by occasional and seemingly random flashes of what she would have said were decisions but in truth were only crystallizations of prejudice, or affection, or expediency. Those were what she ran her life by, and they served, and he had no objection, usually. Now he asked, "What do you think of it?"

"But I simply can't imagine what's got into them. They must have lost their minds."

His eyes went back to his book. "Possibly." He had meant to treat this affair of Agnes and Gino as a joke; any other time it would have been. "Good concert?" he asked, and then without giving her opportunity to reply, "Latham's around here more often than not."

"Oh, heavens *no*," Hennie protested, statistics on her side. "Wasn't it last week? But if you don't like him I wish you'd say so— You were the one kept dinning into me we must have him out!—and if so I'll just have him for tea." She cocked an eye at him by way of the glass-wreathed mirror. There was a long silence. He didn't know if he would answer. He knew it drove her nearly mad when he didn't answer, because she had frequently told him so. "*Do* you not like him?"

"Any reason I shouldn't?"

She was startled. He could see her startled face among the glass lilies and roses and forget-me-nots. "Don't be absurd."

She sailed into the bathroom and instantly he reached out and clicked off the light. He screwed down into bed and lay there thinking about Edward Latham stepping backward and forward behind his neat railing of cultivated clichés, shooting his cuffs and smoothing his hair. "The man's a damned unicorn," Laurence said to the closed bathroom door, and for no reason this somewhat fantastic statement carried with it a ray of comfort.

CHAPTER EIGHT

Next morning early, as Hennie was looking over her summer dresses, deciding which were ripe to be given away, singing, and reminding herself as she lingered over cotton and silk that not once in all her life had she ever regretted giving away anything nor thought of it again, Mr. Tuthill, unannounced, appeared in her doorway, and she greeted him with rapture.

"You've come to put in my bathroom shelf! Oh, good. The bath powder's always springing off the window sill into the air and turning turtle, but *now* it'll have a place of its own."

Mr. Tuthill moved about the earth, somehow managed, without lifting his feet from the floor and now he thus advanced a little into her room, but he did not immediately reply to her enthusiasm and his eyes searched beyond her shoulder. "I leave my folding rule here?" Her heart sank; he hadn't, after all, come for her. But she had not seen his rule; she lacked even the small opportunity the rule would have afforded her to capture him by holding it as ransom. He went on without regret. "That's funny. Well, somewhere. I'm at Lewises, over on Prospect Avenue, on a sagging sink."

She eyed him warily; could he be trying to provoke her past bearing? Surely, surely he had said he would come to her and make a bathroom shelf when he was through with Mrs. Comfit's back stairs and had even admitted, when pressed, that he would put up for her exactly the same kind he had once built into Clare's room, even recalling with a measured relish, the problems and satisfactions of that bit of carpentry, much as Hennie supposed Tintoretto might have referred, in later life, to some not unsuccessful fresco, struck off long since.

"You're through at Mrs. Comfit's, then?" she prodded, trying to catch him out.

"Not entirely. Few little things, here and there. Nothing to signify." He went past her on his big silent rubbers and bending drew from behind the clothes hamper his lost folding rule. "Thought I might've." His smile upon her was very sweet. "Mrs. Lewis's developed this sagging sink, sags a'most two inches," he said, "well, inch and three-quarters, any rate. Noticeable, if you look at it. Frets her, I believe. Or so she says."

"That shelf you put in Clare's room once is absolutely perfect," Hennie said. "Couldn't mine here in the bathroom be just the same, and not be much of a job?"

Was that surprise or was it disapproval, dawning in Mr. Tuthill's pale eye? In a less temperate nature it might even be the beginning of affront, even scorn. "Angle irons in *tile?*"

She hung her head. "Of course. I didn't think."

He drifted past her and down the stairs; she ran to the banisters and was able, his mild mesmeric stare removed, to call, "But you are coming back soon and do it for me, aren't you? You promised!"

The shapeless gray cloth cap vanished slowly toward the shadows of the back hall and a shadowy voice, slow, gentle, "—find the time—" floated up to her.

On her way to the tailor's Hennie stopped in at the bookshop. She ran a finger along the backs of a row of books on a shelf labeled "Bargains; 3 for $1.00." Always she halted before such shelves first thing on trips to bookshops, believing that one day she would be fortunate enough to pounce on the evidence of a wild lapse of judgment on the part of the shop owner. She anticipated the day she discovered first English editions of *The Natural History of Selborne, Out of Africa, Concluding,* and perhaps *To the Lighthouse,* all standing slyly, cheek by jowl, waiting for her to snatch them up, but so far no such miracle had happened and on this day as always waited on this shelf only the worn, lending-library copies of the works of lady novelists who, seemingly, had to get the word "love" or "lovely" into their titles or else die. Hennie's beige chamois fingertips informed her that every single one of these books dealt with an oversensitive housewife with three children and a normal husband, a woman who up till chapter one had been entirely content with her lot but then, owing to some trifling ferment brewed up by the novelist in the double boiler of her imagination, fell into a sad set of circumstances until in the last chapter she saw everything in proportion at last and in a final burst of symbolism bent to pick up the children's blue jeans all tossed in a lovable grubby heap on the bathroom floor. Hennie's fingers went faster and faster and soon she turned away, momentarily depressed as though she had in fact just read them all; she idled along a table of biographies, which she never read, nor wanted to, because as she had explained to Laurence, "How do we *know?* How could we?"

The good thing about this shop was no one tried to sell anything. In fact the owner, a short roly-poly young woman with sandy braids wrapped round and round her head, preferred talking to selling any day, and was even now whispering and exclaiming and darting her eyebrows up and down in company with a customer in a fur jacket. Their low and eager voices hissed in that place like escaping radiator steam. A patient young man hung about near the ornithology shelf, diffident, momentarily hopeful; when the whispers died away he would start up with a book he seemed to have set his heart on and go toward the owner, then become despairing and retreat as the steam started up again. He looked both helpless and in a hurry, and Hennie watched with sympathy. Once he definitely approached the two, but they never saw him at all and the one in the fur jacket tossed back her head and let out a trumpeting "I*ma*gine!" just as he got within ten feet, and he sheered away like a colt. Hennie stood still and directed a stern gaze over at the gossips, trying to conjure the owner into paying attention to a customer who knew what he wanted but not how to make it his own. "—and so she said," came from the two heads inclined near each other; "—so then she said, but I don't see how she could, do you, considering, but she up and said—" They stood absorbed, up to mid-calf in an ever-widening pool of scandal and surmise, its wet poison-tipped waves lapping and splashing wider and wider and deeper.

Hennie couldn't endure it for the young man another minute. She tossed this waiting youth a look of scorn for his weakness and sympathy for his plight and sailed up to confront the gossips and politely, in a sad, hurt, forgiving voice she said to them, "When you're quite through *talking about my aunt,* could you take care of this young man?"

Then she sailed out, her heart thumping at the lie, her cheeks beginning to redden. As she passed the astounded young man she gave him a wild triumphant smile—"I'm just as surprised as you," she wanted to say—but he, staring back at her, never so much as blinked, overwhelmed as he was by a rush of love and admiration and astonishment. He pivoted on a rubber heel and watched her out the door. How much more would he have been loving and grateful had he known she had just put her immortal soul in jeopardy only in order that he might not have to spend the rest of his lunch hour trying to buy *The Lesser Warblers of Southern New England?*

Then with what trembling legs did she pursue her way down the avenue; laughter was shaking in her throat. "So that's what it feels like to lie on a big practical scale. It's absolutely intoxicating. Very likely it's up to the strong to lie on behalf of the weak." And he was weak, that silly young man; why hadn't he stalked up to the proprietress and thrust his two dollars in her pudding face? How flabbergasted the feeble boy had been! How amazed and delighted had she herself been to hear her false and beautiful lie come out in a purr, like Stockinette's at the sight of cream. The fall sky, hot and bright blue, rose up further than the eye could believe, and the gilt-leaved trees, maple and elm and oak, made an archway for her. "If that's lying, then why do I ever try to tell the truth?"

She skimmed away down the avenue. It had been so easy, a serpent's tongue of useful guile had come flicking out of her mouth, pointed like the flickering tongue of a crouched, tapestry beast.

It was the kind of fall day that is so much more promising than even the most promising day in spring. The air was warm but cool around the edges, and Hennie went as though on wheels. The globe of the world had been dipped in a bath of liquid gold and hung up to drip in blue space, but quick gold still ran about, wet, on leaves and into corners of lawns; it pooled up, smiling like water that slips and slides and runs; she could have scooped up a little in her hands, but not much; it was everywhere she glanced. A wind raced up the avenue setting the gilt maple leaves to raining down in showers. She reached out to catch one but it slid past. She wished for the sight of the spare elegant figure of Edward Latham to come up the avenue toward her and knew exactly how it would be—the shock of their meeting eyes. Not love, she thought, but its close cousin; it lays a row of tinsel along every branch; that next hydrant has a halo; there is *no* obligation.

Faute de mieux, she smiled into the faces of approaching, unknown pedestrians; into the faces of children running and un-self-certain young women tripping by, and upon old men she cast a large look of delight. One old man on a cane halted and looked after her, almost raising his stick in a long-unaccustomed hail. She sped on, regardless. "I think Robin Hood should have been canonized, or at least knighted. Protecting the weak is such fun. I'd like to have known him really well. Lady Henrietta; Lady Henrietta Hood," she murmured, going down and up curbstones in a haze of well-being. "Tiles, for God's sake!" she scoffed. But from this instant on she would go about the world leading a perfectly compatible double-barreled life—a cheerful, acquiescent, captive wife's life, and at other moments when no one she knew was looking she would pursue a career of purest mendacity; she would become the secret *dea ex machina* who contrived unexpected happiness for strangers. She wished she were capable of being both kinds of woman openly, but she knew that was not possible. "I am plenty strong enough to lead two lives simultaneously," she said, and turning in at a narrow doorway climbed narrow stairs to the Vogue Tailors and Furriers.

The Vogue Tailors and Furriers was and had always been, only Mr. Speer. Outside the one big dusty window pigeons clattered their wings, descending and taking off on a flat roof, but Mr. Speer never looked out at them. In his hot square room that smelled so strong of machine oil and human hair and human skin and hot irons, he scurried and kneeled and murmured all day. "A liddle paddink not too moch—double-breasted no—you want it should lie fladduh, the colluh?"

"Mercy, no." Hennie, dreaming in the heat above him on a six-inch pedestal, turned slowly as he told her to, keeping her head turned to watch the pigeons, over her shoulder. "Who feeds them?"

"Lady upstairs," he replied coldly, his lips rigid with pins. "Step donn please." But this she was reluctant to do, it brought her so close to his terrible breath. "Your shouldiss is igh you don't need I should give you moch paddink. Some people's sloop away, is somethink awful. Getting stottuh?" he inquired. For years he had been trying to have it she was growing fat, would grow fat sooner or later; only when she had been pregnant had he wholly approved of her.

"No, I'm not!"

"H'hmn." He smiled among his pins.

"I'm not! Go look at my measurements, go way back to that navy tweed I had ten years ago." His smile continued, unbelieving. "Go and look them up," she commanded, now afraid he might be right.

He stepped away into a cubbyhole where he kept a tumble of papers, and presently, sooner than one would have predicted, he came ambling back reading a small bit of pasteboard. "Ips dirty-sigs, vaist tventy-sigs, bust—m'mn—dirty-four, inside omm dirty-one. The same exact figguss," he said, disappointed, and laid them aside. "Now step opp please, I should see about the em."

Very tall, she bent above him, wondering what small miracle she might manage for him. His life must be so extraordinarily dull. "Next time I come for a fitting—early next week, Mr. Speer, if you could?—I'll bring along a sponge cake for your pigeons. Of course I'll have to steal it from my cook!" She didn't think highly of this project, but considered it merely a mild, tentative piece of deception, practicing only, as Agnes would unhesitatingly hand her over the entire contents of the cake box if asked. "Shall I?" There was no reply. What went on in that dark bullet head set low on the white-shirted shoulders; possibly not love of birds. "They look so lovely out there in the sun," she wheedled in a pigeon's own voice.

"Turn please." He swallowed noisily.

Oh, very well, very well, very well. She would find a better recipient for her new benevolence. She wouldn't waste any of her new-found power on Mr. Speer if he didn't want it.

"My daughter's skirt," she said, "the one you just made, the plaid, doesn't that hang a little *straighter* than this one?" But then Mr. Speer had the last word after all. He glanced briefly upward, sighting along the side seam.

"Liddler ips," he said.

The tile-making class dwindled overnight from eleven enthusiasts down to Olivia, Kitty, and Hennie. The instructress telephoned Kitty she had twenty-four-hour flu, thought she might be going to visit her brother in Idaho, was considering taking a course in art appreciation at the museum, had been persuaded to give two hours a week at the Air Force filter station, and had lamed her wrist opening a tin of corn.
"I always say one excuse is much, much better than a lot, even if they're all good," Olivia said with disapproval to her two friends at the zinc table. "I tell my children so, every now and then, so they won't forget. I never believe 'em when people give ten reasons for not coming to dinner, do you?"
The other two didn't either, though Kitty, whose politeness often verged right over into charity, said, "Poor things; and it may just be some one awful reason they can't bear to say."
"But is your life like that?" inquired Olivia, reasonable as always.
At the far end of the big whitewashed room the two black-haired boys went about their work of rubbing pans, shifting large sighing, breathing sacks of flour and now and again opening the heavy soot-black oven door to see to the bed of burning roses within. There was no way of knowing how old these boys might be; their bodies looked young and unformed; they were already round-shouldered.

"Probably ought to be in high school right this minute," Hennie said, bending over her tile with a little tool. "Illegal for them to be working."

"It may be." Kitty glanced searchingly at the two dark creatures and then away. "They look as though they could and should shave though, don't they? I wonder how I'll finish off this edge." She made a row of toothlike marks with the butt of the tool, sat back and considered.

"Gino wouldn't tell Agnes she'd left the vacuum cleaner going in the cold closet, and it ran all night," Hennie said. "She'd darted upstairs to see to something on the stove and then the doorbell rang or something and then Will came in with a cut finger—I wasn't home—and by the time she'd managed to persuade him to let her use Mercurochrome it was time to start dinner and she forgot. We thought for a minute the other day they were speaking, but I guess not."

"Are you sure Gino *knew?*" Kitty asked, peering out terribly fair-mindedly from beneath her pointed hat.

"Must have. The last thing he does every evening before he goes home is lock the cellar door from the inside, so he must have heard it humming away in there like a great, mad bee."

Olivia said she couldn't imagine anyone taking a vacuum cleaner downstairs anyway. Agnes was beginning to make grape jelly, Hennie said, and had thought the cold closet was dusty. "She'll get back at him though, I shouldn't wonder. He brings his own sandwiches for his lunch from home, but she's supposed to make his coffee."

"And she'll pretend to forget to," Olivia suggested.
"No, she'll *burn* it."
"My dear, it's not possible."
"She knows how."

The autumn sun poured down through a row of high windows in one white wall of the converted stable. Motes and beams and infinitesimal flakes of flour slid and floated in this highway of warmth and light. The three women leaned contentedly over their clay, scraping and patting, playing.

"But it's warm as summer." Hennie pushed up the sleeves of her cardigan, took off her scarf, and undid four buttons.

At once Olivia murmured in her prudent tone, "I'd do that last one up again, if I were you. Our two dark gentlemen can't keep their eyes off you."

Hennie gave a delicate hoot. "I never heard such a thing! *If so*, it's only because I'm not dark like you two. Horrible hair like mine, *applesauce* color, always seems to madden Latins and I always get pinched in Italy. Even in the Italian part of Switzerland, as a matter of fact."

Kitty's and Olivia's glances, amused, tolerant up to a point, affectionate, slid together and parted. "Mélisse showed me your new apricot dinner-at-home skirt," Kitty said. "She was putting it in a box with tissue paper. I told her she mustn't show it to me, but she insisted."

Hennie said she couldn't think of a single reason why not; it wasn't a secret skirt in any way. Kitty said oh, she didn't mean to change the subject but everybody knew she had but the brain of a bird and she couldn't think what made her think of it just now but how much money had these two managed to collect for the new boys' washroom at the school?

Hennie suspended her tool. "Why should the new boys need—oh, I see. I was in Long Island on that expedition of mine when you had the P.T.A. meeting, and I didn't know a thing about a new washroom."

"I've taken in about eighty dollars so far," Olivia said. "Three thousand we need if we tile it," she told Hennie. "Now you, you're always saying you don't know what to do with yourself these days, why don't you get onto some rich old—well, bachelors, for instance, and screw a few thousand out of them?"

"If I only knew a rich old bachelor—" she began, but Kitty couldn't wait.

"You know that new man in town, Latham, don't you? Didn't someone say?" She turned with elaborate airiness to Olivia. "And you know him too, don't you?"

"Oh, yes. He came to dinner once. He's very intelligent; quite, I mean. He reminds me of an airedale, for some reason I can't put my finger on. He gets all his clothes made in London so he certainly could part with the price of a washbowl. Or maybe he'd like to give them the hot air blower thing the boys are going to have such a whirl with. Tell you what." She rooted about in her handbag. "Hennie darling, this means you. Here's a list of people not yet approached, and try for a quota of four hundred dollars. Don't look at me like that! Your victims will be, let's see, the Garretsons, who are such awful stinkers about the Community Chest but are said to be besotted about their grandson who's in Will's class so they must have some good qualities, and old, old Mrs. Comfit, who's doddering but so sweet and absent-minded she might give something almost unconsciously, or I wonder if the bank controls her? Laurence will know. How is Laurence by the way, these days? I haven't seen him of late."

"He's become a manic-dyspeptic."

"Oh, too bad; but that will pass. Anyway, about Mrs. Comfit, if necessary, get him to put the screws on her. And all the parents of the boys in Will's class. There! That will keep you busy and happy the whole rest of the fall." Hennie looked at them in honest wonder. How little, how little they knew her. Who did know her? The figure of Edward Latham, that well-turned-out trust officer, materialized before her inward eye. *He* did; he understood her. She bent above her tile, marveling at how little anyone knows anyone else, even though they may be the best of friends.

"Ha!" these two said, low but cheery, to each other half an hour later as the tile-making class dispersed on the sidewalk. Hennie had said she wanted to walk, but before Kitty and Olivia quite parted to go to their station wagons, they hissed a moment together. "You were brave as a *lion*, darling!" Kitty said, but Olivia disclaimed credit. "No, no, it was *you*. You started it." "Ha!" they both said, "we'll see," and nodding, parted.

At one o'clock Laurence telephoned from the bank that he wouldn't get home for dinner that night.

"A fine note!"

He said he knew; there were men from New York hanging around his neck. She suggested he bring them home for dinner, but when she learned there were four of them she said as a matter of fact there wouldn't have been food enough for even one extra anyway. "But I'll give Stockinette your lamb chop, with your love," she said.

"Do," he replied sadly. "I'll break away as soon as I can, but you know what these men are like."

Hennie said thank God she didn't at all.

She and Will, who had been excused from afternoon school for dentistry and shopping, lunched together, Stockinette at the head of the table. Now and then a blunt beige paw exquisitely etched with black made a tentative appearance at the table edge, questing and polite, but at a word from Will it was withdrawn and the little lion head would turn slowly, with a false unconcern, toward the window. "How you wrong me," she would have said.

"Isn't she wonderful?" Will asked lovingly. "Isn't she? Have you ever known a cat like her, in all your long life? Can I go to the movies?"

"When, for heaven's sake? Certainly not on a school evening. You were out at cub scouts last evening and you show it today; you look quite tired."

"That was my duty."

"No fun to it?"

He flashed her a bright dark smile. "It's the one about little wild animals and the school wants us to see it, they said. What if I just went to the six o'clock, I'd be home by eight and in bed almost immediately. Peanut butter sandwiches," he said quickly, making the most of a look in her eye. "Very nourishing. Agnes could make me a tray, couldn't she, with lots of nourishing sandwiches and milk and I'd take it up to bed and we'd be asleep in no time."

"We? You and Agnes?"

"Me and Double-Fatness." He looked languishingly across at his darling's veiled, gooseberry eyes; her nose was an iced mulberry. He had recently heard Agnes refer to her as—the way he heard it—"the altar'd cat." Altar'd, dedicated; somehow she had been rendered more sacred by an early trip to the vet's than most other cats, or anyway she was more so than the ones who had not been altar'd. Perhaps it hadn't taken place at the vet's at all, but in her past maybe there was a little ceremony she had gone through; in his mind was a faint but pleasing picture of a very small ecclesiastical enclosure, flowers, dark paneling, possibly a scrap of floating white veiling above dedicated whiskers. *Spaded* was a word in normal use among his friends, usually employed in connection with dogs, but it had not occurred to him that the two words, such as they were, had anything in common.

"You can stay down after shopping and go to the six o'clock if you take a nap after luncheon." He gave a long howl of disagreement and outrage, but she insisted. When she said, "If you get to a nap early you may get up early," he remained unimpressed, but when she said, "But if you get to your nap late, you'll have to stay there late," he broke into a flood of protests. "Well, anyway, your teeth are going to be cleaned at two-thirty so go give Stockinette her lunch and then come right upstairs; you can lie on Daddy's bed for a while; it won't kill you."

They went out through the pantry, the cat wreathing around his ankles and both disappeared under the kitchen table, nothing showing except Will's sneaker soles, worn, gray-white with much running, side by side exposed to view.

"Stockinette's one fault," he could be heard to murmur.

"What is?" inquired Agnes from the sink.

"Chews with her mouth open."

Ten minutes later, after trying a getaway out the back door, he reluctantly flung himself down on his father's bed, and Hennie submerged all but the upper half of his face with a big blanket. She lay down on her bed and smiled across at him. "Cozy? Now we'll both go to sleep. Shut your eyes." She stretched, relaxed, settled her head into the pillow and closed her eyes, the smile with which she had tried to persuade her child that naps were a delight still about her lips. "Hush," she said, low. "We mustn't talk. Sleep—sleep."

"How long do I have to stay?" he demanded in a fierce whisper.

"Hush—sleep. Half an hour."

Five minutes dragged by, and she knew they were both wide-awake, more awake than before lying down. She cautiously peeked and there was one great glittering bright eye watching over the blue blanket. She quickly closed her lashes and began to breathe deeply, thinking to mesmerize both of them into slumber, but presently from beneath folds of wool came quick urgent whisperings—"One-seven-eleven-nine; get that, team? One-seven-eleven-nine."

"Will!"

"O.K., O.K."

Then real silence descended. Tranquillity flowed down her extended arms and legs. Outdoors no traffic moved on the quiet street; indoors Agnes had left the kitchen and gone to her own afternoon nap. Hennie's mind slowed, slowed, slowed—

" 'While God is marching on!' " yelled Will, sat bolt up, singing, flinging away the blanket, bounding in the bed. "Time's up! Half an hour! Yippee!" His sneakers hit the floor. He wrenched open the door by its flowered handle. He was gone, but the sound of his charging feet on the stairs came echoing back like the sound of thunder to the woman on the bed.

"It's so warm for September," Hennie said to Stockinette. They were out in the back yard, Hennie waiting around for Will to get back from the neighborhood dentist so she could take him downtown for winter shoes, Stockinette seemingly without plans of any kind. Hennie sat in a garden chair, her gloves and handbag on the grass, and in the bag, yet unread, a letter from Geneviève Mésurier, with whom she, rather than Will, was in correspondence.

The lawn was a city lawn, large and flat and square, with thin, city grass and no assurance that the earth went very deep beneath it. In a shed in one corner Laurence kept a chest of tools that had descended to him, inappropriately enough and by devious degrees, from the family home in Center Sandwich. Hennie had never seen him with a tool in his hand. "You could perfectly well fix this with some of those lovely adzes and things you have out in the shed," she sometimes said to him, but he always replied at once what a satisfaction it was to him to know she could, with a slight expenditure of blandishment, get Mr. Tuthill to do it, and be happier in the end.

Unambitious flower beds producing daffodils in the spring and now about to come out in clumps of copper and white chrysanthemums bordered this yard, and near the house on a space of brick flooring stood long chairs and a wooden table. A narrow brick path ran sedately past the budding chrysanthemums, some meaningless groups of small, city evergreens, and a dogwood tree. It was a pretty place. Hennie sometimes thought she must fix it up and give a series of garden parties there or install a longer table and make a practice of having family meals out there in warm weather, as European peasants do. "And a trellis of vines," she said to Stockinette, looking around to see where, "right here. We'll have a carafe of red wine and long crusty loaves someone would cut with great peasant swipes of a knife, and then I can see the knife at rest, after, upright, in somebody's fist. Whose?" It seemed unlikely to be Laurence, who liked melba toast, delicately browned, and kept hot in a covered dish of Georgian silver. "What do you think about it, puss cat?" Will hated to have his darling called *puss*. "Call her by her Christian name," he insisted. That implacably urban cat sat down on the brick path with her back to Hennie, her calm and simple shape that of a fat bottle. "Where is your friend William Stacpole?" Hennie inquired of the unmoving fur back. "He's late. Let's hope it doesn't mean cavities. If he doesn't come pretty soon there won't be time to get shoes for him and a dress for Geneviève as well."

Following the brisk initial correspondence with the *Amis de la France*, off had gone—by air because Hennie had so wanted him to get it—a parcel to André Leclerc of Neuilly, and right back had come a letter on the thinnest of white paper, in the palest of blue slanting writing, saying, "*J'adore les tootsierolls.*" At the same time she had dispatched André's package she had sent an identical one to Paul Mésurier having, ever since the moment of repudiating him as a foster son, so unfairly, she feared—for who can control his own ancestry—been uncomfortable about him in her conscience or her heart or some such troublesome region. "*Mon fils et moi nous sommes tres contents que vous êtes content avec les bonbons,*" she had written back to André, and forced Will to add his signature to hers. "Let's hope the other guy forgets to answer," Will had said. "All this French!" To the first letter to Paul, Hennie had added that benevolent postscript to his sister, informing her in a tortuous subjunctive that if she would send her size, she would send her a warm winter dress, and back by air had come a letter from Geneviève in pale blue ink and a fluent English. "Mammy tells to me I may write you a letter. The reason I write so well the English I have studied it since three years. I have sixteen. I have a gray and white cat since three years." There followed a few lines of conventional, letter-concluding French politenesses rendered into English and, in a shy little gush, "I am forty-three inches, since you ask."

"Forty-three inches!" the man beside Hennie at a dinner party had repeated. "The girl a dwarf!"

"Oh, surely not. I mean, she doesn't say so."

"Must be. Unless she means around her waist, in which case she's a monster." He had tossed a cashew nut up and neatly into his mouth. "Send her a hat," he suggested.

Hennie had immediately replied to Geneviève, complimenting her warmly on her command over an alien tongue, saying no doubt French and American ways of measuring for clothes were quite different, and could she have a few further and more complete figures? It was Geneviève's reply to this now waiting unopened in Hennie's handbag.

She sat daydreaming how she would fetch over this little French girl in a year or so, to live in their house. Some days she daydreamed that Geneviève probably looked like Claudette Colbert and they would present her at the Winter Assembly in a cloud of tulle and admiring bachelor glances, and at other times, more practical she knew, she saw the child sitting happily in the sewing room making exquisite underwear, year after year. "But maybe that's selfish," she chided herself. "Anyway, I can get all the exquisite underwear I need from Bendel.

No; we'll bring her over here and educate her, and then she will be a living international bond." The *Amis de la France* certainly would be surprised and grateful, and all her friends would say, "Isn't Hennie Stacpole wonderful, the way she always does *more* than she's expected to?"

Stockinette's ears moved forward, her round face came into full view, and she smiled around at the back door.

"Here you are at last. Stockinette and I thought you'd forgotten us. Let's see them. Oh, nice and clean and shiny. You *can't* hug her now, darling. No, no, you can't play marbles with her now. Anyway, I don't believe a cat would— Come on, all the shops will be closing."

"She's mad for marbles," Will said. "She makes ab-so-lute-ly accurate strokes every time."

"She does? That must be because you've taught her so well, because actually I'd think she couldn't play games of skill, being about twice too fat."

"Yes, she does!" he yelled. "And she gives twice as much love!" He caught up his darling to his skinny chest and glared at his mother. Then with a calm grace he put her back on the grass. "Coming in a trice," he amiably said. "What is a trice?"

"Wouldn't it be exactly three times as long as a minute?"

"But it sounds much shorter. I think it's three times as short as a minute." He gave her an urbane smile, tucked the striped cotton of his jersey in at the belt of his blue jeans and accompanied her along the path at the side of the house.

In the dress department of the department store Hennie sailed up to a clerk who was sailing up to her. "We are interested in buying a dress for a little French girl," she said.

"We?" Will reproved her.

"We are interested in the children of a little family in France," Hennie went on calmly, covering Will's mutter that he wasn't any such thing, "a sort of foster brother and sister for my son. The boys correspond."

"Oh, that's cute." The clerk loomed, menacing, over Will. "So you can talk in French, sonny, that's just wonderful. So let's hear you say something. Miss Cleary," she called over her shoulder, "c'm'ere, hear this little boy, he talks French!"

Will stamped his foot and shot out of his eyes a dark-brown look of hate to cover all women. "I don't know one single word of it," he said. "Not one single word! *I never heard of French.* I—"

Hennie took him by the shoulder and conducted him to the children's shoe department, leaving him in the hands of an old nameless man in an alpaca jacket who had known the Stacpole children's feet since they could walk, and when she mounted again to the junior miss department she was not surprised the saleswoman was nowhere to be seen. She got hold of another and retained her by dint of a running spate of talk while she slit open Geneviève's thin white envelope with the end of her house key. "You see, I have to buy a dress for a young French girl. Wool, I'd say, wouldn't you, with winter coming? I have her measurements right here so it ought to be quite easy, though she's no one I've ever seen.

Nothing too expensive, but pretty, and warm because of no central heating, or so I suppose. Now let's see—" The first page of the letter, which she murmured aloud in order to keep the captive saleswoman from escaping, dealt politely with return references to the facts of the Connecticut Stacpole family as set down in the recent letter to the St. Martin Mésuriers. " 'I think your fat cat you take less time.' Well, whatever that means. I'll have to read it more carefully some other time. She hasn't studied English very long yet. 'You would like to send a winter dress.' Here we are. 'Thanks you very well. I like a yellow or blue color.' Yellow or blue, you see; blue's more practical, don't you think, though of course their dry cleaning is the best in the world. Now here we are." She flipped over the page and read to the end of Geneviève's letter. "She says, 'I think I understand the manner to take the measure. Buste—16 inches, hips—39 inches, weight—97 inches, thanks you. Mammy sends you her thanks, your little friend, Geneviève.' "

Hennie frowned and read the page again; she held it far off and squinted, thinking that maybe Olivia had been right when she said that when Hennie did admit it was time to get reading glasses it would strike her all of a sudden any day now and be the greatest relief. Then she even looked over at the face of the saleswoman for help, but on that carefully made-up sagging oval she saw only a mild incredulity that faded while she watched into chilly disinterest. If the woman had said aloud, "No sale," Hennie wouldn't have blamed her for a minute.

✦

In the late afternoon Clare and Jo and the eleventh edition of the *Encyclopaedia Britannica* were on the floor in the library. The big slow sheets, the heavy flopping Bible paper so densely printed, poured back and forth over each other, this way and that. "Iran, Irak, here it is," she said. They bent above Irak, their breathing audible. "Are you reading, or not?" she presently asked in a small voice.

"I was looking at the back of your neck."

"Ah-h!" She quickly turned around and kissed him. "—no, no, that's all. Now look, here we are, here we see that Irak is a province of Persia. Was that what you thought or what I did? I haven't told Mummy our changed plans yet, but I'm going to any minute."

They studiously leaned nearer the page, and the print swam. Clare's vision cleared first. "Very interesting," she announced. "Don't you think it is? 'Its greatest income derived from the carpets made in many of its villages.' The first thing we must ask for for a wedding present is the *Encyclopaedia* because we'll never be able to afford it for ourselves."

"This is the best edition, much better than the later ones I've been told, though a bit behind the times on Iran and Irak, I guess. As a matter of fact, I've thought she seemed quite normal and ordinary lately— Well, I've heard people who ought to know say this is the best edition."

"I know." They considered this for a while, letting slide the subjects of carpet manufacture and Mrs. Stacpole's dementia. "Maybe Mummy and Daddy don't know that and don't care much. I'm pretty sure they don't care at all because I *never* see them reading it. We might perhaps— Don't you suppose they would like to have a more recent edition and let us have this one? As a matter of fact that would be quite a practical way to arrange it, wouldn't it, because then we could have that money for something else."

"What money?" he asked, doubtful.

"Why, the money they'd have given us to get an encyclopaedia with! Oh, here comes Mummy."

Hennie came in, carrying a sheet of letter paper. "I have a job," she told them. "Hello, Jo. How are you? The school needs a million dollars more or less for a new washroom and this morning I was given an enormous quota to collect." She sounded very pleased. "It may take me months. Move aside just a bit, dears, so I can get to my desk." She smoothed the paper out on the blue blotter and briskly dialing, asked to speak to Mrs. Comfit. "Oh, I see," she said into the receiver. "Doesn't come to the telephone," she reported to the two on the floor. She made a cryptic wiggle with a pencil beside Mrs. Comfit's name. "That means I must go and call on her, which should make her give a bit more because of the inconvenience, but I hope not *too* much as that would upset my calculations, and throw me out of work too soon. I'll put on a coat and go around before dinner. Old ladies are always downstairs then, if ever."

She dialed again, and then again, speaking into the instrument with great charm and distinctness though at the dialing of each new number she had to rear back a bit and squint. "I am never going to get glasses," she informed them over her shoulder, "no matter what. I am immortal, or so I have always supposed. Mrs. Talbot, please." But Mrs. Talbot was in New York for the day and not back yet, and Mrs. Henderson's line was busy.

Clare should have been glad to have an occupied mother, but it threw her own cherished plan out. Something to channel her energies, her mother now said as she rang Mrs. Walker's house, and Clare's face fell. The nagging irritability her mother's gaiety had been causing her might now disappear and no longer would she find it necessary to keep on interpreting Hennie to her lover. Not that Jo had asked for any sort of elucidation of his future mother-in-law's character; he had seemed on the whole willing to accept her as she was, and this Clare deplored. It seemed unenterprising of him. Now she kneeled up on the hem of her skirt to take a photograph Hennie had come on while simultaneously poking in a cubbyhole and listening to the busy signal at Mrs. Lenox's. Clare fondly scrutinized the picture; it was herself at two with floss hair and a mouth like a bud.

"Isn't she sweet?" Hennie asked him, and Clare handed it to him. He looked, and then burst out thankfully, "Oh, how she's changed!" Clare quickly took it back.

Mrs. Lenox, Mrs. Garretson, and Mrs. Andrews were all out.

"Where do they all go!" Hennie marveled, and Clare predicted Will would be in college before the new washroom was built. Hennie's pencil crept down the list. She murmured, "The committee wants me to ask Mr. Latham for a contribution. I guess I'll ask him up to dinner tonight."

"I'm going to be out; we are," Clare said. "We're going to a friend of Jo's for cocktails and have a hamburger after, somewhere."

"Tell Agnes," Hennie said out of the corner of her mouth at the receiver.

"I have. And she said Will's stayed down for a movie."

"Mmn-hmn."

"And Daddy's having dinner at the club with those New York bankers."

"Now *that* I had completely forgotten," Hennie lied pleasantly. "He will be disappointed." Which he? Clare asked herself. "Is Mr. Latham there?" Hennie asked the telephone. "I'll feed him crepes suzette," she said in her lower, natural voice to the two on the floor, "and break down his resistance. I might get a hundred dollars, or do you think that's too much to expect from a bachelor?"

But Clare would not reply. She wouldn't even look up. Her troubled glances followed along the patterns of the rug and over the spread white pages of the big book she no longer took any interest in, and the photograph of the little girl. She wished she were that child again and safe and had not yet heard of faraway countries that changed their names; nothing had changed while she was two, nor for a long time after. Jo hadn't admired the photograph, so it must be he loved her for other, different reasons than the ones her family loved her for—if they did. She would have liked to cover her ears at the changed tones of her mother's voice and she could see from her place on the floor, how when a voice came quacking through the telephone her mother's suspended slippered foot suddenly moved, the ankle arching; that arching ankle made her ill in the stomach. Then Hennie laid the instrument back in its cradle. "There; that's all the work I'm going to do for now. Clare, you're looking so glum, darling. What is it; a headache, a sore throat?"

"I have, a little. A tickle."

Jo gave an experimental swallow and said, loyally, that he thought he had one too, and Hennie said if he actually hadn't at the moment, he probably soon would have. "Or that's the way it was in my engaged days." The two on the floor looked away at nothing, not liking this touching, this stroking, of their private wonder. "Maybe Clare needs to have her tonsils out," the woman maundered on. "Once I had a beau who swore he'd never, never marry until he found a girl who'd had all her operations and a mink coat. He had hair that stood perfectly straight up like a raccoon, and I've often wondered if he ever did. Clare's always had excellent tonsils, but you never know, do you," she said, folding up her list of names and tucking it away in a hole. "No; you never know. Maybe you'd better have a double tonsillectomy and an adjoining nurse."

Jo cleared the throat, which he later told Clare had begun to ache in earnest. "Mine were taken out when I was four," he said.

Hennie congratulated him. "And *you*'ll hardly need a mink coat, will you?" she said, but Clare jumped to her feet and pulled at him with both hands.

"Oh, please get up," she begged, desperate-sounding though she tried not. "Let's go to that cocktail party, now, even if it would be too early!"

They left quickly and were hardly through the front door before Jo said, "Now I see. I don't see how you put up with it. Does she go on like that *all the time?* I absolutely must get you out of this life you lead here; why, she isn't even serious about anything, is she?" His indignant face turned to her. "Spring vacation!" he promised, like a knight making a definite date to rescue his beloved from dragons or whirlpools, and only sorry he had to put it off another minute.

"Oh, thank you! Oh, I'm so glad! I haven't told you before because it was too gruesome but she wants us to be married with some sort of wild, spring, out-of-doors ceremony with everybody in costume, flittering around, and dancing on the grass, and flutes and so on."

"Oh, God, she doesn't!"

"She does, she does! Oh, she never, never used to be like this. I simply can't control her. Can't you see yourself, kneeling, in velvet pants probably?" The look of torture on his face was enough to satisfy anybody. Hennie, who had never thought again of her festive suggestions to Clare, would have been flabbergasted at such an expression on the face of her probable son-in-law. "If we let her keep on with her scheme we'll have to have a maid right away," she predicted at random, "if only to take care of all the velvet clothes she'll buy me. She's mad for velvet lately, for some reason."

Jo's stern young eyes rested on the smooth top of the

head of his beloved. "We've got to discuss this further. I had no idea. I must think about it by myself for a while, first. I'll come late tomorrow evening after they're all in bed. You let me in."

Sighing with perfect happiness, and hope, Clare said she would.

Sleek as a cat, replete with crepes suzette, Edward Latham lolled on the sofa beside the spread-out fan shape of the new apricot velvet skirt. His empty hand lay near a fold of it and presently Hennie, as though unconsciously, ran her hands down along under the spread edges, lifted them just enough to settle them a trifle nearer herself—a less widespread fan now—folded her hands in the soft glowing copper lap and turned a sweet smile upon him.

"I got you here tonight for a purpose," said she.

"Ah."

Did he sound a breath complacent? Maybe it was only the crepes; he had had so many she had lost count, and been forced to make herself avoid catching Agnes's eye, being afraid one of them might have lifted an eyebrow at the other, and it might have been herself, and caught out in it. "Yes, I did. More coffee? Do, because I want you to be very wide-awake and alert and civic-minded." A black-brown jet arched from the silver spout. "And yet, at the same time, *comfortable*. She indulged in a quick reconnoitering glint at him to see if he looked comfortable. As for her, she was terribly comfortable, billowed up, borne up on an orange velvet cloud. "The thing is, the boys' washroom at the wonderful day school everyone's children go to here is in the most pitiful condition, which incidentally is fine for me because it provides me with a purpose in life. You can't imagine," she said, with an assumption of great frankness, and handed him his cup, "how great wedges of plaster have fallen out all over the place and the plumbing so desperately sluggish I believe it's thought not to be even sanitary any more. We're all quite distraught about it." She tried looking both distraught yet attractive; fifty dollars, she had decided; he could perfectly well, even for a cause he wouldn't possibly have the least interest in. "The washbowls," she told him, "are positively starting away from the wall."

How sleek and well-brushed he was. The angle of his jaw looked burnished like a statue; maybe his man polished him; his blue eyes were clear. Hennie said to herself she could become very, very fond of him; there was the faintest scent of leather from him. How fortunate she was to have found—and so handy, right in the bank!—someone who would release her from her state of captivity.

"More coffee?" she asked, affectionately.

"Your cat there is playing with the whatever-they-are. Should she?"

"The maiden hair ferns?" She looked around over her shoulder. "But she never does. That's most unlike her." Stockinette was sitting, aloof and quite motionless on a table, staring with disapproval at the woman on the sofa.

"She was though," he said. "Batting at them with her paw like Billy-o."

Hennie couldn't believe it. The frail airy green flakes hung motionless; Stockinette looked away and yawned. "Well, to go on," she said, turning back to him, "the washroom *floor* is so old and saturated with generations of boys throwing water at each other there's this real danger it may give way and let them down into the cellar. Think of it, a whole generation of promising young men, just simply gone down through the floor."

He laughed, finished his coffee, and put aside the cup, and then sat, smiling at her, admiring her. She flowered and expanded in the warmth. Strange thing, that all her life long so far she had not realized her own true nature. She had merely gone along acting like everyone else whereas beneath it all, far inside, she had been an enchantress. Even during this past week of revelation she had made the most foolish mistakes about herself. How for instance could she ever have supposed that making tiles, no matter how beautiful, would have satisfied her? The results would have been only a tottering small heap of them, each with a domesticated-looking dragon on it, leaning in the back hall, and eventually Gino would have taken them to brace the tool shed steps with. Anybody could take a bit of stick and outline a dragon on a piece of soft clay, and almost anybody could tell fantastic lies to cheer up people, but it took skill to pry money away from its owners; it took skill and charm. So far she had had only a qualified success, but she believed she could see fifty dollars in Edward's large blue eyes and she flirted out the warm velvet folds again; maybe he would go up to seventy-five. This encounter was better in all ways than her late afternoon call on old Mrs. Comfit, who wasn't half as senile as people said, having parted with a tired grubby five-dollar bill with the greatest reluctance; she had sent a maid upstairs for her handbag and had appeared to entertain a conviction that Hennie wanted the money for herself.

Edward Latham ran his hand along an apricot fold. "Terribly pretty," he said, leaving his hand there.

"Edward," she warned, "I'm thinking exclusively about faucets and linoleum, and automatic soap."

"I know," he peaceably replied. "You wring my heart about it all. I never suspected lawyers' and bankers' sons were so underprivileged. I'd love to contribute a thousand dollars to alleviate their distress."

Then she did scream. It was a scream of purest surprise. It sounded almost like a protest. "*Oh!* But do you think you ought to?"

She said the same thing later, but was less surprised, when he kissed her good night just as the door was closing. He had started out, and returned for the purpose.

"Shall I see you soon again?" he asked.

"Oh, yes, Edward; yes."

After the door had clicked shut on him she ran upstairs with the great skirt swaying side to side and by then she was laughing. She zipped out of her clothes and tossed them into a colored heap. "Oh, my job, my poor dear job!" she said, waving her arms into the top of a pale blue nightgown. "So now what has become of my job and my quota!" She was stricken with love at her own beauty in the big mirror, all soul alone, barefooted, hair on end. She gazed admiringly, and then sprang into bed, and when Laurence came home not long after, she was lying motionless, making the kind of breathing sounds a good wife does when she is asleep—long, slow, regular, passionless, with now and then, intermittently, for realism, the little catching noise normal in a woman of forty-three who might be dreaming: Are the children in their beds warm and is tomorrow perhaps the cook's day off?

If Laurence noticed the bright heap of clothes he said nothing, and presently he was flat and breathing steadily. She reached out a silent hand and touched the switch and soon he was so deeply sleeping his breath was inaudible. She reared up on an elbow and tipped an ear toward him. Yes, he was breathing; he was alive and all right. As for her, she flung herself back on the pillow and lay awake for what she thought of as hours and hours, smiling into the dark tent of the night.

CHAPTER NINE

Thursday morning at breakfast Laurence said the days were drawing in; there was chill in the air; winter was just around the corner. Hennie told Will if this were so he'd better wear a flannel shirt to school instead of his cotton jersey, but Will assured her he was boiling. He said the Greens had to play the Reds in basketball that afternoon and how would he look jumping around in a shirt?

Hennie poured out three cups of coffee and slid lumps of sugar into two of them. "Nobody minds me any more," she sighed. "I wish I had somebody still so small I could dominere over them. In fact, the fact is there aren't nearly enough people in this house anyway. So much of the day it's practically empty, if you don't count our silent pair out back. I'd love to live in a huge great house full of people the whole time."

Over their shirred eggs her children regarded her tolerantly. Clear as through glass they all had the same picture of her she had of herself, as the chatelaine of a great estate, surrounded by revolving humans, all with jobs of their own for her to direct—hewing wood, drawing water, embroidering firescreens, and roasting oxen—but all dependent on her, coming up every so often, every half-hour, to reach out a finger to touch her, for renewed strength.

"And guests," Hennie said. "Many, many guests, all coming and going."

"How would Agnes like that?" Clare was laughing at her mother, but she admired as much as Hennie did the picture of the tall woman walking about her mansion. "With a big bunch of silver keys clanking at your waist, I suppose." Hennie smiled at her over her lifted cup and said yes, exactly.

"We could begin in a small way," she went on, just as they might have supposed the subject was as good as finished. "I mean with a small guest. I might ask your cousin Susan from Boston down for the week end." She turned to Will, freezing him with the treachery of her smile. "Just your age."

"But she's a girl!"

"That's very true, she is, but she's not a leper. There are girls in your class at school."

"But I *know* them! I've always known and hated *them!*" He put down his fork. "I'm going to be away when Susan comes."

"Where would you be?" she gently scoffed.

After breakfast Will mounted to his room.

It was quite clear to him that home had become, though only recently, quite unbearable. He stood in the center of his room, frowning, glancing about from under dark brows. The wonder was his father didn't stand up to her. "What she needs is a good sound spanking. That's what would do her the most good." He added a few words to which he was not entirely a stranger—"I don't enjoy doing this but you've been asking for it." But then he knew very well no one was going to discipline her. It should be his father's duty and pleasure to spank her hard, but Will knew he never would, wouldn't dare to. "Sissy!" he hissed, between his newly cleaned teeth.

He heaved a sigh as the truth came to him—he would have to go away, alone, and far, and—might as well—why not?—everything at home being so awful—forever. He realized he had always meant to run away. "I just never got around to it, but now's the time, boy." Nobody could be expected to stay in the same house with a woman who did and said the dangerous things she did and said, getting her own children all mixed up with a lot of French ones and now Susan! "Why'n't she leave me alone?"

He stalked over to his desk where he had a tremendous amount of money hidden, dollar bills laid between the pages of an old coloring book. He never spent his allowance, or hardly ever, preferring to have the weekly quarters changed into new bills. "But got to think of Christmas coming," he said, provident if not logical, and laid back a few bills between crayoned pictures of hens and apple blossoms and sailboats and turkeys. He packed most of the money into his blue jean pockets, slipped down the back stairs, and out the kitchen door.

He was without plans. The day was rather cool as his father had said, and he moved along briskly, looking for all the world like a boy going to school.

He arrived downtown sooner than expected, and slowing his steps began looking at the town of his birth as though he had never seen it before, as though he were a tourist and this town Rome. "H'hmn," he said, aloud, "very interesting." He felt himself to be the best possible kind of tourist, polite and observant. He went up to a hydrant. "H'hmn," he said, bunting it with his sneakered toe. "Pretty good hydrants they have here." He strolled on, easy and free. How sensible he had been not to pack a suitcase. He wasn't carrying anything, didn't need to. "Because I'm so rich." The massed dollar bills crackled against his narrow hips.

Noon found him in a part of town he had never seen. The street signs said Salisbury Square, and he pronounced it to himself as spelled. It was a very large square and must once have been the home of wealth and fashion. Vast shabby Classic Revival houses with beautiful ruined porticoes and façades, smoke and time and rain-stained and with their paint peeling, or, worse, painted vulgar orange-yellow and a terrible cabbage green, enclosed a wide stretch of grass and trees. Beneath the porticoes of every house massive wooden columns leaned a little; they looked as though they might slowly, slowly fall over if a boy put both hands against them. Dirty papers were drifting in the gutters. In the square, lengths of railing were still standing, but by no means all around the grass plot. Some houses had the lace of ironwork across their wide verandas, and Will thought they looked like houses where many parties had once been given but now it was obvious that the people living in them had other matters on their minds. It was now a swarthy race who inhabited Salisbury Square. Old women in black bought grapes and bananas off barrows at the curb. Old men with sticks, like old propped apple trees, leaned against the walls of small shops that had been built out at the front of some of the big houses. Unlighted neon signs swung from these shops, saying Pizzeria or Pasticceria. The sun warming his back, Will idled along, enjoying freedom and strangeness, giving no thought to home.

A rusty young cat sped out of an alleyway and halted suddenly at an old bit of food on the pavement. Will was concerned to see she had a tight string around her neck, but when he squatted down to untie it a second-floor window rattled up and a billowing, black-dressed woman leaned out over him and screeched, "*Va via di quà!*" From his crouch he turned and looked up at her. Terribly fat, she was, with a tiny, bright-red mouth.

"It's hurting her neck," he explained, and at that moment a boy his own age burst from the sagging front door and hurtled down the flight of steps, a sudden emissary from the woman in the window. Dressed identically in jersey and blue jeans the two boys confronted each other over the animal who was delicately eating the scrap of food. "*Va via di quà!*" the boy cried, and Will, still crouched, looking up at him, wished for the first time he had paid attention to his French lessons.

"This string's too tight. I should think you could see that." He stood up.

"Cris'sakes." The other boy spat, and aimed a large kick at the cat, but Will took it on his hip. The edge of a crisp new dollar bill sprang from a pocket at the blow and the pasty-faced boy's black eyes popped. Will negligently stuffed it back. "If I had my scout knife," he began but the tremendous woman, whose eyes were sharp as jet, billowed even farther out the window and called to her child, "Bring'm in, we got something good to eat, tell'm. Bring the cat," she added with cunning.

The room this woman lived in had such a smell as Will could never even have imagined, a smell so strong, comprised of so many drifting, interlacing strata, that he didn't know if he liked it or not, or if he could stand it.

"Sure, sure," the woman said out of the tiny scalloped mouth painted on her wide pale lips, "sure, sure, string's too tight. I fix." She got a knife from a drawer and sawed the string while the cat protested. "Cat she lika string lika this maybe." Will said he didn't think so, and was relieved when it parted. The horrible wee mouth smiled at him but her coal eyes were never changing. "Nice kind boy. You got something nice in your pockets?" she inquired, offhand.

"Oh, no. Not specially." Will stuffed his noisy wealth deeper, but when his hands came out so did a stray bill. He retrieved it from the filthy floor. "Here, you might as well have this for helping the cat," he said. It would have seemed churlish to put it back in his pocket in the face of all her interest. He laid the bill on the table and said he'd be going along now, but the other boy was hanging around just inside the doorway, eyeing Will with his unfathomable eyes. "So I think I'd better be on my way," Will said, and looked at the boy to see if he were going to move aside. The boy stepped one step backward and put both hands out to the door jambs, making of himself a wiry barrier. Will thought them a disagreeable pair, and when she opened her false little lips, like a bowknot of wet pinkish-red satin and asked him where his father worked his patience was at an end.

"He's just an old banker," he said—knew at once it was the wrong thing to have said—turned and sprang at the boy and pushed him aside and thundered down the stairs. He heard the woman yelling, a shocking big yell to come from that tiny hole, and then, a nightmare, the sound of the boy's pursuing feet. In spite of his pasty face and the circles around his eyes this boy was fast. Will had to exert himself to the full. He ran like a demon but the nightmare feeling was intensified by the tightness of his pants, so rigid were they with currency. "I'm not going to stay and settle down in this part of town," he decided as he flew.

He darted across a street at the top of the square, under a red light, felt the traffic change behind him, and took a split second to look over his striped shoulder. The other boy had been halted by the traffic; past cars and trucks Will saw him make a gesture he did not yet know the meaning of and perhaps never would. Breathing hard, his heart thumping altogether too hard under the jersey and in the soft triangle at the base of his throat, and massed dollar bills expanding and tightening in his hip pockets, Will went on.

"Some other part of town," he panted. "Boy, was I kidnaped there! But I got away." To the end of his days he would believe his life had been menaced in Salisbury Square. "Anyway I guess I'd rather live in the country somewhere," he now decided. "A little cottage would suit me, me and Stockinette—" and at the thought of Stockinette love struck him a blow so fierce and strong he staggered, and stopped.

Where was she, his darling? Miles and miles away across the sprawling city. Folded and patient, would she be waiting for someone at dusk to give her her supper? What if it were Agnes's day out? Oh, God, it *was* Thursday! With an accuracy unshared by the other Stacpoles, Will and Stockinette always knew Agnes's days out. That fiend, his mother, more often forgot Thursdays than not and the way she was these days she would probably forget to feed her own husband, much less remember to set down the saucer of Cat-Smack and milk. A worse picture, Susan with Stockinette in her beastly lap, rose to torment him. "Well then, damn it to hell, only for that I *can't* run away!" He stamped a sneaker. "I will too run away! I've made up my mind and I mean my mind!" He went on a few more yards of pavement, but in the end, with the fall afternoon cooling about him, leaves falling, breezes running at him out of alleys, he made his way back to the part of town he knew. It proved to be a long walk, and not without detours taken in error.

As he went he brooded about his day. The pallid boy grew and grew and the woman lolled in his recollection like a horrible soft doll. "Brother, was I kidnaped!" he said several times. Not that his mother would have cared; not she. She would have been perfectly happy all day gushing over the intolerable Susan. By now Susan would have been given his room and all his things. She would mince about the house all day, dressed in frills. She hadn't been invited merely for a visit; she had come to live. He saw her flouncing along the halls. "I'll pinch her bottom," he whispered. "Every day harder and harder, every day till she's absolutely black, right through her pants." None of the girls in his class at school had ever been guilty of a single ruffle, but he knew for a fact the kind of clothes Susan wore.

He entered his home at dusk by the back door and encountered his mother in the front hall. "Now where have you been? Aren't you late?" she genially inquired. He looked up at her out of the tops of his eyes, marveling how she did not know his heart to be crammed with terrible thoughts and intentions and his blue jeans with all his allowance since April.

"Nowhere. Has she come?"

"Has who come?"

His mouth was down-curved like the mouth of a frog. "Susan," he spit out of this unbecoming orifice.

"Oh. Oh, yes. Well, I did call her mother after breakfast." Maddening, casual, she straightened the mirror over the hall table, peered at herself, and lifted the lock of hair above an ear. "But she couldn't because she's going to a dancing-school party, and I didn't really expect she would."

Now he hated the faraway Susan worse than the one he had supposed he would find waiting. "I hope there isn't a single guy dances with her once," he said with swift malice, poised on his sneakers ready to fly. "I hope she has to go around all by herself and *dancing with mid-air!*"

"Goodness, you're a vindictive child, aren't you?"

"*Yes!*" he cried, never having heard the word, but he clutched it to him with passion and sprang up the stairs.

For a time in that house the two people who least deplored Hennie's week-old euphoria were Hennie herself, who loved it, fostered and fed it, and Gino, who hadn't noticed it until the evening, three days before, when Agnes had startled herself and him both by saying aloud as he passed through the kitchen to the cellar to hang up a trowel, "The goings-on in this house!"

"Hunk?" had been shaken out of Gino, and it had been this encounter Laurence witnessed and reported to its cause and source, his feckless wife. Gino and Agnes had, of course, at once, shocked at their lapse, returned to Stygian silence, only to betray themselves again that morning when, after her telephone chat with Laurence's sister in Boston, Hennie asked Gino to deliver a note for her, downtown.

Gino had delivered notes before this, but never to a

bank, never to an officer in a bank. While she had dashed off two or three lines and signed it he had stood by the desk, appalled at the thought of making his way across all the marble flooring and past secretaries and stenographers, through wickets and little swinging gates. He was so disturbed that when he went through the kitchen toward the back door he paused.

"Now what," Agnes said, and he tipped the note so she could read the address. An angry sad look flowed down over Agnes's face. "Lost her mind," she said, and Gino silently agreed.

So her afternoon off found Agnes bolt upright in one of Mrs. Platcek's stiff chairs.

"Now let's see," said Mrs. Platcek, pleased, opening the large book on the desk. "Agnes MacGilvray. Cook-general." She looked over at Agnes. "I don't seem to remember ever seeing you in here before."

Agnes bowed, as at a compliment. "I'm not one to chop and change," she said, and when Mrs. Platcek asked her how long she had been with Mrs. Stacpole Agnes was able to tell her exactly, down to the week and minute, and it was a very, very long time indeed, so long that Mrs. Platcek gave a gasp of admiration, but then she shook her head, because after all what would become of the employment agency business if that kind of record were at all usual? "I see," she said. "My." With nods and becks she attempted to draw from Agnes her reasons for leaving after all these years, but Agnes sat stiffer than ever.

"A lot to put up with, probably," Mrs. Platcek suggested. "A family like that, they get so used to you they begin to impose on a person. Little ways."

"Not at all. There is not a thing wr-r-r-rong with the household. I simply desir-r-re to make a change."

"Perhaps you want me to see if I can get you a place where they pay a bit more?"

"I am pair-r-rfectly satisfied with what I make, thank you."

Mrs. Platcek, a miffed oracle, returned to the scrutiny of her large book, and meanly she murmured, "It's a real pity you aren't a couple." Agnes had no reply for such a remark. "M'hmn, m'hmn. It isn't a good time now for making changes. No. Let's see." She scanned her hen-tracked pages. "You wouldn't want restaurant work. Now, here we are, maybe something." Her finger gave a skip and settled at an entry. "Mrs. Comfit."

Agnes said she would prefer not to take a job with any of her present employers' friends or acquaintances. Mrs. Platcek peered over at her; such fine feeling was not often expressed in her stuffy waiting room. "That makes it harder. I don't see how we're going to avoid that. Aren't your Stacpoles friends of dozens of the best families in town?"

"Hundreds," said Agnes, complacent. "All of them."

Mrs. Platcek sighed and flapped shut her book. She had no patience with the woman. "You can come in to-morrow about this time," she said, "if you can get off for an hour or two. I might have something for you."

✦

All at once the days had grown colder and darker; in the living room Will turned on the lamp; the dark curtains that descend the end of afternoon in the dark months would from now on sway every day closer to noon, veiling as though slyly a few more minutes, cutting off time.

Stockinette came in and jumped to a front window sill, sank down on the white enameled wood, folded away her paws, softly flung down her tail to outline her hips and thigh, closed her eyes and was asleep. Will in the room behind her embarked on a little somewhat overdue homework, a blue and yellow map of the Nile, the wide river blue, the surrounding countryside as yellow as he could make it. The crayon went fiercely sideways and with every stroke he saw not simply an additional stroke of ocher but fields of standing grain, tall, undulating in a hot wind, and long-legged brown people with stone-bright eyes set sideways in their faces, striding the perimeter of the harvest. Stockinette drowsed awake from time to time; she was too middle-aged and settled to chase the point of his crayon as she had when, in kindergarten, he had been forever coloring pictures of holly berries and Virginia creeper. Her whiskered face turned from time to time out toward the darkening street. The world is full of hopeful little dogs, she observed to herself; damn them.

In came Will's mother, and soon after his father, and Hennie as she ran down the blinds, told him to take his homework upstairs, to run along like a good soul because she and Daddy had something private to talk about. "Private and not in the least interesting," she annoyed him by saying. Laurence wore a nimbus of cold, outside air, pungent as though he had kicked through leaves on the pavement, provocative and sharp. It gave Hennie a glinting preview of winter to come, the long, cold, secret, white and exciting season. This year she anticipated it more than usual, believing that by, say New Year's, her double life would be swinging along on well-oiled tracks.

"More lights on," Laurence suggested, and her vision melted. "Days are getting shorter." He tripped another switch and all over the room the lamps came on, and Hennie let run down yet another blind through which she had never, would never, see Venice. Very, very slowly Will gathered up his colored work, fitted the crayons back into their box as maddeningly slowly as possible. "No, I guess *this* way would be better," he murmured, unnecessarily changed the position of the purple, sighed, let fall a few papers, trailed to the door, returned in a rush and scooped up his fur love from the window seat; her great tail waved down in a festoon and her smiling sarcastic face bobbed at them over his jersey shoulder as he ran out.

"Oh, the skinny elegance of little boys," said Hennie.

Laurence inquired amiably, "Have we a secret, or are you just allergic to the smell of crayola."

"No, no, I love that crayola smell, but I thought you'd like to know as soon as possible that I have a real job on my hands at last—don't interrupt! It's getting Clare married by Christmas. Jo, too, of course."

"*Oh* no." He sat straight up, ignoring the knife stroke in his sacroiliac region. He smote down his hand once, in the gesture Joseph Wood so much admired. "That is too much!"

"But why too much, darling?" She looked as honestly surprised as complete deep awareness of duplicity let her; she widened her eyes to the point where she couldn't focus at all, convinced this gave her expression an utter candor. "I'm sure I can do it if I try."

The pain in his lower back flowered, shrank, flowered again. He spoke very patiently. "You know what I mean as well as I do. Anyway, why?"

"We're having a very bland dinner tonight; you'll love it; creamed chicken and rice. Because she wants to be married *so much*, poor lamb."

"We haven't brought her up to think she can have something simply because she may want it."

Hennie made a face and asked if there were any better reason for going after something. "Anyway, this is different."

"Damn right."

There was a long silence while they severally contemplated within themselves the undeniable fact that Laurence had right on his side, but presently he roused himself from this, to him, agreeable occupation and reminded her in a kind voice that she already had a job; had she forgotten? Was she neglecting her fund-raising?

"Oh, you mean the boys' washroom. Oh, I did have, yes. Yes, but I got my quota, so—"

"You never told me. Congratulations."

"Yes, it is nice, isn't it? And anyway I didn't think that project interested you much."

"It doesn't, deeply. You would be amazed at some of the washrooms I've managed to survive, man and boy. But this business about Clare and Jo, now, I mean it. Hands off. Leave it."

"Darling," she mourned, "I *don't* see why anybody as handsome as you are has to have dyspepsia."

Because Hennie forgot for a few moments that it was Thursday, they went up to change for dinner. She had been pleased and surprised by his forcefulness in forbidding her to help Clare; if only he were always so domineering and fierce her life would be much more delightful; if she could only be a little bit afraid of him, what fun it would be. She sat at her dressing table and held out her hands to him, but just then he looked down to button his braces to the waistband of flannels back from the cleaner. When he did look up, she had picked up her comb.

"I've come to a conclusion about how I'm going to live," she said. "I'm not going to tell you because, well, I merely believe it will work out better if I don't." She watched him in her mirror, smiling on him via the silver-shadowed glass. He moved about, but always within the frame of her big stoppered scent bottles, curling snapshots of the children and Stockinette, sconces of twisted blue and green glass flowers. "You're very handsome, aren't you?" she asked calmly.

"Is that what you weren't going to tell me?"

"Of course not. Back up a minute; there's a thread on you. No. The thing I'm not going to tell you, I'm not going to tell you. But you well know how astray I've been the last week and you've been very good about it and I want to thank you; Clare and Jo have been good about it too, though actually I don't suppose they've noticed. But now I believe I've come to the end of it. I just thought you'd like to know. You don't have to worry about me any more."

She paused, waiting for him to come round into her vision out of the mirror, but instead of revealing normal curiosity. Laurence disappointingly went back a notch in their conversation. "I don't pretend to understand women, and never have, but I knew if I let you alone you'd swing around in time."

Her comb clicked as she put it down. "I don't know what there is to be so proud about, not understanding women!"

"I'm not proud." But she did not believe him. He went away entirely out of her frame of sparkling glass lilies and into his closet for shoes.

She sighed and began again. "What I am trying to say is this: For days now, ever since I threw what's-her-name's alarm clock at the tree I've had this terrible strength in my arms and legs and emotions. It's only since I threw the clock, though that isn't in the least important."

"But my darling, it wasn't like you."

"I know. But it did somehow set me to wondering why I have been so discreet and quiet and underdone all my life. We take too much for granted."

He gave an acquiescent hum and then denied it. "Not really." She watched him, now at his chest of drawers, taking cuff links out of a little leather box, hooking them out absorbedly, fitting them into buttonholes. "I'd say our life was pretty good."

"Of course it is. It's perfect." She watched the reflection dealing with its cuffs. "Shall I help you?"

"I have it, thanks."

"We've always been so completely well-fixed yet all the time we might have been insecure—so—" she faltered, meeting his sardonic eye in the glass. "Well, isn't there just too much of everything, things, people, doings? For people like us, there is."

He opened a little drawer, peered intently within as though he expected treasure, and closed it.

"I think maybe I should have had lovers?"

"Ah-h-h, for God's sake." He turned away and picked up a necktie.

"I'm that hungry age," she informed his back. "Forty-three and upward is terribly hungry." She could scarcely bear his tolerance. She didn't believe it was tolerance; it was complacency. "Second wind!"

There was no answer to this. She couldn't see him clearly enough in her mirror so she swung around on the dressing table bench and observed him widely and insistently. "Don't tell me bankers are different from the rest of the human race of men," she said, and he laughed a little, shook his head a little, peered into the small top drawer again, shook his head, shut it. A jet of suspiciousness began bubbling up from the sand bottom of a clear pool, that clear pool of her heart. What had he been before she had known him? He hadn't had long to be anything. What was his young past before they married? It couldn't have been very flamboyant; there hadn't been time, and perhaps not opportunity either. Westminster and Yale and a job and marriage had followed each other in ordered train, but maybe there had been moments, dreams, that he still privately dredged up and gloated over. Maybe in bed at night when she supposed him to be so safe asleep under heat-speed number 4 he was really lying treacherously silent, dreaming awake, regretting the passing of what she had never known. She sat with her hands in her lap, scrutinizing, speculative. Even the back of his head was handsome. Had she been deluded all these years?

"What have we got but intuition to go by?" she inquired, plaintive.

"Who's we?"

"Women. Women go skating along with only the very thin silk thread of intuition for a guard rail between themselves and *pits* of trouble! What do we know about anything?"

"No different from men."

"Oh, it *must* be." Then, "You have a very handsome back-of-the-head," she reluctantly told him.

"So my mother always said," he replied, and now she could see he was laughing at her and watching her in his own austere mirror that had only a calendar stuck in its rim. He brushed his hair quickly, thrust a handkerchief into his jacket pocket, tweaked down his chamois-colored vest, and charged out the door, calling, "Last one to touch the cocktail shaker's an old maid!"

The Stacpoles sat around the kitchen table. As a family, they enjoyed Thursday night, especially if Agnes, as she had tonight, had left everything ready. "What a treasure she is," Hennie said.

"What is real estate?" Will inquired as he slid into his chair. "I keep hearing about it all the time but I don't know what it is at all. Hey, let me tell you about basketball this morning, how I made four baskets. We have to play awful fast because they don't give us half long enough recess, so we absolutely have to whiz around and I was playing forward this morning and way up at the end of the court and I ran and I ran—" With a craftiness he had not believed himself capable of he minutely described day before yesterday's game. It did not occur to him that he need not say anything at all about basketball, only what a fine way this was to conceal the fact he had not been at school that day.

His parents nodded and ate and thought of other things and exclaimed "Wonderful!" whenever a pause occurred in his account of his triumphs on the court.

"But *then* what should happen but Spike made a basket!"

"Wonderful, darling," Hennie murmured.

Will turned to look at her. If he had been telling the truth, that he had been kidnaped, he believed she would have said the same. "Spike is a Green," he said coldly.

"Oh, how awful, then."

"Yes, it was. But matters improved, because the Reds won. Let's say this salt cellar is Andy—"

"Darling!" cried Hennie, but not to her son. Her eyes widened and she stared at Laurence's hand that held a fork. "Where did that terrible great scratch come from?"

Laurence's instant look of pleasure that she had noticed it was followed by one of mock modesty. "I cut it on my safe deposit box," he said, and then they both burst out laughing. She cried, "I can't bear it!" They laughed and laughed; he tipped back the kitchen chair on two legs the way they always told Will not to, and she bent above the table edge. "Occupational hazard," he got out, and they hooted at each other while Clare gently smiled to see them so silly. But Will took the opportunity of their being nearly speechless to continue. "Well then, Andy comes up fast alongside Spike—say Spike is this knife," and he unended his knife. But his foolish parents were still looking sideways at each other through half-shut eyes. Will thought how hard it was, when he was trying his best to deceive them for their own comfort, that they weren't even listening. "Spike is this knife," he reiterated with a relentless voice, but Laurence cried out, "You know what that box did? It bit me! Bit the hand that feeds it! Oh, that box has got *the jaws of a crocodile!*"

Will sighed, and laid down Spike. "But in afternoon recess," he sadly said, his eyes watching his parents' faces for some sign, any evidence at all, of returning quiet, and indeed soon Hennie fetched the long, notched sigh that is the end of a good laugh, turned to Will and said, "Tell me."

"The Greens won then," he said, sounding as though it had been her fault.

"Oh, dear," breathed Hennie with the very last breath of her laughing. "I'm so sorry. Better luck next time, and it wouldn't be fair if one side always— Who wants coffee? Clare, coffee? Then Daddy and I'll take ours into the other room."

Left at the kitchen table, Clare and Will, those two reasonable beings, angled for the bits of pineapple in the silver bowl of stewed fruit.

Will was very tired after his extraordinary day. It seemed the very least his mother could have done was listen to the fabrications he had so painstakingly created. But no. "I hate anybody calls me Willie," he remarked.

"Does anybody?"

"They better not." He didn't know when he'd been as tired as he was now. For once, the thought of bed was not intolerable. He got up to go, but at the door he was taken with a pleasant conceit and turned back to inquire of his sister, "On your wedding dress when you get married are you going to wear a trail?" He grinned tiredly within, knowing better; it satisfied him to simulate ignorance. "I think trails are disgusting, myself. Are you?" He blinked at her like a polite bird awaiting a reply to a polite question, but she merely whispered, "Little Willie Stacpole," and it sent him out of the room yelling.

I believe I gave you every opportunity to ask me, she silently said to Laurence's back when, four and a half hours later they were reversing the scene of before-dinner. She was brushing her hair for bed now instead of combing. Off peeled his comfortable old yellow waistcoat and he tossed the cuff links back into their little leather box. Both were sleepy. The evening had been quiet, spent reading. Hours ago Will, perched up on a sofa arm, had been heard his spelling for the morrow.

"Aren't these the same words you had the other evening?"

"Review," said Will, quickly. He was torturing an elastic band in his brown fingers, hesitated over the number of *m*'s in *amount* but was abnormally self-assured, confident, and brisk when it came to *receive*, and went without nagging off to bed, with Stockinette heavily doubled over one arm, her rear end hanging awkwardly down, waggling, her whiskered face looking back at the grown ups defiantly. "I wouldn't let *you* do this to me," was in her feral, milky-green eyes. Will was reminded he was not to take his love to bed with him, and he smiled tiredly back. Laurence and Hennie had sat on, reading until ten.

"Lights no more. Lock the door. Burning log," Laurence had then chanted, in words Hennie had made up for him so long ago they were now partially obsolete. He had brought the fire screen and opened it across the chimney mouth. "Burning log. Outdoors dog. Bed for cat. Thermostat." They hadn't had a dog since Mrs. Comfit's chauffeur had run over their old setter.

Upstairs they had dragged Stockinette out from Will's tight warm clutch—she made a soft furious sound in her throat at them, enough to let them know what she thought of them, too low to wake her god—and had deposited her in her basket in the hall. There had been a time when Laurence would get into bed with his book, turn the lamp away from her closed eyes, and lose himself in the history of the American Civil War, and when after the whole of Antietam or Bull Run he would shut the book and yawning great square yawns turn out the light, he had at once fallen into a deep snore, and this had enraged the dozing Hennie and she would rouse enough to ask in a hiss, secret-sounding to show how late it was, how very late, "Have you seen to the thermostat?"

Now Hennie brushed, yawning, ready for sleep.

"Rain tomorrow," Laurence predicted, going past her into the bathroom.

"D'you think?" She leaned and pulled the cord opening the Venetian blind out horizontal, but it was impossible to tell if there were stars or not because now out there was a lighted room hanging complete and unsupported in the autumn dark. Hollowed out in black space, she looked into their bedroom reversed, hanging complete; if she swayed even slightly, further details sprang into view. Blandly the bedside table would appear, with its four books on it; she knew which books; and a small chair covered in yellow chintz, its seat softly concave where someone had sat in it not long since; one of the three bears, she thought, or me putting on slippers before dinner; I'm the fourth bear and live out there. She moved again and could see the half-closed door to the bathroom and the chest of drawers. It is our lives, hanging out there, she thought, and wondered if in her present condition of incomplete grace she didn't belong out there too, and whether anyone would notice if she went out there to stay. She could leave a bolster in the bed here. "But I haven't laid eyes on a bolster for twenty years," she said aloud, and surprisingly from beyond the bathroom door in the room outdoors, came Laurence's mild voice; "No, neither have I," it said, "but I bet they use 'em still in Center Sandwich."

"Through a Venetian blind, darkly," she murmured, and stood up to look and see if that other pale-blue bedroom had a floor, and at once she could see a safe, a reassuring rug was there too, a rectangle the color of blue plums.

"But I don't happen to want safety," she said to Laurence returning. "I want strange things to happen."

"I don't see it," he said, and sprang into his pajamas. As he tied the strings he cocked his head. "What do I hear?"

"That's Jo, coming to call. Clare said he might be, after he got some necessary work done. We didn't tell you because we hoped you might have got to sleep and not know a thing about it."

"Hell of a time of night to go calling. What if I stalked downstairs and forbid him the house?"

"What indeed? Forbade, it is. She'd be thrilled. Oh, yes, she would! Remember, you're the man who doesn't bother to understand women." Ten minutes later in the darkness, she said crossly, "Oh, go to sleep and stop yawning!"

In the grip of a deep, deep gaping Laurence managed to say he was going to as soon as he could stop yawning.

Two hours later, some time after she had heard Jo go home, she was still awake. Lying in bed like a great cat, wide-awake, she had heard twelve strike and with the third bell note she had invented a game, the flashing recall of the day. It had been at three in the afternoon she had had the telephone call from Edward Latham in reply to her carefully airy note of the morning thanking him for his washroom contribution, at four she had walked downtown to meet Clare and look at fur jackets; Clare hadn't cared for beaver; at five she had come home and met Will in the hall; at six Laurence had come in and told her so brutally that she must not conspire with Clare for a Christmas vacation wedding; at seven sat down to kitchen dinner, at eight convinced Will there was an *a* in *weather*; at nine—nine—nine what had she been doing? Reading; at ten put Stockinette in her basket and given her her pretty duck and here it was twelve o'clock and she was as wide-awake as a fox. Her long legs went thrusting about under the covers, tingling, restless. Her unbearably nervous, tremulous, tremorous ankles twisted together, much against her wish, beneath the thin wool and silk. She thrust her legs in all directions, seeking peace.

She wished Edward Latham would come flying in at the window, doing a splendid breast stroke, and his two admiring blue eyes, like headlights, glow on her. He would sit on the edge of her bed and they would talk, in witty whispers, about—about what? "About me," she said aloud, and rose at once on an elbow to lean across the dark and listen, but she hadn't waked him. The only sound in the room was his purring breath and an occasional, irrational click from his blanket switch. "Purr-h, purr-h," and again "purr-h, purr-h" he went; heavens, how regular; the first beginnings of snoring. She leaned further and switched him up one more degree for good measure before flopping back on her pillow to try to sleep.

She must have slept, but the next thing she knew she was in the kitchen, under the beating bright ceiling light, confronting on the table a pile of cookies and a glass of milk. She looked at the milk a while, then returned it to the bottle and made a trip to the dining room for the brandy decanter. "That's better," she said, "healthier," swished the pale blue warmth of her dressing gown skirts about her knees and legs and sat down again. The kichen was as glaring bright as an operating room. Whenever a bulb burned out in the working part of the house Gino took pleasure in screwing in a twenty-five watt one and then Agnes would wait until his afternoon off before she substituted a hundred watts. If he did not actually see her balancing on the stepladder he could not be sure that one of the Stacpoles had not had to do it, and this, Agnes hoped, would give him a momentary twinge of guilt. Hennie was glad to see, as she sat dipping her tongue in the brandy, that Agnes had left the broom where he would trip over it first thing, and her practiced eye traveling about the bright, white, hot, impersonal cube of room also observed that Gino, in returning the scrap basket emptied, had pushed it so far under the table no one could throw anything in it; evidences of normality, these things were, and as such she welcomed them. She had no wish nor intention to extend the habit of sideways-living to the staff.

The brandy made a warm track a long way down inside her. "I feel fur-lined," she told the insubstantial but amusing figure of Edward Latham, which had only that minute taken a seat across the antiseptic white table. She smiled bewitchingly at him. For some reason which did not seem too strange at that strange hour he was wearing a pale gray tail coat and a pleated shirt.

"How do you suppose my Agnes can bear to spend all her life in this kitchen?" she inquired of the amiable shade. "Everything's so sterile. You wouldn't think a mere icebox would be fit company for a woman all day, would you? But she likes it like this. She's perfectly contented. Once I put up an oil painting on that wall, a cheerful red and gold and green portrait of a hen, most appealing, but I never saw it again after the next spring cleaning. She works here all day and then every evening she wrings the necks of the faucets, picks up her alarm clock, and off she goes upstairs to bed, alone. Isn't that sad?"

She poured and drank a few more drops of brandy.

"Well," she said, yawned, got up and carried the heavy crystal bottle by its neck back to the dining-room cupboard. If, as Laurence had so disturbingly pointed out, there did occur an occasional armistice belowstairs, it might be that tomorrow in the early morning—today!—but before the Stacpoles were even up, if Agnes came down to find the decanter in the kitchen she might jerk a not entirely hostile thumb in its direction, and Gino might then smile, though it had been years since anyone in that house had seen such a thing. When she returned to the kitchen, Edward Latham and his pleated shirt had gone.

Next morning Laurence said he had been too hot all night. "I dreamed I was redigging the Panama Canal," he said, and turned to look at her, as though he wondered.

Hennie bent forward and selected a pin for the neck of her dressing gown from the irregularly jeweled bristling back of a blue velvet heart. "You did? But it wasn't a very hot night actually, not for the time of year, with winter coming, as you keep on saying."

CHAPTER TEN

Clare lay alone in her bed at some anonymous dark hour, her blood trembling with glee and triumph. That she was about to be named Wood instead of Stacpole brought her whole life to a peak, and tied an iridescent bow on the tip. "Divine. Divine. Divine," she sang under her breath, kicking around in the sheets, bouncing and flouncing. At moments, she squealed silently.

"And Mummy brought us *to* it," she said aloud, accenting the *to*.

What a born diplomat she must be to have so easily at last, persuaded him. She would never tell anyone how she had done it, no one; especially she would not tell her mother. She quieted for a moment, trying to catch back something from her very distant childhood, something last evening's triumph over Jo reminded her of;

the feeling she was having now was the same as one she long ago had had—when she was very small she was given a box of jackstraws in the shapes of little tools, stiff pieces of wire with heads of color-stained wood, minute blue hammer heads, yellow hoes, cerise axes, and acid-green rakes, and once in a while she had been able, crouching and kneeling above the nested heap, to draw out of it most delicately, with a very small magnet, the one desired jackstraw, and it had been exactly like that, last evening. Without troubling or trembling the rest of the jangled heap of Jo's young prejudices, the one most inimical to her, that acid-green prejudice she had abstracted with a magician's touch, and as she lay now remembering how it had been done she saw extremely small flecks of color, purple, cerise and hyacinth-blue, in a floating dance, in a *mobile*, behind her closed lids.

They had had the living room to themselves. Hennie and Laurence, Will and Stockinette, were all asleep upstairs. She had been lurking about downstairs and had the door open before he set foot on the step.

She had begun the visit with a good many deep long sighs, sad distracted glances and above all a kind of polite inattention which soon, though he had arrived in hopeful mood, affected him so he begged for an explanation. This elicited the largest sigh yet and a murmured, "Oh, nothing; nothing new; only Mummy's terribly high spirits, which I supposed you were here to discuss, but if it bores you—" Here she appeared to be unable to continue, for pressure of private worry.

"If it's that flowery wedding you told me about, I've

thought that over and I don't believe she'd press it. I believe it was just a temporary whim." But she rolled her eyes and shook her head. "Well, then, tell me," he commanded and presently they were facing each other from the ends of the sofa like two solemn limber puppies and in fierce whispers she was pouring out a detailed synopsis of how she now deeply feared her mother must actually disapprove of their engagement because how else to account for the strange, strange way she was behaving.

"I don't quite get all this," he said.

"She's so gay! So sort of wildly gay, you must have noticed, and what I'm so afraid is that she's being brave about it and this effort has somehow unhinged her a trifle."

"I may not amount to much yet; I haven't had the time to! But I'm not all that objectionable, I should hope."

"Oh, darling, it isn't *you* at all. Any young man would do this to her. You don't understand. Oh, darling, I'm not blaming you, so please don't go making that huffing sound. No, it's something I've just learned from Mrs. Comfit's niece who's visiting her and she told me—I was so surprised, but she's seen it happen over and over again —that women, mothers, become *queer* when their daughters get engaged. I suppose it's some form of jealousy, so maybe what you ought to be is very much flattered. But unhinged, almost, as I said."

"Not when their sons do?"

"No, I guess not, as a matter of fact. Mrs. Comfit's niece didn't say about that, though they may."

"My mother hasn't. I wrote her all about it and she wrote back a perfectly—"

"Don't boast." She gave a wailing whisper. "*Oast oast oast*" came whispering back at them from the dark empty rooms around; upstairs the rooms would be dark too, cool with their windows open, silent. In the cave of light made by the one lamp the young ones crouched, almost hopeless. "Help me to think what to do because I don't see why, unless there's something like that the matter with her, she feels so well. Help me to think."

"It's only a matter of waiting until April; April's not so far off."

"No." One finger tip drew designs on a sofa pillow. "No, I suppose it isn't. It might get to the point where we'd have to find her some nice sanatorium for the winter months, though, mightn't it?"

"I suppose," he said slowly, "a really scientific way to go at it would be to break, to appear to break it off, and then observe her closely and see if she improves any."

She looked so alarmed he repeated, calmly, he meant only to appear to break their engagement.

She did not look as though she thought highly of this scheme. "Yes, I see." She looked a thoughtful ten or eleven years old, one plotting to get her own way, temporarily blocked. "That would be rather too drastic, though, don't you think. I don't believe in drastic measures except in awfully drastic situations. You see, you couldn't come here any more."

"Maybe. But if she then returned to what you would recognize as her normal self—I don't suppose *I'd* know the difference—then we could go at being engaged differently somehow."

"Yes, I see." Tears slowly, miraculously, came to her aid and brimmed over and down. "Oh, it's so sad."

His mouth tightened for a minute and then he said, "I promise; spring vacation."

She gave a sob. "That's nice," she said.

He looked down at his own folded hands and said well then, Christmas vacation.

It was like turning all the lights on, on a Christmas tree. Her tears sparkled and winked; she put out her pink tongue and caught them. "Ah-ha! That's better!" She came along the sofa to him and hugged him, rearing back for only a moment, to say. "So we'll humor her by letting her do a great big velvety wedding, which ought to be enough to keep any middle-aged woman completely and fully occupied. And it's a funny thing, Mrs. Comfit's niece says that when the child, the daughter, actually marries, then all this queerness—just passes off! Isn't that strange!" Her eyes filled again with bright crystal tears. "I'd love to see her happy again," she said, "sensibly happy, once more, before she gets too terribly, terribly old."

"Then tomorrow, by special license," he said, and quoted the Connecticut statutes. "In case of emergency. Because I simply cannot go through a big lot of wedding parties at Christmas time, with January tests coming. I have to spend all Christmas vacation studying. I *have* to. If this isn't an emergency, I don't know what is. Trust me. I'll manage it."

Thus had she withdrawn the sharp-headed jackstraw and now she could lie in bed and gloat.

"Divine, divine," she sang. "Divine, divine." But in the morning she soberly descended to breakfast, a Stacpole still, the round white collar of her dress a baby-nun's frame for her demure face, her soft, hanging, brown hair.

What moleskin-headed grandchildren we're going to have, Hennie thought; nary a curl among them. The more she saw of her serious son-in-law-to-be the more fond of him she grew, and she had even begun to experience short spasms of amused love. Contrary to her first impression she now found him handsome, and took frequent opportunities to say so to Clare, though not more than once, early on, and into the face of instantaneous opposition, had she ventured her opinion that she hoped some day he would be moved to give up his crew haircut.

"A poached egg, darling?" she now offered her daughter. "Toast. Daddy has the marmalade. D'you know, when I was young my nurse told me if you blow on sealskin, on that soft straight short fur, you can tell if it's real by its being a different color at the roots; reddish, sort of."

"I knew that," Laurence surprised them all by saying. "I used to do it every Sunday to the tippet or whatever it was around the neck of the woman who sat in front of us at church. Now what in thunder was her name? The Congregational Church in Center Sandwich," he added. "Willard? Bollard? Dollard, that was it. No, no it wasn't. Dullard? Mallard? Pritchard?"

"*That* wasn't a very nice thing to do in church," said Will. "For instance, it might have cooled off her neck."

"Might have been just what she wanted," his father said, and turned to ask Hennie what on earth had made her think of sealskin at this hour of the morning?

Hennie started to smile. "Something made me think of moleskin," she began, "and so I—" but then she happened to catch her daughter's eye and a warning look was gathering there, a protective, suspicious, mother-hen expression that caused Hennie to drop her own eyes and set to smoothing her napkin with meek, mild hands. "I can't *imag*ine what," she meekly said.

Laurence, selecting his final piece of toast, said winter was coming, and they all said yes, and suspended their forks and gazed out the windows. The world did not look copper and gold this morning; there were low fast-moving clouds, gray uncertainty in the air and against the window panes, tentative but unmistakable, a scutter of old leaves. Laurence yawned and Will said he wondered if his father had gone to bed on time the evening before. Laurence yawned again and said no, it wasn't that; yes, he had; it was only he couldn't help thinking how tired and sleepy he was going to be by bedtime tonight; the New York train always made him drowsy.

"New York!" Hennie said sharply. Her hands went still, in her lap. "What do you mean, the New York train?"

"I told you. Didn't I? Meant to, anyway. All day long, damnation take it."

Surprise caused her to glance aside. "Not a word. Well —home when?" She had intended to inform him casually, as he was in the act of departing for downtown, that they were to drop in at Edward Latham's for a drink, the end of the afternoon, and in his call yesterday he had said, "And perhaps you could stay on afterward for cold meat and salad? My man's got to be out," he had gone on, "visiting hours at the hospital—his mother's hip —but he leaves everything ready."

"Home when?" Hennie asked again, "because—"

"Oh, God knows. Dinner at the Century and when men get to talking there's no knowing, but I'll try to make the ten o'clock. I only hope it won't mean oysters."

"I see." A delicate tide of apprehension lapped across her stomach. Panic and gaiety and anticipation chased each other in ripples along her skin. She smiled tremulously at him. "But then *don't* eat oysters, darling," she said. "You won't, will you? There's no law makes you."

He grumbled he might have to, pushed back his chair and departed, a possible martyr.

After he had gone Hennie hung around upstairs in her dressing gown, idling hither and thither, stopping and starting. She was waiting for the exact moment to arrive when she would telephone Edward and say how terribly sorry she was but they couldn't come. "I'll call in exactly ten minutes," she decided, "nine-thirty on the dot," and stooped to tree yesterday's shoes. Downstairs the piano tuner whose name she was forever unable to remember arrived and went to work. Agnes, who had surprisingly asked for an hour or two off that afternoon, a thing which had not happened before in all the years, could be heard following her vacuum cleaner about in the back part of the house. Hennie carefully folded a blouse into a drawer before snatching it out and tossing it in the laundry basket above which Mr. Tuthill had not returned to install a shelf. Infinitesimal pleated shivers ran about in her insides; she knew they looked like the inch-high crystal waves that, summers on the beach at Flanders Point, portended the turning of the tide.

Clare could be heard coming down the hall singing, trying to drown out the piano tuner. She stopped in Hennie's doorway. "I've been calling you," she said, smiling on her mother with the smile one gives to heedless, much-loved children.

"Oh." Hennie paused in her picking up, and by a considerable effort salvaged a word or two. "I heard you. Your coat, you said; but what about it?"

"Yes. Shall I?"

"Shall you what, darling? You mustn't expect me to be clairvoyant so early in the day."

"*Wear* it *today*, I said. My raincoat, because it's so dark and cold. I'm going out. Out for luncheon."

Hennie sighed. "Really is it? I'd thought it was quite warm." I'll telephone when the piano tuner has finished; not before; but the exact instant he closes the front door I shall dial the number. Clare withdrew, looking reproachfully over her shoulder, and hung her raincoat back on its hook, and Hennie swooped to the hamper, snatched out the blouse which she now knew she had always disliked and threw it into the scrap basket; Gino would find it and take it home to his mother, who would be unable by six inches to get it to button across her Tuscan bosom.

No one had ever known a piano tuner to stay so long. It really could not be necessary, all the reiterated plunking, like a mourning dove on an opal-colored evening, in a faraway wood. "I'm *so* sorry, Edward," she was going to say, "but the fact is—" She must be careful not to gabble; nervousness leads straight to gabbling, as she was well aware. Then his calm voice might reply "But *you* will come." To that she must reply no, no. *Oh*, no, she couldn't possibly. "Not *pos*sibly, Edward—" and he would wait, and smile, until her voice, the traitor, gave out and then say, "Why not?" One thing she did know, only one, and that was if she went she would wear the new blue silk from Bendel.

After all, sooner than she had expected, downstairs the piano tuner began on the terrible, sweet, mellifluous, suffering piece he always played when he was through. It was his invariable reward for all the conscientious plunking, the sugar lump on the tip of his nose. "The minute he's through with that awful thing I'll call," she said, but knowing from of old that this might not have to be for some time yet as, other falls, other springs, how backward and forward and sideways this man swayed in his final throes and was often carried away nearly to tears by the sweetness of his own performance—then off he would stalk, stern and cold, clapping on his hat as he went, looking coldly before him after his moment of emotion, and leaving all the piano ornaments for Agnes to put back.

"I'll just dress first," Hennie said.

Presently she ran down the stairs. Agnes was restoring the Lowestoft bowl to the piano top. In came Mrs. Stacpole, flying.

"Oh, there you are, Agnes. Look, I'm late to the hairdresser, somehow. I'll stay downtown for luncheon which will be nice for you if you want to be out for a little, but will you do just one thing—call Mr. Latham at the bank for me and tell him I'm afraid we can't come this evening after all because Mr. Stacpole has to be in New York." She turned the Lowestoft bowl on its teak base. "You will remember, won't you? Just those two things, one really, that we can't come because Mr. Stacpole is in New York for the evening."

Gino knelt on the library hearth, his flat basket of polishes and brushes beside him, and slid pink paste into the flutings of the poker handle. He had done this about five hundred times before and would have looked sharply up, turning his smooth black head like a startled bird, if anyone had asked him if he did or did not intend to do it another five hundred. Any other future but that one, that sure one, would have frightened him. Sometimes but not often he considered plans for leaving the Stacpoles. He would have thought better of himself if he had worked in a big garage or a factory with other men and sometimes as he washed windows in the white clapboard house or weeded or swept the walks, he would think he would leave next year. "But they pay too good. But factory work," he told himself as he meticulously, deftly, burnished the handle of the poker better than anyone else could have done, "that would suit me better'n this. Housework! I'll get a job with the railroad." But then he bent his head, frightened. He scared himself, when he talked to himself like that.

He heard the bell at the front door, and Agnes rustle through to open it. He polished softly, looking like a black bird huddled and absorbed over some object it had found, a stick or a pebble.

The woman at the front door was from the lending library.

"It would have the red ribbon marker in it," she was saying to Agnes, and Agnes, with a mere breath of reproof in her voice said, "I *know*, madam," and looked for it in the living room, and then glanced in at the library door but encountering Gino's bird eyes withdrew as though the air in there were tainted.

"They've had it three weeks, so I feel they must be through with it, and Mrs. Comfit's had her name down so long."

Agnes said she would just run upstairs, so she just ran upstairs and down and said no, nowhere; should she telephone the hairdresser where Mrs. Stacpole was having her hair washed this morning, and ask?

"No; oh, no." But the voice was dissatisfied, and Gino in the library, who could see the book from where he was kneeling, with its tongue of red satin lolling out at him, smiled. "But Mrs. Comfit is particularly anxious to read it."

Agnes said she would ask Mrs. Stacpole about it when she came in and then no doubt the man who worked about the place, she said, could perfectly well run over to Mrs. Comfit's with it; perfectly well. The voice implied this man was precious little use but he could do that. The woman hung about for a minute, then the door was clicked shut on her, very politely, and Agnes without a turn of the head, sailed past the library to the back hall door and slammed it.

Silently Gino rose and laid the book in question in plain view on a table in the living room, returned, sank on his knees, finished the poker, and started in on the andirons; these had fluted pineapple shaped knobs too and he polished the backs of them as beautifully as the parts that showed.

The chief reason why he worked so well was his loathing of Agnes. Oh, to have a dark waistless woman to go home to every night! Not quick, like Agnes; not clever; someone of no particular age but smelling heartening and warm of sweat and garlic, somebody solid and slow, not like Agnes. Agnes was the perennial enemy, who darted and sped in pursuit of her flying duster. He hated her for being so disgustingly odorless. With his waistless woman he would work his way down between sheets, under many, heavy blankets, but he knew for a fact nobody in the world had ever wanted to go to bed with Agnes. "I'd rather have nobody than her," he said, laying aside the fact he had nobody. Sometimes, behind lowered lids, he speculated about Mrs. Stacpole, but the scent of her Chanel 22 sent his thoughts and imaginings all skittering off in a panic. He had always shied away from the mocking sharp expensive smell that moved with her, a gauzy gold nimbus through which her blue eyes regarded him. "If I were you, Gino," she often began her orders, "I'd cut the grass today." He disliked her being tall and himself short; the woman he would have liked to go home to would rub garlic on her skin and never go out of doors and be divinely squat.

He heard the enemy come through the swinging door from the back hall, pause by the hall table, and then go out by the front door. "Hunk!" he said in surprise. He reared up off the hearth and slipped into the hall. There on the table he saw a narrow curled strip of paper from the wall fixture in the kitchen, inscribed in her loathed writing. If there was one thing about her he hated more than another it was the way she stood before this fixture writing nearsightedly, her lips pursed. He smiled and stepped to the front door and held it open long enough for the slip of paper to be found by the foraging autumn wind. Smiling across his shoulder, he watched the paper blow away behind the glove box and then behind the bowl of chrysanthemums. It had said:

> Mr Latham
> called
> back he
> says Mrs
> Stacpole
> you

> should
> go to his
> house
> anyway.
> Agnes

He closed the front door and passed quietly on into the living room where he knelt and soberly went to work on the handles of a chest; painstakingly and well he dealt with them; nobody could polish better than Gino.

Gino was nowhere around when, about five, Hennie came, walking quickly, back from her hours away from the house. She looked searchingly about in the hall, then moved toward the kitchen, then remembered Agnes was out. Her breath was uneven, her cheeks pink, and her eyes bright. She stood looking about, listening, listening. Nothing. No message. The house was empty.

Clare flashed in at the front door like a kingfisher, her blue clothes sleek to her sides like feathers. She sped past her dallying mother and up the stairs; Hennie had scarcely reached the point of wondering why the child looked so happy when she flashed down again, rushed to her mother and kissed her, made for the stairs, hung across the banisters halfway up enveloping her mother in a warm regard. "I'll see you soon," she cried.

Hennie laughed at her, absent-mindedly. "I should hope so."

"But not dinner. And don't worry if I'm late, really *quite* late tonight. You won't, will you? Promise me?"

Hennie moved to the hall table and ran her fingers

along the edge of it. It was not like Agnes to have left no note, unless, of course, there had been nothing to say. She touched the chrysanthemums, lifting their heads. She heard Clare go on upstairs and then come darting down. She did not observe the very small overnight case her child was carrying under her far arm but thought how like a blue kingfisher she looked, launching itself blindly and brightly from its branch. "Will *you* be out tonight?" Clare called back, but with the front door closing.

"In, I guess," muttered Hennie. And in she was. She stood a while longer in the hall. She heard a fierce fall wind run once around the house and off up the street; it would return. She stood motionless, one hand against her cheek; there was something she had forgotten, or lost. There was something she was trying to remember, something connected with her childhood; probably nothing much. She felt sad and comfortable. The golden-faced grandfather clock struck five-fifteen. Out from the shadowy corners of the hall stepped veils and wisps and wreathings like blue gauze; they advanced on her slowly, floating and wreathing, and watching them come, she yawned profoundly. Far off she heard the soft silver crash, the airy cascade of something breaking. "Oh," she said. "I'm tired."

She went early to bed, not noticing just then the loving short note skewered down so firmly to Clare's pincushion with corsage pins from flowers other boys than Jo had once sent her; she was a careful child, on the whole. In the dark hall Hennie's foot scraped against Stockinette's basket, making it creak. "Excuse me," she said to a cat she could not see, to a cat who was not there but in bed in Will's room, clamped under his elbow.

She crawled her way into bed, beat her pillow, and laid down her head. Much later, after calm sleeping, she heard the shower bath water rushing into its tiled pool. Presently the line of light under the bathroom door was clicked off and she heard him come back into the bedroom. "I didn't hear you come home."

"Been in bed long?"

"Hours."

"*You're* tired?" he asked with amazement. In the dark he came to the side of her bed. She felt his eyes turned down on her.

"Yes, yes," she murmured. "I'm exhausted."

She could feel him smiling in the dark. His knees were at the edge of the bed. "That's too bad," he said, his voice contented. "Move over."

"Yes, yes." She turned and wrapped him in her long arms. "Oh my," she said, admiringly, "just exactly like a great big, cold, wet lizard."